Readers Love Cardeno C.

Strong Enough

"Cardeno has written such a feel-good story, and it's wonderful watching sweet, deserving Spencer finally believe he's strong enough and deserves this treasure of Emilio and his family"

—Happily Ever After (*USA Today*)

"The author's voice (new to me) was lovely, the writing crisp and still emotionally charged. A great book with which to spend a few hours escaping from your own life."

—My Fiction Nook

"Whenever I'm craving a really good dessert, I'll be reaching for this story again."

—Hearts on Fire

A Shot at Forgiveness

"A great story by Cardeno C. The perfect bite to escape from the worries of the day and allow a little romance to help you smile."

—Gay List Book Reviews

Until Forever Comes

"If you love paranormal romance, read this book. If you like Cardeno C.'s other work, read this book. If you are new the m/m scene and are shopping for new authors, read this book. When you are done, bet your bottom dollar, you will go out and pick up Cardeno C's backlist."

—Gay List Book Reviews

By CARDENO C.

THE MATES SERIES
Until Forever Comes
Wake Me Up Inside

THE HOME SERIES
He Completes Me
Home Again
Just What the Truth Is
Love at First Sight
The One Who Saves Me
Where He Ends and I Begin

THE FAMILY SERIES
Something in the Way He Needs
Strong Enough
More Than Everything

OTHER TITLES
Eight Days
Places in Time
A Shot at Forgiveness

Published by DREAMSPINNER PRESS
http://www.dreamspinnerpress.com

MORE THAN EVERYTHING
CARDENO C.

A BOOK IN THE *Family* SERIES

Dreamspinner Press

Published by
Dreamspinner Press
5032 Capital Circle SW
Suite 2, PMB# 279
Tallahassee, FL 32305-7886
USA
http://www.dreamspinnerpress.com/

More Than Everything
© 2013 Cardeno C.

Cover Art
© 2013 Reese Dante.
http://www.reesedante.com
Cover content is for illustrative purposes only and any person depicted on the cover is a model.

ISBN: 978-1-62798-260-3
Digital ISBN: 978-1-62798-259-7

Printed in the United States of America
First Edition
November 2013

To Rachel and Selina: Thank you for all of your hard work on the Facebook page and the Goodreads group. I'm endlessly grateful for your help, support, and cheerleading/mothering.

L.A. Borgaard: Thank you for all your help with this book and all the others.

To Kelly Shorten: Thank you for all of your website help and blog help. I hope you enjoy the fish!

To Mary Calmes: Thank you for being a wonderful friend and writing partner.

To Reese Dante: Thank you for another amazing cover.

Prologue

Charlie ("Chase") Rhodes

IT'S funny how when you're a kid you think you have it all figured out. You think you know who you're going to be when you grow up, what you're going to do. And yet, you can't actually see yourself as a grown-up. I mean, grown-ups are *old*. And they're constantly saying shit we think we'll never say and doing shit we think we'll never do.

When I think back to how many times I said I'd never do this and I'd never say that, I want to cringe. Because you know what? I do all of it now.

Just this morning, when I was getting the kids off to school and they were fighting with each other over who got to hold a spatula—yeah, I know—I told them to stop talking to each other. No, really, I did. This was me: "Bobby, Stephi! You put down that spatula right now and go wait for me in the car. And I don't want to hear you say a word to each other! Do you understand me?" Um, yeah, excellent life lesson: don't talk to your sibling.

It was only a step above my useful "Because I said so" conversations. "Why do I have to eat the peas? I hate peas." And I'm thinking, I fucking hated peas when I was your age too, kid. Still don't love them. I'm just waiting for you to go to bed so I can eat ice cream straight from the carton. But what I say is, "Because I said so, Bobby. Now eat your peas."

So, yeah, I'm doing all the things I never thought I'd do, saying all the things I never thought I'd say. But you know the really crazy part about it? I'm happy. I mean, like deliriously fucking happy. And I figure happiness like this needs to be documented.

Thankfully, the PTA was selling these scrapbooks as a fundraiser last fall. Because when I decided to become a suburban housewife, I was told there were two requirements: learning to scrapbook and having a vagina. I was fucked on the second one, obviously. I mean, I can rock a pink sweater and low-slung white jeans better than some trophy wives with the most expensive racks money can buy, but a vagina? Thanks, but no thanks. I'm pretty attached to my dick. But I've always been creative; hell, I was a dancer and choreographer for years, so I was sure I could zigzag scissor and star-stamp just about anybody under the table.

So here I am. Eight thirty on a Friday morning—a time when, in my old life, I would have been sleeping off the bender from the postshow party the night before, and instead, I'm sitting in my bright-yellow kitchen, at the round wooden table I got at this amazing antique store that opens only one weekend a month and I'm always there when the doors open, like clockwork. Anyway, I'm sitting at my table, drinking my nonfat, sugar-free, extra-caffeine (okay, I'm making up the last one, but don't you wish it was an option) latte, and I'm putting together an album of the life I never saw coming. The life I never knew I always wanted.

Confused? Well, hopefully I can help clear it up for you. Oh, and don't freak out about flashbacks, okay? Think of it more like you're hearing a story from beginning to end, with a little bit of narration in the middle. It'll be okay; I promise. Just follow along.

Chapter 1

INTRODUCTION

Charlie ("Chase") Rhodes

THE first time I saw Scott Boone, I knew the bisexual label I'd been trying on for size in my head was bullshit. I was gay. It wasn't a total shocker or anything. I'd asked my parents for an Easy-Bake Oven for my eighth birthday. By the time I turned twelve, I knew asking for the Barbie Styling Head I actually wanted was a straight shot to strange looks and "Shh, he's walking up" conversations, so I asked for money instead. Then I bought the hairstyling Barbie toy I actually wanted and hid it in my closet. Someone should put that story on Urban Dictionary as an example of irony. But I digress.

Scott Boone was everything I wasn't. He was tall, broad-chested, athletic, überbutch, right-handed. Again with the digression.

Anywho, I was a scrawny fifteen-year-old, sitting in my bedroom in my mother's second-story Brooklyn apartment—my father had moved out by then—and I was *not* teaching myself how to do a new french twist on the Barbie Styling Head, which I'd dyed an amazing shade of auburn, when I saw a truck piled high with furniture pull up out front and the most gorgeous guy I'd ever seen hop out.

I can't say for sure, but I think I might have started drooling. I definitely sprung a boner. Because, here's the deal: it was summer in the city, so it was hot as a motherfucker and Mr. All-American was wearing cutoff jeans, Pumas without socks, and *nothing* else. I almost broke my neck running to get my camera so I could snap a picture of the wet-dream-come-to-life who was moving into my apartment building.

Since starting at the beginning seems like as good a place as any, that's the first picture I'm putting into the album: Scott Boone at age sixteen, blond hair cut jock short, no shirt, shiny with sweat, and the fodder for almost all of my masturbatory fantasies for years to come.

Chapter 1

Charlie ("Chase") Rhodes

"HI, UH, hey, uh, hello," I smoothly said to Scott as I came running down the stairs. "Do you want some he—"

And that's when I really kicked the seduction strategy up a notch by managing to slip on thin air and then land ass-first at the bottom of the stairs, knocking over some of Scott's stacked boxes in the process. I sort of froze then, just did the slow pan up to him to check whether he'd noticed my snafu. Because, you know, it was totally possible he'd somehow missed someone yelling out to him, then screeching while falling down the stairs, and finally banging around boxes loud enough for deaf Mrs. Winters in 3E to hear.

He was staring at me, mouth gaping, hazel eyes wide. Yes, hazel. Death-defying accidents and unbeforeknown humiliation weren't enough to prevent me from inventorying everything I could about his appearance. In case you're interested, his nipples were tiny and pink, and I had this strange urge to feel their texture. With my tongue. And my eyes are blue. Just thought you might want to know.

I assume there were other noises around us. Probably cars driving and honking, people shouting, a kid playing hopscotch, birds chirping, a mugging; whatever, you get the idea. There were noises. But the thing was, I couldn't hear any of them. It might have been head trauma from my fall, I'm willing to remain open-minded about that possibility, but as I sat there and locked gazes with Scott, everything went quiet, everyone around me disappeared, and he was all I saw.

"Are you okay?" he asked me once he finally closed his mouth.

His lips were really nice. Not too thin, not too plump, and a great shade of red. I wanted to kiss him. I'd never kissed anyone. I wondered if I'd be crap at it.

Was I supposed to stick my tongue in his mouth and twirl it around his tongue, or what? I thought about asking Loose Linda on the fourth floor, but there was a higher than likely chance she would have wanted to take a hands-on, or in this case lips-on, teaching approach and I wasn't up for it. Let's take a moment to think of all the double entendre jokes we can make about that last comment. Okay, moving on.

"Hey, can you hear me?" Scott asked, sounding worried.

I could hear him just fine but I decided against mentioning it because he was rushing over to me and, as I might have mentioned, he wasn't wearing a shirt. He squatted in front of me, brow furrowed, chewing on his bottom lip.

"Should I call an ambulance?" he asked. "Do you need anything?"

And just like that, he'd handed me the perfect opening.

I pushed my brown hair out of my eyes and said, "CPR."

He raised both eyebrows. "What?"

I did that fake cough thing that never sounds convincing because it's all dry.

"CPR," I repeated. "I think maybe I need CPR."

"CPR is for people who aren't conscious or breathing," he patiently explained.

I doubled up on the fake cough and added a dramatically hoarse voice to complete the picture. "Are you sure?" I asked as I rubbed my throat. "Shouldn't we go ahead and do it just to, you know, be safe?"

Scott shook his head. "I took a babysitting class from the Red Cross when I was thirteen," he said, sounding very earnest. "And I have to do annual refreshers to keep up my certification. I know what I'm talking about. You're breathing on your own and conscious. That means CPR is not indicated."

Damn Red Cross, cockblocking me. I dropped my hand from my neck and let out a sharp sigh of disappointment. "Yeah, okay." I looked down and tugged at a loose thread in my jeans.

"I'm Scott Boone," he said.

That was the point in the conversation where a light gust of wind should have made my hair blow just so, a guy on the corner should have started playing a violin, and those chirping birds should have flown around us and landed on a shoulder, or, at the very least, a dinged-up box. Alas, none of that happened. Instead, I dragged my gaze up to meet his and proceeded to ramble like an idiot.

"Hi, Scott. I'm Charles Rhodes but everyone calls me Charlie. Well, not everyone. In third grade Maxwell Jacobs used to call me Chase. Chase Rhodes, get it? 'Cause people get chased on the road. Not that anybody chases me, but I never complained because it could have been worse. The girl who used to sit next to me? Her name was Sandra Butts. She used to beg people to call her Sandra but it was third grade, so even the teacher called her Sandy and—"

Thankfully, Scott's father saved me from the certifiable-worthy ramble. Well, technically he shouted in frustration, but the result was the same.

"Scott! Quit chit-chatting with your friend. We have four more truckloads to bring over, and I'd like to get this done before sunset."

Friend was good. I was happy to start with friend. I'd be even happier if Scott could become the kind of friend who liked to spend time naked in my bed when my mom and my sister were out. Excellent. Now I had something to work toward.

"Sorry, Dad," Scott said without moving his gaze away from me. "Be right there."

But he didn't move. He just kept staring at me. I swallowed hard and tried to think of something interesting to say, but couldn't come up with a single thing that wouldn't risk a black eye. Then a loud crash sounded from the truck and Scott's father started cussing up a storm, so I figured it was time to get up off the sidewalk and lend a hand.

"I'll, uh, help with these boxes," I said as I climbed to my feet.

"Yeah?" Scott asked, smiling brightly. "If you're sure you feel okay, that'd be great."

"Great," I said as I rubbed the toe of my shoe back and forth across the concrete.

"Great," he said as he stuffed his hands in his pockets and dragged his waistband dangerously low.

"Great," I said as I looked up at him from underneath my lashes and chewed on my bottom lip.

"Scott! Dammit, come on," his father yelled.

That broke our *great* standoff. Scott hustled over to his father, I scrambled to pick up one of the displaced boxes, and, together, the three of us moved a truckload of stuff into the apartment directly next door to mine.

When we were done unloading, Mr. Boone rushed Scott out of the apartment.

"Let's go. We have to load the truck and do this all again," he said.

We both followed him out the door and stood in the hallway as he locked up.

"Will you be around later?" Scott asked.

My nonexistent social life was finally panning out to be a good thing. "Yeah," I said. Then it dawned on me that instead of sitting around thinking about my new friend, I could actually be with him. "I can go with you guys and help load if you want," I volunteered.

Scott's whole face lit up. "Did you hear that, Dad?" he said. "Charlie said he'd help us."

Mr. Boone started booking it down the stairs, and Scott and I followed.

"Your parents are okay with that, uh…."

"Charlie," I reminded him.

"Right, sorry. Your parents okay with you coming along, Charlie?"

My father was long gone—I hadn't received so much as a postcard in more than a year. And my mom was picking up a bunch of overtime at the hospital, so she'd be at work until close to eight. Lord knew where my sister Rachel was. Probably spending the night with her latest future ex-boyfriend.

"Yeah, no problem," I told Mr. Boone.

He nodded and grunted, and then all three of us squeezed together into the cab of the truck.

"DO YOU want me to help you unpack?" I asked Scott once we were done dragging all the boxes into his bedroom.

I was exhausted, my arms were so overworked my muscles were twitching, and I was putting odds at sixty-forty that my legs were going to collapse at any second. But I focused hard on mind over matter and told my body to buck the fuck up because being helpful-friend guy meant I could look at Scott.

Scott, whose cheeks were flushed from hours of lifting boxes and walking up and down stairs. Scott, who was so tall I had to tilt my head all the way back to see his face. Scott, whose arms were bulging with thick muscles I didn't normally see on boys our age. Scott, whose legs were covered in downy hair I wanted to caress. *Scott,* said in a dreamy, wistful voice, and followed by a long sigh. Okay, so maybe the last one was overkill, but you get the idea: I wanted to be with Scott, and if manual labor was the price of admission, well, I was willing to pay for my ticket.

"Nah, that can wait until tomorrow." He flopped down on the extra-long twin mattress we'd dropped in the corner of the room. "I'm beat."

Seeing him lying down almost made my knees buckle and, that time, it wasn't from arousal. I figured my body was just envious.

"C'mere," he said as he patted the spot next to him. The mattress was pretty narrow and he was very broad, but he scooted all the way to one side and I was but a wee lad… no? Okay, I was a skinny little runt, so there was plenty of room for both of us on the mattress. Better?

"You sure?" I asked as I moved forward.

He grunted his assent and tapped his hand again. I plummeted onto the mattress face-first, making us both bounce.

"Sorry," I mumbled into the fabric under my mouth.

He raised his arm, dropped it on me, and landed a few halfhearted pats on my back.

"'S okay," he slurred. Then he tossed his other forearm over his eyes and sighed.

We lay in silence for a while. I might even have dozed off for a little bit. Once my body had a chance to rest and recuperate, though, my brain kicked on and I remembered some questions I'd filed away throughout the day, intending to ask Scott for answers when we were alone. There were lots of voices and noises coming from the next room, but technically it was just the two of us in the tiny space. That counted as alone. I flipped onto my side, propped my elbow on the bed, and rested my head on my hand.

"Scott?"

"Huh?"

"What's the deal with your parents?"

"My parents?"

"Yeah."

He moved his arm off his face, rolled onto this side, and then mimicked my pose. "What do you mean?" he asked.

I chewed on the side of my lip, feeling uncomfortable all of a sudden, like I was prying or overstepping or generally clueless. But he didn't seem upset, so I decided, what the fuck, and charged on ahead. "Well, your dad was helping us load the truck and stuff, right?"

"Uh-huh." He bobbed his head.

"So then who was the other guy? The one, uh—" I tried to figure out the right words to ask about the man I'd seen groping his mom's ass in the kitchen. She had been packing boxes. He had been feeling her up. I had been mortified as hell. I finally settled on, "—with your mother."

"Oh!" Scott said. "That was Dave."

Right. Okay, not helpful at all, then.

"Dave?"

"Yeah." He nodded. "My stepfather."

"Your parents are divorced?"

"No, not divorced. Just not married to each other. Never have been."

"Huh," I said. "And that woman who was at your old apartment? The one packing up the bathroom?" And having a conversation about feminine products with Scott's mother that made me wish I could plug my ears with supersize… damn it. Still thinking about those products. Horror.

"That was my stepmom, Julia."

Since my parents split, I'd had maybe a couple of phone calls from my father. No way was my mother going to start dating one of his buddies or exchanging recipes… or other things… with whoever my dad was banging.

"It's cool," Scott said, making me realize I must have looked as confused as I felt. "My dad and Dave are, like, best friends or something. They all went to high school together: my mom, my dad, Dave, and Julia."

"Oh, that's, uh, nice." Weird. Totally weird. But lying as close to Scott as I was at that moment, his scent seemed more important than his family dynamic. He smelled good. Seriously good.

"What're you doing?" Scott asked.

I snapped my head up. I'd somehow managed to get my face oddly close to Scott's chest. And by oddly close, I mean I was a tongue-length away from making contact with his skin. I hoped he couldn't hear my heart beating louder than a conga drum and tried to come up with a viable excuse for almost licking the guy. My initial thought was to go with seizure, but Lord knew what they taught him in that Red Cross class, and I didn't think a hard-on was a believable side effect of that particular condition.

So instead I rolled onto my stomach, propped my chin up on my hands, and said, "Nothing." Then I chewed on my bottom lip and looked up at him from underneath my lashes, hoping against all hope that he wouldn't call me out on the obvious lie or shove me off his bed.

Thankfully, he did neither. He rolled onto his stomach, mimicking my position once again, and continued our conversation from what seemed like hours earlier, even though it couldn't have been more than a minute or two.

"So are your parents married to each other?"

I had never been more grateful for a distraction, even if it meant talking about my parents' ugly divorce. Scott met my gaze the entire time I spoke. He looked sympathetic, nodded at all the right times, and asked follow-up questions. And suddenly, I realized he was listening, really listening, which was when I knew I was in big trouble.

Super-hot neighbor guy was enough to make my dick hard in close quarters. Add in nice and compassionate and an entirely different organ was on the line. After witnessing the pain that resulted from a crushed heart firsthand, I didn't think that was a good thing. So I answered his questions and told him about my fucked-up family, but instead of thinking about how good it'd feel to have him wrap me in his strong arms and hold me tight, I thought about how good it'd feel to wrap my hand around his dick and stroke him hard.

Having sex fantasies about the jock next door struck me as much safer than hoping to find something the grown-ups in my life didn't seem capable of achieving. So much so, that I wouldn't even let myself think the word. I had a hot new friend. End of story.

Chapter 2

INTRODUCTION

Charlie ("Chase") Rhodes

THE more I got to know Scott, the more I realized he was a case of the cover perfectly matching the book. What I mean is, his kind eyes, warm smile, and wholesome overall appearance weren't hiding someone who secretly yanked kitten tails or listened to death metal. When school started that fall, Scott joined Model UN, Key Club, and the football team. The first two were very impressive and civic-minded and blah, blah, blah. But have you seen those football uniforms? The pants are super tight in all the right places, and Scott had a body to die for.

And that right there, folks, brings me to the second picture in the album. It might be a little unorthodox, but fuck it, I love this shot: Scott in a huddle at the homecoming game, bent over, white pants, backside view. I didn't miss a single game all season, but to this day, I have no idea how that game is played or what a down is—in a football context, anyway. I am, however, intimately familiar with going down in the way that counts. Sorry, got distracted. Back to the picture.

Chapter 2

Charlie ("Chase") Rhodes

"HEY, homo, are you actually wearing girls' clothes now?" a nasty voice boomed from behind me. I tried to place it without turning around.

The words weren't anything I hadn't heard before. A lot, actually. But knowing which particular asshole said them generally helped me assess whether I should respond, duck, run, or a combination of all of the above. I thought about how depressing it was that there were enough candidates for this job at my school that I was struggling to identify the culprit. And that even accounted for the fact that I was now a sophomore, so one class of bully prospects had already graduated. That was, unless the new freshmen were going to make my life miserable too. I was so distracted being horrified at the idea that kids younger than me might give me a hard time that I forgot all about the guy currently giving me a hard time.

"Are you deaf, Rhodes? I asked you a question."

Right. Asshole asking what I assumed was a rhetorical question and apparently not having anything better to do than stand behind me and look at my ass while I got my books out of my locker. Hello, irony, pleased to meet you.

My friend Selina was at her locker right next to mine, and the two of us had frozen in concert. "I'm sorry, Charlie," she whispered to me without moving any part of her body.

Apparently, we were both going for the "if I can't see it, then it isn't real" approach to dealing with the situation at hand.

"It's okay. Hang tight. They'll leave after I'm gone."

I sighed deeply and stuffed as many books as I could fit into my backpack without damaging my brand-new-to-me ballet shoes. I had found a class at the youth center not too far from my apartment and I'd been spending every free minute practicing, which impressed my teacher so much that she found me the shoes. If I wanted to get in some practice time that afternoon, I'd have to avoid a broken leg. Taking a deep breath and holding the books I couldn't fit in my backpack against my chest like a protective shield, I turned around and appraised my bully du jour.

The sneering face was familiar, but I didn't know the guy's name. Ditto for the two guys standing behind him looking vaguely uncomfortable and yet amused. It was a hard combination to pull off, but brothers were making it happen. Go them. I darted my gaze around, trying to chart an escape path around the three big impediments that had me somewhat trapped against my locker.

"What kind of guy wears a pink sweater?" Asshole Number One asked.

Uh, one with a cool skin tone and great fashion sense. That sweater made my blue eyes pop and my pale skin look creamy and glowy. And side note, the jeans were hand-me-downs from my sister but the top was from the men's section at Filene's Basement, thank you very much.

Because he was new to my harassment scene, I wasn't sure whether this guy was the violent type. I did like that sweater, though, and I wasn't inclined to get blood on it, so rather than telling him he was way off base, I avoided eye contact and said, "Excuse me" while I tried to step around him.

"No," he said as he crossed his arms over his chest.

"Seriously?" I sighed tiredly.

"Yeah, seriously," he said as he stepped forward, looking two parts menacing and one part ridiculous.

I hadn't intended to say that out loud. Damn.

"Come on, you guys," Selina whispered. "Just leave us alone, okay?"

"You don't need to worry about that, porky," he said disdainfully. Then he dragged his gaze from her feet to her face and sneered. "Unless you stop stuffing your face and lose a ton of weight, you can count on a lot of alone time."

His buddies giggled. Selina blinked away tears. And I got pissed.

"Look"—what the fuck was his name?—"uh, whatever your name is, we're suitably scared or impressed or intimidated or whatever. But we need to get to class now, so move."

On the plus side, my comment got him to move. Unfortunately, rather than moving away from me, he moved toward me. Or, more precisely, he moved his hand toward my shoulder, connected hard, and shoved even harder. My books crashed to the floor, I went tumbling back against the locker, Selina grasped my arm to steady me, and Asshole clenched his fist, seemingly readying himself for the next round.

"Hey, Charlie. How's it going?" I tilted my head to the side and saw Scott Boone walk up behind and slightly to the left of Asshole. "Nicolas, right?" Scott said to Asshole, clueing me in on his name. "And you guys are"—he squinted and looked at the other two guys—"Troy and Steve?" he said as he patted their backs. Two bobbleheads nodded, and Scott somehow managed to smoothly move his huge frame between them and over to me. His gaze moved to the books at my feet. "Oh, your books fell," he said. Then he squatted down and stacked my books up. Once he had them neatly arranged with the largest on the bottom and the smallest on top, he straightened up. "We need to make sure this never happens again, Charlie." He said my name, but he was looking straight at Asshole Nicolas, who was standing there, slack-jawed.

"You know this guy, Scott?" Nicolas asked.

Scott shifted my books into one arm and wrapped the other around my shoulders. "Sure, I do," Scott said. "He's my next-door neighbor and a good friend. Hey, remember how Coach said the team is like a family?" He paused. "No, maybe you guys weren't there. I think he said it during varsity practice. Well, anyway, the team is like a family, so we need to have each other's backs on the field and off. Since Charlie's sort of like my family, I guess that means the team will have his back too." He took a step forward, keeping his arm around me. The three guys stepped aside to give us room. "Coach feels pretty strongly about that kind of thing. If you move up from JV, I'm sure you'll hear the speech."

The three big menaces nodded some more, mumbled, and then scattered. I stared up at Scott in awe.

"Aren't you going to introduce me to the guy who just saved your life?" Selina asked.

Scott blushed. "I'm sure you guys were fine. I didn't do anything," he said.

But he had to know that wasn't true. Scott had been in our school for less than two months, but already he was Mr. Popular. Making the varsity football team had helped with that, but mostly I chalked it up to his always present smile, upbeat personality, and dick-hardening good looks. He was the kind of guy everybody naturally gravitated toward, and frankly, I was constantly surprised he still gave me the time of day.

It had been one thing when he was new to the neighborhood and didn't know anybody. But once Scott got settled and made friends, I was certain he'd stop spending time with a scrawny sophomore who hung out with the theater geeks and the art dorks. But counter to my predictions, he never tried to put any space between us. If anything, we'd become even closer as we'd spent more time together.

"Scott, you remember my friend Selina, right?" I said. "Selina, I *know* you remember Scott, the guy who might not have saved my life, but who definitely saved me from another black eye or fat lip."

Scott's distressed gasp took me off guard. "Do you really think they would have hurt you, Charlie?" he asked. "I thought they were just screwing around and being jerks." He cupped my cheek and gently ran his fingers along the edge of my eye while he traced my bottom lip with his thumb. "If they give you any more trouble, you let me know right away, okay?"

A dip of my head was the best I could give him. My tongue suddenly felt thick in my mouth, and I was busy swallowing. The warning bell rang—I'm talking actual school bell here, not anything in my head—and Scott dropped his hand. "Gotta go," he said as he handed me my books. "My next class is on the other side of the building." I took my books and watched him jog away. "See you tonight," he shouted over his shoulder. Then he turned the corner.

"Wow," Selina said. "He's—"

"Yup." I sighed wistfully. "He sure is."

FRIDAY nights that fall consisted of football. Yup, I just wrote that sentence. Never in a million years would I have thought I'd be spending my free time at school, but there I was every Friday, climbing the bleachers, sometimes alone and sometimes with whatever friend I could wrangle into joining me. And it wasn't because I liked the game. In fact, the game made no sense whatsoever, the scent of hot dogs and processed cheese made me want to vomit, and more often than I care to recount, there was actual vomit from drunk classmates who liked to drink behind the bleachers. Sounds like good times, right? Strangely enough, I had fun at those games, despite all the olfactory horrors I just described.

Given all the time I'd been spending with Scott since that summer, I'd gotten to know his mother and stepfather pretty well. They were nice people, easygoing, and generally upbeat. Very much like Scott. I didn't know much about his father and stepmother other than what I heard from Scott, because they had moved to Nevada the week after we'd met. It turned out that was part of the reason Scott moved into my building. His parents each had an apartment in the same building for years and they hadn't left because they'd wanted to stay close together. But when Scott's stepmother took a position out of state, his mom decided it was time to relocate closer to her husband's job, which was around the corner from our building.

Anyway, I knew Scott's mom and stepdad, so I sat with them at the games and heard all sorts of adorable stories about Scott as a kid or Scott playing sports or Scott breathing or whatever. I took any grain of information thrown my way and tucked it into the place inside that lit up when I thought about the boy next door.

"Third down," Scott's stepfather said during the last quarter of the homecoming game. He leaned forward and rested his forearms over his knees.

I followed his gaze to the field. The players were huddled together, rehearsing for a porn shoot or exchanging hair tips or whatever the fuck they did when they were all sweaty, pressed close together, and bent over. I tried to adjust myself without being obvious and then picked up my camera and stood.

"I'm going to snap some shots," I said.

Whenever Scott saw my projects for photo class or art, he always said they were gorgeous and that I had a great eye. So I had taken to bringing my camera to the games, figuring it was a good opportunity to take pictures of him without coming across like a stalker. The party line was that I was taking pictures to send to Scott's dad. The behind-the-scenes truth was that I got a lot of personal satisfaction from these pictures. I was still trying to figure out how to justify a request for a shoot in the locker room.

"Thanks so much, Charlie," Scott's mom said. "Scott's father hates that he lives so far away now and can't see him play. The pictures help, and yours always turn out better than mine. Plus, you save me from having to lug a camera around."

"I'm happy to help," I said. *And also happy to use my zoom lens to zero in on your son's ass wearing those ridiculously tight leggings they call pants.* The wardrobe designer for football uniforms should win a fashion design award for pulling that shit off.

I walked over to the railing, lifted the camera to my eye, and moaned. Scott was directly in front of me, bent over, ass high. Good thing I'd packed an extra role of film, because I used up the rest of the one in the camera documenting Scott's fine posterior.

"Hey, Charlie. What'd I miss?" Selina asked as she sidled up next to me and took a noisy sip of her soda. "Ohhh, I see." We stood hip to hip and watched the game as we shared her drink. "Do you think he knows?" she asked me eventually.

"Knows what?" I asked nervously.

She raised one eyebrow.

Yeah, okay, so she realized I had a thing for Scott. I'd have had to be dead not to. Well, dead or straight.

"How long have you known that I'm, uh…." I licked my lips nervously. I'd never said the word out loud. What if she didn't actually know? What if she was talking about something else and once she found out she'd hate me? What if—

"That you're gay? I think you sealed the deal when you insisted on doing my hair and makeup for Todd Green's bar mitzvah," she said. "I'm still getting compliments about that, by the way. Everyone thinks I had it professionally done."

"So you don't mind?" I asked quietly.

She turned her head to look at me. "About the hair?" she asked, looking confused.

"No," I said. "About the, uh, about me being… you know."

"Gay, Charlie. You've gotta learn how to say it because the awkward stammering is just, well, awkward. And why should I mind? Who you like has nothing to do with me. Plus, this way we can ogle football players together." She turned back to the field. "Have you noticed those pants they wear? Oh my God."

"Yeah," I said as I lifted the camera back up. "I know."

Chapter 3

INTRODUCTION

Charlie ("Chase") Rhodes

AT THE risk of making you think I was a total stalker, I once took a picture of Scott from the street outside his bedroom window with my zoom lens. But it wasn't stalkery, honest. Okay, maybe a little.

Here's the deal: it was my sophomore year, his junior year, and I was coming home late one night. I glanced up and saw Scott opening his window. It was dark outside and he had his light on, so I could see him perfectly: every line of muscle on his chest, the way he filled out his white briefs, his tousled hair, like he hadn't combed it after his shower. I had a zoom lens on hand and I wasn't afraid to use it, so I quickly snapped the picture. The lighting wasn't great from that far away, and I wasn't holding the camera perfectly still in my mad rush to get the shot, so it turned out grainy. The picture quality wasn't even good enough for stroke-off material.

Now I bet you're wondering why I'm including it in the album. Well, it's because Scott opening his bedroom window at night was the backdrop for some of the most personal conversations of my life. We didn't need to see each other to talk. Hell, I think it actually made it easier to put it all out there when we didn't see a face reacting, judging.

Anyway, that's the next picture going into the scrapbook: a blurry Scott seen through a window. Oddly enough, it was this fuzzy image more than any other that I went back to over the years when I craved human connection, when I wanted to feel like I mattered to someone. No matter where I was, when I looked at that image, I could hear Scott's voice in my head, and every once in a while, I'd feel like I was falling in love for the first time all over again.

Chapter 3

Charlie ("Chase") Rhodes

SCOTT and I shared a wall. His bedroom was at the end of his apartment and mine was at the end of my apartment. We both had our beds adjacent to that wall, with the windows right above our heads. So when the weather was decent, we'd open our windows and lie in bed at night, talking.

Our bedroom windows were so close together that we shared a fire escape and when there was no traffic noise, we could just about hear each other whispering. Even with ambient noise, we could talk quietly and still make out every word. Sometimes, I'd close my eyes and pretend the wall was gone and Scott was right next to me, speaking intimately into my ear. I'd fantasize that any minute, he'd wrap a long arm around me and hold me close to his broad chest.

"Charlie? Are you awake?"

Something settled in my chest when I heard him calling out to me.

"Yeah," I answered.

"Oh, good," he said, sounding relieved. "Everyone went out after the game, and things ended up dragging longer than I expected. I was worried you'd be asleep."

"Nah," I answered. "I was up sketching until a little bit ago." The truth was, the drawings were just a way to occupy my time while I waited up for him. I'd gotten used to hearing Scott's voice every night before I went to sleep, and I didn't want to give that up.

"Cool. I'm gonna hit the head and brush my teeth and then I'll be ready for bed. Just wanted to make sure you were up."

I warmed inside at the knowledge that the first thing he thought to do when he got home was check in with me. I heard two thumps that I'd come to recognize as Scott's sneakers hitting the wall when he kicked them off, then the rustling of clothes being removed, and finally the scrape of Scott's bedroom door opening, telling me he was heading toward the bathroom. Just the sound of his familiar nightly routine was enough to make me relax. My eyelids had just drooped shut when I heard the squeak of his mattress springs.

"'Kay, I'm back," he said. "How was your night? What'd you do after the game?"

The last football game of the season had been that evening. Our school won, which was great. Everyone was excited and worked up. One of the players was having a house party to celebrate, and though Scott had encouraged me to go, I'd passed.

Being his friend meant I was no longer being cornered against my locker, but it didn't mean the jocks actually liked me or wanted me around. Sweet Scott didn't realize that. In his mind, I was his friend and they were his friends so it made sense for us all to hang out together. But I knew things weren't that simple, so I'd begged off the house party.

"I went for pizza with Selina and a couple other girls."

"That sounds fun," he said.

I shrugged even though he couldn't see me. "Yeah, it was okay."

There was a long pause and then Scott spoke again, his voice suddenly sounding strained. "You spend a lot of time with Selina," he pointed out.

"Yeah. We've been friends forever. How was the football party?" I asked. "I'm imagining that one scene from *Sixteen Candles*."

Scott chuckled. "The one with the guy trapped in the glass table and the toilet paper in the trees?" he asked.

I smiled at his amused tone. "Yup, that's the one."

"Uh, no. It wasn't like that. First off, Granger doesn't live in a mansion. Plus, he has common sense. And even if he didn't, he has neighbors who know how to call the cops."

"Okay, fair enough." I pulled my sheet up and shifted on the bed, trying to get comfortable. "So what was it like?"

"I dunno. It was a party. People sitting around talking and drinking beer, some token idiot crying about his girlfriend, a couple thinking they're being discreet when they sneak into a bedroom but everyone sees them. You know, a party."

I wasn't on the popular kids' party-invitation circuit, so I didn't actually know. But it seemed sort of pathetic to admit that, so instead I said, "Sounds fun."

"It was okay," he said and then gave one of his "I'm relaxed now" sighs, which were different from his "you're being ridiculous" sighs and his "I'm so tired I can fall asleep standing up but I still have more homework" sighs. Yup, I could differentiate his sighs. Quit judging me. He had golden blond hair, warm hazel eyes, and muscles fucking everywhere. You'd have memorized his sighs too. Trust me.

"So," he said quietly and paused before adding, "you went for pizza with Selina?"

"Yeah, Selina and these two other girls."

Another pause. "So it wasn't, like, a date?"

Uh, one moment to be shocked at the idea of dating my best friend, who I thought of like a sister, and then I started laughing hysterically at the thought of what Selina would say when I told her this story.

"I take it your uncontrolled laughter qualifies as a no?"

I gasped for air. "Of course not!" I said.

"Okay, okay. It's not, like, a crazy question or anything. Geez, you two spend a bunch of time together."

"She's my friend," I said as I tried to catch my breath. "And it's not *that* much time. I spend more time with you than I do with her."

"Yeah, but that's different. I'm a guy."

And that's when I lost the ability to breathe for a whole other reason. He was right, of course, but not in the way he meant. Actually, the difference he had pointed out was the exact reason I could never feel the way he was implying about Selina and the reason I felt exactly that way about him.

There are moments when you're suddenly and unexpectedly faced with a life-altering choice. You go one way and things continue as they are. You go another and, well, they don't. I was smack dab in the middle of one of those moments.

I could have told Scott right then. I could have said I was gay. I could have explained I didn't feel that way about girls. I could have admitted I felt that way about him. None of those confessions would have taken a lot of words, but they took more courage than I seemed able to muster. Because even though I like to go on and on about how hot he was or that I wanted to make out with him, the truth was I loved being Scott's friend.

He was always a great listener. We joked around and laughed together. Even watching TV or some goofy movie was more fun when I was doing it with Scott. So, yeah, my friend was hot and droolworthy and all that, but most of all, he was my friend. And I couldn't bring myself to risk losing any part of that.

"Charlie? Did you fall asleep?" Scott asked, making me realize I'd gotten lost in my head. Again.

"No, I'm up." I didn't even smirk at the potential double entendre.

"'Kay, good. 'Cause I'm not ready to crash yet and I didn't get to talk to you all day. Hey, did you see me make that touchdown?" He sounded so damn proud. It was cute.

"'Course I did. I even got a great picture of it."

"Yeah? Cool."

"I snapped one of you being pummeled too," I told him.

"Very nice, Charlie," he said sarcastically.

"Hey, you were flying through the air like Superman. It'll be a great picture," I said with a snicker. Then I turned on my side and settled in for a night rehashing the last game of the season and listening to Scott's voice and laughter.

"ARE you excited for tonight?" I asked Scott, trying to sound upbeat.

I was glad he was focusing on his shirt as he was buttoning it because if he had been looking at my face, he would have been able to read me well enough to know I wasn't at all happy about his plans for the that night. It was senior prom and Scott had a date.

I'd been lucky up to that point—Scott wasn't much of a dater. It was funny, actually, how oblivious he was. I'd always tease him when yet another girl would try to get his attention and he'd totally miss it. One time, and I swear this is true, he offered a cheerleader a tissue to help wipe whatever was in her eye. The girl had been twirling her hair and batting her eyelashes, and he implied she had some sort of medical condition. I'm damn proud of the fact that I managed to hold in my laughter until she was out of earshot.

Anyway, I was no longer laughing, because *my* Scott was going to be getting all touchy-feely with Melinda. Not that there was anything wrong with Melinda. And not that Scott knew I thought of him as mine. Mostly because I still hadn't gathered the courage to tell him. But regardless, I hated the idea of him going on a date.

"I don't understand these stupid tuxedos," Scott grumbled into the mirror. He had gotten his shirt buttoned up and tucked in and now he was fiddling with his cummerbund. "What is this thing? Is it like a belt? Why do I need a belt?"

I was sprawled across his bed, lying on my back and propped up on my elbows as I watched him. "What on earth are you doing?" I asked.

"I'm tying this belt thing," he grumbled as he wrapped the cummerbund around his waist and tied it on the side like a sash.

"What are you, a pirate?" I said with a laugh. I got up and walked over to him. "Why are you doing it like that?"

He shot his hands up in the air in defeat, the black fabric dangling from his fingers.

"How am I supposed to tie it?"

"Here." I swiped the cummerbund from his hand. "Let me do it." I shook it out and then held it up straight in front of him. "See, this part goes in the front and the clasps go in the back." I pressed it against his belly and wrapped my arms around him to close it.

Scott was much bigger than me, so for my arms to reach around him, I had to stand really close. I had been so amused by his helplessness with the tuxedo it took me way longer than it normally would have to realize I was pressing my body against his and I could feel his rapid breath on my head, my face so close to his body that his scent surrounded me. I moved my lower torso back, not wanting him to feel my reaction to being so close to him. My hands started shaking and I was having trouble fiddling with the clasp.

"You got it?" Scott asked, his voice sounding huskier than usual this close up.

"Uh, yeah, almost," I answered breathlessly. "I think this would be easier if I was behind you." I took his big hand in mine and pressed it against his belly. "Hold this in place." I stepped behind him and took in a deep, calming breath, then lifted the fabric and connected the clasps. "There you go," I said as I stepped a bit to the side and flattened the pleats while we both looked at him in the mirror. "You look amazing."

I had my right hand on his lower back and my left on his belly, flattening the cummerbund. He covered my hand with his larger one, stopping my movement. I raised my gaze, and our eyes met in the mirror.

"Yeah?" he asked. "You think I look good?"

I wanted to tell him he always looked good. I wanted to say "good" was an understatement. To me, Scott Boone was gorgeous, whether in wrinkled pajama pants or cutoff jeans or a fancy tuxedo. His sparkling hazel eyes, his dirty-blond hair, his golden skin, his broad frame, all of those things did it for me in a big way. So big, in fact, it was a wonder he hadn't yet picked up on my feelings for him.

Scott could read me so well, it was only a matter of time before he realized my reaction to him wasn't exactly buddy-buddy. It would be better if I told him, I realized, but not then, not right before he was leaving for prom, not until I had a little more time to figure out the right words.

So instead, I took in a deep breath and smiled broadly. "Yup," I said. "You look like James Bond."

He arched one eyebrow. "James Bond, huh?"

I grinned and bobbed my head. "Boone. Scott Boone."

"You're a goofball." He smiled fondly at me and then let out a loud breath. "Okay, I have to go pick up Melinda." He looked around the room. "Where'd I put the corsage?"

I saw a clear plastic box next to his bed. "Is this it?" I picked it up and looked at the blue flower inside. "It's pretty." I ran my finger over the box. "What's it called?"

"What? The flower?" Scott shrugged. "I don't know. Hydrangea or something." He took the box from me and said, "Grab your camera. My mom's gonna want pictures before she lets me leave the apartment. She promised my dad she'd send enough that he'd feel like he was here in person. You know how much he hates missing this stuff."

He picked his jacket up from the back of his chair, I snagged my camera from where I'd left it on the bed, and we walked toward his bedroom door. Suddenly, he paused with his hand on the doorknob and looked at me.

"Charlie?" he whispered.

"Yeah?"

His gaze locked on mine, but he didn't say anything for several long seconds; he just licked his lips and furrowed his brow. "Thank you," he said eventually.

I wasn't sure what he was thanking me for, but it didn't make a difference. My response would have been the same no matter what.

"Anytime," I said.

$$Chapter\ 4$$

INTRODUCTION

Charlie ("Chase") Rhodes

THIS one isn't a picture, but it's still going in the album. I'm not usually one to fixate on dates or times. I've been late to enough parties and meetings and missed enough flights to prove that fact. But there are a few things, a few dates, I'll never forget. The very first one was Scott's prom night. Well, technically, it was the next day, because midnight had passed.

When the year ended, I tore the page out of my calendar and I've kept it ever since, folded into a tiny square and stuffed into a pocket in my wallet. It traveled with me as I moved from apartment to apartment, from city to city; it kept me company in cars, subways, trains, airplanes, hell, even on a cruise ship. It's all creased and worn, but I still have it—the piece of paper marking the date of my first kiss. Our first kiss.

I've gotten more skilled at using my lips and tongue since then—we both have. But that first kiss... there's never been anything else quite like it.

Chapter 4

Charlie ("Chase") Rhodes

"YOU were out late," Scott's disembodied voice said the second I opened my window.

"I saw your light on when I was walking up, but I was sure you'd left it on or something," I answered. "It's barely midnight. What are you doing home?"

"What do you mean? Prom ended at eleven."

I smiled. "Well, yeah, but usually people go out after. Are you already in bed?"

"Yeah," he answered. "Just reading a little."

"Okay, give me a minute to get washed up." Less than five minutes later, I was in my boxer shorts crawling under my blanket. "I'm back," I said as I flicked off the light on my nightstand.

"Where were you?" Scott asked.

"Uh, the bathroom." I furrowed my brow. "I told you I was going to get ready for bed."

"No, not just now. Where were you tonight? You never stay out this late." He paused, and when he spoke again, he was so quiet I almost couldn't hear him. "I thought you'd be here when I got back."

He sounded sad or disappointed or something. I wondered if he'd had a bad night.

"I went to a movie with Selina and then we got some pie at the diner on the corner. Is everything okay?"

Truthfully, if I had known Scott was home, I would have wrapped things up earlier. Selina had been exhausted, but I didn't want to go home and obsess about when Scott would be back or what he was doing or whether he was going to follow the time-honored tradition of boffing his prom date. And because she was a good friend, Selina kept me company and distracted me with funny stories about her family in Puerto Rico, where she planned to spend the summer.

"Yeah," Scott said. He was quiet for a few breaths. "I just missed you tonight."

My heart came crashing to a stop and then started jackhammering in my chest. Scott and I were friends—close friends, even. We spent a bunch of time together, laughed a lot, talked. But saying we missed each other because we were apart for a handful of hours? No, that was outside the bounds of our relationship.

"Did something happen tonight?" I asked as I tried to work out what was going on with him.

"No," he answered. "Melinda wanted to, but I... no."

I pushed down the queasy feeling in my stomach that came when I was forced to think about Scott touching someone else and focused on being a good friend. Scott was forever there for me when I needed to unload about my dad, and he was endlessly supportive of my ever-increasing interest in dance; it was my turn to lend a shoulder.

"So, uh, you guys were making out and she wanted to take it further than you were willing to go?" I asked.

"No!" he yelled loud enough to wake up his mom and stepdad. "No," he said again, more quietly this time. "She wanted to make out. I wanted to come home." There was a short pause and then he said, "To be with you. I wanted to come home to be with you."

"You wanted to be with me instead of making out?"

Though he didn't answer, I knew Scott hadn't fallen asleep because I heard his sheets rustling, then him walking around his room, and finally a clanging sound. It took me a few seconds to register what it was—the sound of footsteps on the iron fire escape. I jerked my head up and sure enough, Scott Boone was standing outside of my bedroom window.

"Scott?" I said as I scrambled up to a sitting position in my bed. "What's going on?"

"It's not that I wanted to be with you *instead* of making out." He gulped and chewed on his bottom lip as he dropped his gaze to the floor. "The thing is, I, uh—" He took in a deep breath. "I wanted to make out, but not with Melinda." He raised his head and locked his gaze with mine. "I want to do that with you, Charlie."

For the first time since I'd met Scott, I suddenly had the feeling that maybe my crush wasn't so hopelessly one-sided. That realization was only a little less surprising than if Scott had announced he was a demon from the planet Herpes coming to kidnap me at gunpoint. Wait. Do demons come from planets or do they come from hell? And would I get extra credit in health class for naming my imaginary demon after an STD?

"Charlie?" Scott whispered hoarsely, redirecting my attention back to him. He was standing at my window wearing cutoff sweats and looking about three shades paler than normal with the moonlight glowing behind him.

"Do you want to come in?" I asked him.

"Come in?"

"Yeah. I mean, it's, uh, windy out there or noisy or freezing hot or freezing cold." I stopped rambling and smiled at my friend, hoping that even in the low light he could see the happiness in my eyes. "I'm no expert, but I'm pretty sure that whole making-out thing you mentioned will be much easier if we're in same room."

He looked equal parts relieved and nervous as he crawled over the window ledge and onto my bed. I was already sitting. He knelt in front of me with his backside resting on his heels. And we looked at each other. Just looked, for the longest time.

I remember that his blond hair was slightly disheveled and sticking up on the right side. I remember that he had a bed crease from the corner of his eye down across his cheek. I remember that he had more silky blond hair on his chest than the last time I'd seen him without his shirt on. And I remember that he was looking at me like I mattered, like I was important, like he wanted me.

"Scott," I finally choked out, and then he lunged. He tangled his fingers in the back of my hair, clasped my shoulder, and pressed his lips to mine. It wasn't artful—our noses bumped, his tooth snagged on my lip, and I sort of licked his chin. But, oh Lord, was it ever hot. And I'm not going to qualify that by saying it was hot to my sixteen-year-old self, because that level of raw, unadulterated need is sexy at any age. And to know that the boy I'd wanted for so long felt the same about me, well, let's just say that with our first kiss, Scott Boone captured a part of my heart, and no matter what happened after that day, that part of me would always belong to him.

"HEY," Scott said, and then he rubbed his nose back and forth against mine.

We were sitting in his room, on his bed. He had his back to the wall, legs spread and stretched in front of him. I was sitting between his thighs, my legs draped over his, my arms flung over his shoulders. We were supposed to be doing homework, and we had been, for a while, until we got distracted and started kissing.

We had both had summer jobs that summer—me working reception at dance studio that let me take free classes, and him handing out towels at a local gym. But whenever we weren't working, the two of us had been together. In some ways, it was exactly like it had been before. We'd laugh and joke around. We'd talk about our families, our hopes for the future. But in other ways it was different. After that first kiss, it was like the walls came down and we were always touching each other, smiling at each other, kissing each other.

"Hey," I answered and grinned.

"I love kissing you, Charlie." He nipped my chin. "But we have to take a rest and work, okay? I have a calculus test tomorrow, and I got through the last one by the skin of my teeth."

"You got a 90 percent," I scoffed.

"I know," he said with a solemn nod. "One more wrong answer and I'd have missed my A."

One corner of my mouth tilted up, but I held back my laughter. To me, a C was good enough, but Scott had a 4.0 grade average, and in his mind, if he got less than an A on anything, he might as well have failed. We were a month into the new school year, and he was busy with football again, so his studying time was limited as it was. He didn't need me to make it worse.

"Okay," I said as I scooted off his lap. "I'll take off and you can call me when—"

"No." He grasped my knee. "You don't have to go. Don't you have homework? Bring it over and we can study together."

"I was just gonna practice a little." I had moved just about everything other than my bed out of my room and Scott had helped me screw a pole into the wall horizontally so I could use it as a dance bar. We hung a bathroom mirror someone had pulled out of their apartment behind it and I was set.

"Perfect." He beamed. "I'll pack up my books and come over to your apartment."

My heart thumped harder in my chest. It happened every time I was reminded that Scott wanted to be with me. "Yeah?" I asked quietly, feeling pleased deep down.

"'Course. You know how much I love watching you dance. It'll be perfect."

I did know. Scott had always been supportive of what was quickly turning into my obsession. He would sit and let me show him some moves I'd learned, listen to me talk about what I thought would make a great show, and sometimes I'd walk out of class to find him waiting for me outside the windowed wall. "Thanks, Scotty," I said.

We packed up his books and walked out of his room.

"Where are you heading, boys?" Lauren, Scott's mother, asked.

"We're going to Charlie's. He's gonna practice and I'm gonna study." Scott walked over to his mom, leaned down, and kissed her cheek. "What're we having for dinner?"

"I was thinking taco night," she said, and then she looked over to me. "Are you joining us for dinner, Charlie?"

"Yeah, he is," Scott answered before I could. He came back over to me, rested one hand on my lower back, and led us toward the front door. "We'll be back in a bit."

My mother worked nights and my sister had gotten a job waitressing at a local bar, so she rarely got home before three in the morning. As a result, I was usually home alone in the evenings, and Scott's parents had taken to including me in their family dinners.

"Does it bother your mom that I'm always eating your food?" I asked as soon as we closed the door behind us. "I can stay home tonight."

Scott had his backpack flung over his right shoulder, and he wrapped his left arm around me. "My mom loves you. No way would she let you stay home alone instead of eating with us."

I pushed my key into the first of the locks on the front door. "You sure?" I bit my bottom lip nervously. "I don't want to overstay my welcome."

Scott pressed his front to my back and dipped down, nuzzling my neck as I finished unlocking and opening my front door. "Yeah, I'm sure," he whispered roughly. "Besides," he added, "you're not exactly eating us out of house and home. I've seen birds with a higher caloric intake."

I walked into my apartment with Scott right behind me. And I mean that literally—he stayed close enough that I could feel his breath on my neck. I shivered and swallowed hard. "Caloric intake? Is that one of those fancy terms you learned in AP Bio, smarty-pants?"

He skated his hand over my ribs, down my side, and over my ass. Then he pinched me and bounced away, raising his hand in front of him protectively.

"Hey!" I yelped and rubbed my abused butt. "What'd you do that for?'

"Well, mostly because you were teasing me, and also because I could." He was grinning, his eyes twinkling. He was so damn cute I couldn't even pretend to be mad.

"Nutball."

"I'm a nutball, am I?"

"Yeah."

"And what, pray tell, is a nutball?" he teased.

"Shut up."

"Is it like one of those cheese balls coated with nuts that Hickory Farms sells at Christmastime?"

"I'm going to smack you," I said, feigning anger.

"What if I like that?" He waggled his eyebrows at me.

I shot forward, trying to get to his ribs, knowing how ticklish he was.

He let his backpack drop to the floor and jumped back. "Ooooh, close but no cigar. Better luck next time."

I squinted my eyes and clenched my fists. "That's it, Boone. You're toast."

Before I could do anything, he turned and ran into my bedroom. I gave chase and caught up with him at the foot of my bed and we went tumbling down, him flopping on his back, me landing on top of him. He cupped my ass

34

with one hand and tangled the other in my too-long hair. "Hi," he said and then pulled me down for a kiss.

I immediately melted against him and moaned as he pushed his tongue into my mouth and slid it against mine. When we finally separated, long minutes later, I tilted my head to the side and looked at him. "Did you plan this?'

"Me? Never."

But he pulled my face down again, kissing me harder, and this time he rolled his hips up and pulled my ass forward, encouraging more friction.

"I thought you had to study," I panted.

"Later," he said.

I kissed my way across his jaw and over to his earlobe. "But your test."

He thrust up, letting me feel his erection. "Charlie," he whimpered. "I'm so hard."

I almost came in my pants. "Oh, God," I said. Then I buried my face against his neck and rolled my hips, giving us both what we needed.

Scott gasped, moving his torso up and down as he caressed my ass and said my name over and over again. I rutted against him, whimpering and sucking in air.

"Gonna," I said. "Scotty, Scotty, I… gonna…."

"Me too." He thrust up hard and held me in place as he shouted out, "Charlie!"

That was all it took for me to lose it. I clutched his shoulders and groaned as I coated my briefs.

"Oh, wow." I let out a deep breath and settled on top of him, my muscles feeling warm and loose.

He petted the back of my head and combed his fingers through my hair. "Yeah," he said. "Exactly."

We lay together, our hearts beating in sync. I kissed and nibbled on his neck and ear. He massaged my nape and rubbed my back. It felt so good and so right, I was willing to deal with sticky underwear if it meant not having to move away from Scott.

"Charlie?"

I flattened my hands on either side of his shoulders and straightened my arms, raising my upper body so our eyes could meet. "Yeah?"

He grinned, reached up, and pushed my hair out of my face. "I might have planned it a little."

Chapter 5

INTRODUCTION

Charlie ("Chase") Rhodes

FAMILY is a funny thing. Our parents, our siblings, they're always there, you know? Deep inside of us. We don't choose them, we get mad at them, and sometimes we feel like we don't want them. But we always, always need them.

I know guys who haven't talked to their parents in decades, some because they passed and some because they're bigoted pieces of shit. These guys are doing fine without Mom and Dad around. They have successful careers, great friends; some even have families of their own. But no matter what they've accomplished in their lives, no matter how many people are around who love and cherish them, there's still an empty hole that long-gone family left behind that nobody else will ever fill.

Don't get me wrong; it's not like they're crying into their soup every night. Like I said, they're happy with their lives, with who they are, really happy. But no matter how old we get, no matter what we achieve, we always have that little kid we once were somewhere inside of us. And that kid, well, that kid can't help but love his mother and father, and even that pesky sister or brother.

When it's bad, family can wound you so deep, you're sure healing from a combination herpes infection and skydiving accident would be easier. But when it's good, when you feel that love and know it's always going to be there, no matter what, when you have a strong net underneath you every day, ready to catch you if you fall; well, then there's nothing better than having family. And that, my friend, is the thing about our parents and siblings, annoying though they might be—even if we don't always like them, they're ours and we can't help but love them.

Which brings me to the next pictures I'm putting into the album—a collage of our families, mine and Scott's. My mother worked a lot after my father left. She didn't burden me with the details, but I pieced together some things—money that should have been going to bills went to girls and gambling, and by the time he walked out, there was nothing left except a huge amount of debt and a good dose of betrayal. But even though she was gone most of the time and exhausted when she was home, I always knew my mom loved me. Same with my older sister, Rachel. And given how much time I spent at Scott's place, his mom and stepdad became almost like a second set of parents to me.

All those years living a few feet away from each other, and I don't have a single snapshot of the six of us together. But I have a great picture of my mother and Scott's mom, taking a rare break to sit down at the kitchen table and drink tea. I have a picture of Scott with his stepdad, at the edge of their seats, their faces tense, and fists clenched as they watched the end of what I'm guessing was the most important sports game of all time. I have a picture of me and Rachel, sticking our tongues out at the camera and giving each other bunny ears. And I even have a picture of Scott with his dad and stepmom when they came into town for Christmas one year.

Stepparents, divorce, sibling squabbling, money problems, long-distance separation. Family. All in all, I'd say Scott and I both won the lottery in that department.

Chapter 5

Charlie ("Chase") Rhodes

"ARE you hungry, Charlie?" I looked up from the doodle of a pirouette I'd been drawing and raised one eyebrow in response to my sister's ridiculous question. She snorted. "Of course you are. I swear, ever since you turned seventeen you've been eating more than Mom and me combined, and for the life of me I don't know where you put it."

I shrugged and said, "I get a lot of exercise. Dance isn't just spinning around in circles, you know."

Rachel pushed her pointer finger on my right bicep. "Okay, let's see the muscle," she said. "Flex."

I raised both arms and tightened my muscles.

"Holy shit," Rachel said. "Wow, little brother. For a small guy, you are seriously ripped. No wonder Scott follows you around like a lost puppy."

"Hardy, har, har."

She ruffled my hair. "I'm making spaghetti and meatballs. You want some?" I nodded. "So did Scott decide where he's going to school next year?"

"Yeah, he's going to SUNY. It's close enough that he can live at his mom's and save money."

My sister rolled her eyes and smirked. "Yeah, that's why he's going there. It has nothing to do with staying close to you."

I blushed. "It's a good school," I insisted.

"So is UNLV, and his father lives in Nevada, so he can get in-state tuition and get the hell away from miserable winters and snow."

"Since when do you know so much about Nevada?" I asked with a scowl.

"Since Christmas, when I heard no less than five conversations between your boyfriend and his father where the man practically begged Scott to move closer to him after graduation and Scott stammered and came up with the most ridiculous bullshit reasons ever why he wouldn't go." She paused and looked at me with a suddenly serious expression. "You need to tell him to be careful. Seriously, that boy cannot tell a believable lie."

"In some circles that would be considered a good thing, Rachel."

She shrugged. "Speaking of Scott, where is he tonight?" she asked.

"Some graduation run-through thing." I twirled my ballpoint pen like a baton and wondered whether I could fashion some sort of flame add-on for each side. Maybe Q-tips would work.

"I'm surprised his mom didn't insist you eat dinner with them anyway."

"Lauren and Dave are going out with people from her work," I answered. If they had been home, my sister would have been right. Scott's mom was really good to me. She'd been treating me like part of their family almost from the first day I'd met Scott going on two years earlier.

"Mmmm," my sister said dreamily as she stirred the sauce. "Dave is soooo sexy."

I threw my pen at her back. "Dave is sooooo married. Say it with me now: *married.*"

She looked back at me over her shoulder and scowled. "I know. I was joking around." She paused. "Well, not about the sexy part, because that's true, but you know what I mean."

My sister's last two boyfriends had been, and I quote, "in the process of getting a divorce." I can't tell you what that means because I didn't meet one at all and the other I spent about thirty seconds with when I ran into him with my sister on the street. But I'd overheard conversations between my gorgeous sister and my angry mother, and the word "homewrecker" was thrown around more than once.

"Hopefully you don't mean what I think you mean, because, again, he is married. Also, he is twice your age. And he lives next door. With his wife. You remember Lauren, right? Dave's wife, also known as the woman he married."

"Cut it out, Charlie. I get enough of this shit from Mom. At least she has a reason because of all of Dad's crap. Besides, I know Dave is off limits and I have no intention of coming on to him." Her back was to me so I couldn't see her face, but I could tell from her tone that she was more hurt than she was angry.

I got up, walked over to her, circled my arm around her belly, and rested my chin on her shoulder. "Everything okay?" I asked quietly.

She sighed and I felt the tension leave her body. "Yeah, I'm fine. I just get sick of being judged all the time, you know? So I'm into guys in their forties instead of guys in their twenties. Why should that matter? I'm twenty years old. Why can't I date whoever I want without getting shit about it?"

Rachel had always been supportive of me. When we were younger, we went to the same school, and though I had always been one of the social outcasts, Rachel had been Miss Popular. With her long auburn hair, bright-blue eyes, flawless skin, and early-to-curve figure, she was the girl all the boys wanted to date and the one who had invitations to sit at every girl's lunch table. And she had never, not once, complained about being saddled with a little brother who didn't rank in the same social circle. She used to let me hang around with her, glared at anyone who even thought of making fun of me, and generally took care of me. She was a good sister.

"I didn't mean to judge you," I said. "I'm sorry."

She patted my arm with her free hand. "It's okay. I'm probably being a little hypersensitive because I found out Rodney's wife didn't know anything about their pending divorce."

Rodney was the current boyfriend. Age: unknown. Marital status: uh, yeah.

I stepped away from her, planted both hands on the counter behind me, and lifted myself up so I could sit down next to the stove and talk to my sister while she cooked. "So he lied to you?" I asked.

She took in a deep breath. "Yup. He lied. Shocker there, right? I should have known I was nothing but a piece on the side. Why else would a successful ad exec want to spend time with a big-chested bimbo?"

"Hey, now," I said. "You are not a bimbo. You took AP classes in high school."

"I took AP Spanish," she said as she looked up and met my gaze. "Did I ever tell you that Mr. Ramirez was going through a divorce?"

My jaw dropped. "Shut up! He's, like, a thousand years old."

"He was forty-seven and he was fit for his age." She went back to stirring the sauce.

Yeah, I had to give her that. The Spanish teacher had a smoking body for an old guy. "Hey!" I said excitedly. "I just remembered something."

"What's that?"

"Mr. Ramirez is divorced. Like, all the way divorced. I heard him saying something about his ex-wife last fall."

"Great," she said with no conviction whatsoever. "I'm no longer a hussy because the teacher I was banging senior year actually ended up with a failed marriage. Go me."

I chuckled. "Nice use of 'banging.'"

My sister grinned. "Thanks. I might have done better in my English class if I'd been asked to use bang or blow in a sentence instead of blithe."

"What does blithe mean?" I asked.

"Uh." Rachel furrowed her brow and chewed on her bottom lip. "I still have no clue."

"Huh." I swallowed hard and steeled my nerves. "And what about blow?"

She froze and panned her gaze over to me slowly. "You're seventeen years old and you're asking me what it means to blow someone?"

I rubbed my lips together anxiously. "I'm not so much asking what it means… more, uh…." I gulped again and tried to figure out how to articulate what I wanted to know.

Rachel turned off the burner, carried the pasta pot to the sink and poured it into the colander, and then walked back over to me and hopped onto the counter so we were shoulder to shoulder.

"So you're looking for tips on how to give a killer BJ?" she asked, grinning wickedly.

I buried my face in my hands and mumbled, "Oh God."

My sister cackled. "Well, you've come to the right person. I just happen to be a subject matter expert." She elbowed my ribs. "And if you're lucky, deep-throating might run in the family."

The heat radiating off my face was so intense it was a wonder my skin didn't melt off. "Oh God," I said again.

The laughing stopped and Rachel nudged my shoulder with hers. "Hey, Charlie," she said.

"Uh-huh." I still didn't look up.

"Sex isn't anything to be ashamed of. It's natural and beautiful, and don't you let anyone tell you different or make you feel guilty for enjoying it, okay?"

I dropped my hands and met her gaze. "Yeah?" I asked shyly.

She dipped her chin. "Definitely. Now, blowjobs. The secret comes down to angles."

"Angles?"

"Yup," my sister said. And then she started explaining something way more critical than high school English.

MY BACK hit Scott's bedroom wall, and then he slammed his mouth onto mine and shoved his tongue inside.

"You're sure your parents are going to be out late?" I panted when we separated for a two-second air break.

"Uh-huh."

The break was over and our lips met again. Scott had my face cupped in his hands, I was gripping his shoulders, and both of us were rubbing our groins against whatever part of each other's body we could reach. If we didn't stop, I was going to cum in my pants. Again. Normally, that wasn't a bad thing. I mean, hello? Orgasm equals good, right? But I had been wanting to try out my new hard-earned (pun intended) BJ knowledge, and with Scott's parents out of the house, the time was right.

I pulled back and breathlessly said, "Scott."

He licked and nibbled his way across my jaw and over to my ear. "Uh-huh." His hot breath on my sensitive skin made me shiver, and when he took my earlobe into his mouth and sucked, I bucked forward and cried out. It took every ounce of self-control I had not to spend myself right then.

"Scott," I said again. He chewed on my neck, rubbed his erection against my belly, and dropped his hand from my face, somehow managing to touch every part of my heated body at the same time. My shoulders were squeezed, my nipples pinched, and my shirt lifted, exposing my skin to cold air and hot hands. "Scott," I repeated breathlessly.

"Yeah?"

With one hand, he rubbed up to my chest, while he played with my belly button with the other. All the while, he continued rocking, making me feel how hard he was, how long, how desperate.

"Ungh, seriously, Scott, we need to stop before it's too late."

The rocking got faster, his caresses rougher, and the biting along my neck and jaw turned into hard, frantic sucking. "Too late for what?" he gasped out as he finally pulled his face back and met my gaze.

"I—" My eyes rolled back and I moaned in response to a particularly well-placed thrust of his pelvis, and then I swallowed hard and looked him in the eyes. "I want to taste you, to suck you."

His eyes widened and his nostrils flared. Those motions that were driving me to the brink sped up. "Suck me?" he said, his voice sounding deeper than usual.

Somehow I managed to make my hands move and I gripped his hips, trying to still his movements. "Your dick, Scott. I want to suck your dick."

"Charlie!" he shouted. Then he ground against me one last time and yelled so loud I was sure my mother would hear him next door. "Ah! Charlie!"

He slumped over me and gripped my waist, his entire body trembling as his breath drummed against my neck. I was so needy by that point, so primed for it, I thought I would die if I didn't get off right at that moment. But with his body blanketing mine, holding me in place, I couldn't reach my dick, couldn't give myself that last bit of friction I needed to take me over the edge.

"Scott," I whined as I wiggled.

Before I could say another word, he had his big hands at my waistband. He unfastened my jeans, shoved his hand inside, and wrapped my shaft in welcome warmth. "Come on," he said. "Give it to me, Charlie." I looked up and met his gaze. "Give it to me," he said again. So I did. My cock swelled and pulsed white, hot seed all over his hand and my stomach, making both of us moan.

I dropped my forehead onto his heaving chest, leaning on him as I inhaled his scent. He pressed his lips to the top of my head, wiped his sticky hand on his shirt, and then wrapped both arms around me, holding me close.

"Charlie?" he whispered.

"Mmm hmm."

"I love you."

For a few long seconds, all I could do was clutch him like a lifeline and blink unwanted wetness out of my eyes. I took in a few calming breaths, swallowed down the emotion clogging my throat, and finally answered, "I love you too, Scotty." He hugged me even tighter and I took a shaky breath. "Love you so much."

Chapter 6

INTRODUCTION

Charlie ("Chase") Rhodes

ARE you ready for the next picture? Well, doesn't matter either way because it's going in the album regardless. There are three reasons why I'm choosing this shot: (1) for the first and only time in my life, I'm taller than Scott in it, (2) I have rockin' abs, and those puppies are on display, and (3) Cher. Really, I could have just gone with the third one and left it at that. I think we can all agree it would have been reason enough.

Halloween is my favorite holiday, bar none. This isn't a huge shock, I know. I mean, it is the gayest holiday of the year. But somewhere around age twelve, it was no longer socially acceptable to wear costumes unless you went as some sort of a bloody dead thing, which... ewww. So I couldn't dress up, which sucked the big one. But then the most amazing thing happened—I grew up and suddenly there were Halloween parties I could go to. And the best part was they involved costumes.

The first time this happened was my senior year in high school, which was Scott's freshman year in college. A bunch of his buddies shared a run-down old house near campus, and the tradition was that whoever rented that house had to throw a bash on Halloween. They'd kind of go with a creepy haunted house theme, which, given the condition of the place, didn't take much in the way of decorations. And everybody would dress up, show up, and get wasted. Normal college party stuff.

If there had been a contest for best costume, I'm sure Scott and I would have taken it. I worked my ass off for the better part of two weeks putting together a replica of Cher's Oscar outfit circa 1986. You remember the one—beaded black skirt hovering just above the pubic area, a barely there top with a grid of black bands going up the neck, and the pièce de résistance: a headpiece with two-foot black feathers coming out in all directions like a lion's mane.

Look, I don't want to brag, but my kids win best costume at every fucking Halloween carnival around. When I first started out, I designed costumes for some off-off-off Broadway musicals that were low-budget enough to require dancers to work production. I know how to make kick-ass costumes. And I got my start that Halloween, so I think documenting it is important.

This picture is of me and Scott standing on his buddy's front porch. I'm channeling Cher with one hand on my hip and my best sultry expression aimed at the camera. Scott has his arm around me and he's wearing his trademark grin, a tux, black wig, and fake mustache. It's a great picture commemorating a fun night. And, side note, that night I made Scott promise to never, ever grow facial hair.

Chapter 6

Charlie ("Chase") Rhodes

TWO knocks on our shared wall, a pause, and then three more knocks. Now that Scott and I were in different schools, it wasn't as easy to line up our schedules, so we had implemented that code to let each other know when we got home.

I was in my final year of high school. Moment of silence in honor of the upcoming ending of that horror. Seriously, I couldn't wait to be done with school. My brainy, beautiful Scott, on the other hand, actually enjoyed homework and books and even math, so he had started college at SUNY in September.

"You rang," I said in my best Lurch voice as I did a stiff-legged limp into his room, completing the impression.

Scott was pulling books out of his messenger bag and then stacking them on his desk. His hair was messy, his clothes rumpled. When he heard me come in, he looked up, grinned, and his eyes sparkled. Damn, but was he ever gorgeous.

"Hey, baby," he said.

"So?" I asked. He shook his head. "No?" I sighed and flopped onto his bed. "Scotty, the party is in two weeks."

"I know."

My guy leaned against his desk, crossed his arms over his broad chest, and looked at me appraisingly. I stuck my tongue out at him.

"Well, if you know, then help me. I'm not a miracle worker and you already told me a zombie was no good, same with the Joker, and now Lurch. We need to figure out costumes now or it'll be too late."

"Too late for what?"

I raised both eyebrows. "Uh, too late to get our costumes together for your friend's Halloween party," I answered. "Do you know what you're going as yet?" Scott shook his head. I scowled. "Don't pretend like you forgot. I've been reminding you constantly."

"I haven't forgotten," he answered as he walked over to the bed and then draped himself over me, supporting himself on his knees and elbows while he gazed into my eyes. "I'm just waiting for you to decide on yours first." I huffed and he smiled. "You're cute when you're pouty."

"I'm not pouting."

"No? Well, this lip sticking out right here—" He dipped his face and pulled my bottom lip between both of his, licked and sucked it gently, and then released me. "—says otherwise." I shivered. One corner of Scott's mouth tilted up, and he gave me a heated look. "I love that," he whispered.

"What?" My voice sounded like it was being dragged over gravel.

"The way you respond to me," he answered. "Your cheeks get red, your heart starts racing, and you get hard." He rolled his body so his belly dragged against my erection. I whimpered. "Yeah, see? That too. The noises you make, baby. And your eyes... I love your eyes. I'd say they're like the sky, but I've never seen the sky look so blue, and when you want me, they get darker. Did you know that? Like, right now, they're almost navy."

I licked my lips and gulped as I tried to catch my breath. "I always want you, Scotty."

He rested his forehead against mine. "I know," he said as he rubbed our noses together. "That's another thing I love." He paused for a minute and then spoke again, his breath ghosting over my lips. "You know what else I love about you, Charlie?"

"What?" I asked quietly. We were the only ones home, but there was something painfully intimate about that moment we were sharing and I didn't want to disturb it with a loud voice.

"I love that you don't let anyone scare you away from being yourself. Like some of those jerks at school used to give you a hard time about your clothes, but you're still dressing exactly the same, right?"

I didn't correct his use of the past tense. No sense in letting him know about the sneers his old teammates had continued giving me until they'd graduated. It'd only make him mad. Besides, as a senior, people pretty much left me alone. That, and I stopped caring, stopped noticing. I was almost out of that place, anyway, and then I'd never have to see any of those assholes again. They didn't matter. No way was I going to let them change who I was.

"The purple V-neck cashmere sweater I'm wearing right now confirms that, yeah."

He dragged his hand down my side. "It looks good on you, and I like how soft it is." Scott looked deep into my eyes. "I always like how you look, Charlie. That hasn't changed just because I'm in college now, and it won't change in front of my new friends. I love you exactly the way you are."

I'm not as smart as Scott, never have been, so he always figures things out way before me, even when those things *are* me. But I was slowly catching up.

"Is that what I've been doing?" I asked him. "Trying to be somebody else?"

"Well—" Scott kissed me gently. "You love Halloween more than anyone I know, and the past couple of years you've complained about being too old to dress up. Now we're going to a party and everyone will be wearing costumes, so you can finally go all-out." He kissed me again, longer this time, nibbled on my lips and swiped his tongue into my mouth. "Do you actually want to go as Lurch?"

I blushed and shook my head. "No. His clothes are awful, and I don't want to limp around all night."

Scott cupped my cheek. "Yeah, I didn't figure you'd want that."

"I don't want to go as a zombie or the Joker either," I admitted. "They're ugly."

"Okay."

I chewed on my bottom lip and looked up at him from beneath my lashes. "So you really don't care what I go as at all? I mean, they're your friends. I don't want to embarrass you."

"You could never embarrass me, baby. Besides, no matter what you wear, I'll have the hottest date there."

When Scott said things like that or when he looked at me like I was funny or special or something, my heart felt like a balloon with a pump

50

inside, like it was growing and growing and it wouldn't stop until it filled me completely, until he filled me completely.

"Well, then," I said. "It looks like I have some thinking to do."

He kissed the tip of my nose. "Sounds good."

"Hey, Scotty?"

"Yeah?"

"When're your parents coming home?"

Just like that, his gaze turned carnal. "They're having dinner at their friends' place tonight. They usually stay out late when they go there."

We both stayed perfectly still. He stared at me. I stared at him. Then we both flew into action.

I clawed at Scott's shirt, pushing it up his chest. He went for my jeans, yanking them open and then shoving them down to my thighs. Then he pulled his shirt over his head, tossed it in the corner, and started working on his jeans. At the same time, I tugged my sweater over my head and wiggled and pushed my jeans down to my feet, where they got stuck on my shoes. Then we were both sort of stuck. Me: naked from neck to ankles, but my jeans, briefs, and shoes still on. Him: naked from neck to knee, kneeling, with the same items bunched together.

We looked at each other and, at almost the same moment, cracked up laughing.

"What?" Scott chuckled out as he wiped tears from his eyes. "Don't I look sexy like this?" He swayed from side to side, making his semihard dick swing lewdly.

"Cut it out!" I gasped. "I can't breathe."

"What?" He shook his ass, and everything else. "I'm dancing!"

There was only one way to stop the insanity. I did a crunch so my face was level with his groin, then I grasped his ass and pulled him forward until his dick connected with my lips. The crown slid across my lower lip, over my cheek, and pressed against my ear. It wasn't the smoothest move, but it managed to make Scott stop laughing and start panting. I leaned back, reached for the hot, hard shaft, and brought it to my mouth.

"Charlie," Scott moaned as he tangled his fingers in my hair.

I had about six months of blowjob experience under my belt, and, if the noises Scott made when I went down on him were any indication, I wasn't too shabby at it. It was a good thing Scott enjoyed it so much, because taking his throbbing erection into my mouth was one of the great joys in life. I loved the taste of him, loved how he stretched my lips, loved his scent, so I sucked the man down with gusto every chance I got.

The first swipe of my tongue across Scott's glans made both of us groan with arousal. I lapped at his slit, taking his moisture into my mouth, loving his flavor; then I suckled gently on his crown and rubbed my fist up and down his shaft.

"You're so good at that." He rocked his hips forward, pushing more of his erection into my mouth.

I sucked harder, encouraging him to move as fast as he wanted. No discernible gag reflex meant I could always take whatever Scott wanted to give me. After a couple of thrusts, that turned out to be all of him.

Scott moved in and out until his balls were smacking my chin. "God! I don't know how you do that." He pulled out a couple of inches and then pushed right back inside my mouth. "Feels so good, baby." He tightened his grip in my hair and increased his speed. "So good, so good, so good," he chanted.

I knew what was coming next and I wanted to join him, so I moved one hand to my own shaft and kept the other on his hip for support.

"Can't last, Charlie," he said, sounding almost pained. "You're so good. I…. Oh God, I… Charlie!"

My own cock was pulsing streams of ejaculate over my fist just as Scott's throbbed and shot onto my tongue. I waited until he was done and then I swallowed down his offering as he petted my hair.

"Charlie," he sighed. "Love you so much."

I leaned back and pulled him down on top of me, whimpering happily when the weight of his nude body pinned me to the bed and he nuzzled my neck. I was sated and content, even if my shoes were still on and my now wrinkled jeans were tangled over them.

I felt Scott fidgeting above me and then his shoes clunked on the floor. I followed his lead and toed mine off before pushing my jeans and briefs off with my feet. Once we were both settled, I took us back to the conversation we'd been having before our heated interlude and asked, "How about a theme costume?"

"What do you mean?"

"I was thinking that you don't have a costume picked out yet either, so maybe we can choose something that goes together."

52

"Great idea."

"Yeah?"

He lifted his head and met my gaze. "Totally. I think it'll be fun. Do you have anything in particular in mind?"

"Well, I have one possibility," I said nervously.

"Lay it on me."

"It's fine if you don't want to. No big deal. I can think of something else."

"Charlie." He raised an eyebrow and smiled encouragingly, telling me without words that I had nothing to worry about. Of course, he had used actual words to convey the same thing earlier, and I knew I could always take Scott at his word. If he said I could choose any costume I wanted for his friend's party, that he wouldn't be uncomfortable no matter what I wore, then I trusted it to be true.

"Sonny and Cher," I blurted out. "I'll be Cher."

When he didn't say anything right away, I worried he'd think it was weird for me to want to dress in drag for Halloween. But then he beamed and said, "That's a great idea, baby. You'll make a smokin' Cher."

"Well, you're much better-looking than Sonny, but I still think it'll be fun."

Scott traced my eyebrow with one finger. "I'm glad you like how I look." His cheeks reddened. "Remember that first day we met? I was outside the building. You walked out and I felt like someone punched me in the gut." He took in a deep breath and looked into my eyes. "You're so beautiful, Charlie."

"I took a picture of you," I confessed.

"You've taken lots of pictures of me."

"That day, I mean. I saw you from my window and took a picture."

He looked immensely proud. "Oh yeah?"

I could have teased him, but Scott always made me feel so wanted, so good about myself, I didn't want to hold back my feelings for him. So I nodded and said, "Yes. Then I ran outside so I could meet you and... well, you remember how smooth I was after that."

"What I remember is the most gorgeous guy I'd ever seen came tumbling down the stairs and wanting more than anything to be the person who got to pick him up when he fell."

I swallowed down the emotion in my throat and met his gaze. "You are that person, Scotty."

He dropped his forehead against mine and whispered, "Good. That's all I want to be."

Chapter 7

INTRODUCTION

Charlie ("Chase") Rhodes

SHOES. Pregnant pause while you read that one-word sentence and wonder what the fuck I'm talking about. Okay, that was fun.

Now, here's why I'm bringing up footwear. First off, I like it. I don't waste a ton of money on clothes, but I don't enjoy looking like a slob, so I probably spend more than I should, and that includes investing in a nice pair of loafers. I have a friend who jokes that you can tell a guy is straight by looking at his shoes. Basically, his theory is that if a man's shoes are awful, he likes boobs. It's pretty funny watching him point people out and make his assessments, and I'm going to admit that he's pretty spot-on most of the time. Now, my guess is that right about now you're wondering where I'm going with this little anecdote. The answer is: nowhere. I just think it's a funny story and talking about shoes made me think of it.

Back to my reason for this topic, I'm a size eight and a half. Scott is a thirteen. You stopped paying attention, right? At this very moment you're thinking about our dicks and if the old adage about dick size being related to shoe size is true. Cut it out. That's a bunch of bullshit perpetrated by NBA stars. And I'm not just saying that because I measure in at barely five feet six inches.

Anyway, I'm smaller than Scott. He is taller, broader, thicker, just bigger, and his shoes are no exception. Now, I know some guys might be intimidated by someone who is a solid nine inches taller, someone whose body can wrap around theirs so completely that almost no part of them, front or back, is exposed. I'm not one of those guys. I have always found Scott's size a huge turn-on. And that (finally) brings me to the next photo in the album.

At eighteen, I wasn't quite brave enough to venture into sex videos or pictures, but one evening, when Scott went into the hall to talk to his father on the phone, I noticed our shoes. They were in a pile in the corner of his room where we'd kicked them off before sprawling in front of the TV and playing video games—my All Stars and his Nikes. Seeing the difference in the sizes of those shoes immediately brought to my mind the difference in the sizes of our bodies.

I ignored my sudden erection, grabbed my camera, and snapped a picture. And that's the next picture in the album—our shoes standing proxy for our very different body types. Almost twenty years later, I still get hard looking at it.

(By the way, going back to that whole shoe-size-dick-size thing, Scott has a good three inches on me in the dick department. Three long, hard, satisfying inches. Just saying.)

Chapter 7

Charlie ("Chase") Rhodes

THE shouting woke me up. My mother and my sister were being so damn loud, they probably woke up the whole building. They fought a lot, had always fought a lot, but not like that night. I was about to put the pillow over my head to block out the worst of the noise when my door slammed open so hard it bounced off the wall.

I shot up, gasped, and said, "What's going on?"

Rachel was standing in my doorway; the low light coming in from the front room let me see her face, so I knew she had been crying. "Sorry," she said. "I didn't mean to wake you up, but I wanted to say good-bye."

We both flinched when we heard my mother's bedroom door slam. Wow, looked like we were the drama family that night.

"What do you mean good-bye?"

She walked over and sat down on my bed. "I'm moving to Vegas with Rodney."

"But you guys broke up last year. And he's married. And Vegas?" I sort of screeched the last one.

"Well, his divorce is going to be final next week, he's moving, and he wants to take me with him."

"But... Vegas?"

Rachel bobbed her head. "There's no snow there, lots of jobs, he already rented a nice house with a yard and trees. I've seen pictures; it's perfect. I just know I'll like living there."

Great. She saw pictures of some house on the other side of the country and the next thing you know she was going to drop everything and go there with a guy who had done nothing but lie to her, the woman he was married to, and probably everybody else in the greater tri-state area, which was why he needed to move out west. No wonder my mother had been yelling. I wanted to do the same thing but forced myself to act calm.

"And what about Rodney?" I asked. "Are you sure you trust him after everything that happened?"

She shrugged. "He says he loves me, told me he'd marry me once everything was settled with his ex, but—" She sighed deeply. "You know I haven't been happy here for a long time, Charlie. I'm sick of fighting with Mom about every part of my life. It's too damn expensive for me to move out. Everything is gray and dirty. You can only see little bits of the sky above the buildings. Even if things don't work out with Rodney, this is my chance to get out." She met my gaze. "Tell me you understand."

I got all of that, I did. Rachel was twenty-one years old and she had to live her own life in whatever way she wanted. I loved my sister and I didn't want to lose her, but if moving to Nevada was what she wanted to do, I wouldn't try to guilt her into staying. I blinked away tears and tried to think of something supportive to say. "I'll miss you," was all I could get out.

Rachel threw her arms around me and buried her face in my neck. "I'll call you all the time, and maybe you can come visit in the winter. We'll wear shorts and jog outside."

"Okay," I said and then sniffled as I returned her hug, squeezing her tightly.

After a few minutes, she sat up, cleared her throat, and wiped her palms over her eyes. "Now I'm all puffy and red."

"Just a little." I smiled faintly. "But you're still the prettiest girl around."

We looked at each other for another few seconds, and then she took a deep breath, got up, and walked out of my room.

I'm not going to say that my sister walked out of my life that night, but I will tell you that phone calls and rare visits aren't the same as living together under one roof. Rachel never moved back to New York, and to this day, I haven't stopped missing her.

"CHARLIE! Scott's here and I'm leaving for work," my mom called out.

I walked out into the front room and found myself smiling just at the sight of my boyfriend. He always did that to me. Scott caught my gaze and beamed. "Hey," he said.

"Hi," I answered. My mom was digging through her purse. "When are you getting home?" I asked her.

She located her keys and then put her purse and another bag over her shoulder and reached for the doorknob. "I have a twelve tonight and then I'm doing home care so I won't be back until late tomorrow."

I walked over and kissed her cheek. "You look tired, Mom."

"Don't worry. I'm fine. Lock up after me, okay?"

"Sure."

She left and I closed the door with a sigh.

"Your mom does look beat," Scott whispered into my ear. He had walked up right behind me and pressed his chest to my back. He was big and warm and strong and hard. Always hard.

I ground back against him. "Yeah," I said. "She works so much. I don't make enough at the dance studio to pay for more than just my own clothes and food and stuff."

Scott kissed the back of my neck. "Someday you will. You're really talented, baby. Someday you'll be dancing on Broadway. You'll see. People are going to pay tons of money to watch you."

"I hope so."

He rubbed circles on my stomach and kissed his way from my earlobe, across my jaw, to my chin. I leaned back and he supported my weight easily. It felt good—his touch, the sound of his breath, the feeling of his heart beating against me—and I let myself relax. Like they so often did, those gentle caresses got lower and lower until Scott was rubbing his palm against my groin and cupping my balls.

I was hard because, well, I was eighteen and my boyfriend was in the room so, yeah, instant erection, and I thought I knew where things were going, but then he surprised me and said, "You wanna watch a show or play Mario or something?"

I glanced back at him over my shoulder and furrowed my brow in confusion.

Scott raised one corner of his mouth. "I promise to ravage you later, but I think maybe you need to unwind a little first. You've been working a lot too and studying for finals."

"I'm fine," I said.

"You sound like your mother," he pointed out.

"Mario sounds good."

Scott chuckled. "See that? I'm a master persuader."

"Whatever." I rolled my eyes.

We had just settled in for the game—me lying on the floor in front of the TV, Scott sprawled on the couch with the controller in his hand—when there was a loud, fast knock on the door.

"Scott!" his mom shouted.

He jumped to his feet and rushed to the door, opening the three locks in fast succession before swinging it open. "Is everything okay?" he asked.

She held the portable phone out to him. "It's your father," she said. "He has news."

From the smile on her face, I knew it was nothing bad. Scott put the phone up to his ear and said, "Hello?" Then he covered his other ear and stepped into the hallway. Lauren followed him.

Our apartments were close enough that the phone worked sometimes, but it was usually pretty spotty, so I figured he was going to walk a bit closer to his apartment. I paused the game and scrambled up to get a drink. On my way to the kitchen, I noticed our shoes in the corner of the room under a window. They were in a pile, but you could see all four and a ray of light was coming through the window and hitting them just right. It struck me as a good shot, so I got my camera and snapped a few pictures.

By the time I was done, I'd decided to put an end to Scott's mission to cheer me up through electronics and instead ask him to cheer me up through ejaculation. I had just put away my camera when I heard Scott walk back in. I strutted out to him, ready to pour on the seduction, but I stopped short when I saw how pale he looked.

"What's wrong?" I asked and then rushed over to him. "Did something happen to your dad or Julia?"

He shook his head slowly, paused, and then nodded. "Nothing is wrong, but something did happen. Julia is pregnant." He smiled broadly and made a sound that was dangerously close to a giggle. "I'm going to have a sister!"

It took me a minute to catch up and then I hugged him. "That's great!" I said. "But I thought you said they couldn't have kids."

"I did. That's what they thought too. And she's almost forty-five, so they gave up on it a long time ago, but somehow it finally happened. My dad said Julia is doing well and the doctor said the baby seems healthy, so in four or five months, I'm getting a baby sister."

It was exciting for a while. After she hung up with Scott's dad, Lauren came running in cheering and bouncing about the new baby being added to their family. By then, I was so used to his parents and how close all four of them were that it didn't even strike me as weird that the woman felt so connected to her ex's upcoming birth.

Anyway, I understood how wonderful it was to have a sibling. Even though she now lived thousands of miles away, Rachel was still my confidant and, along with Scott and Selina, one of my best friends. And besides, Scott was happy, so I was happy. But, as I was often apt to do, I didn't think through the details of the Scott-having-a-sister thing. Maybe if I had, I would have been better prepared when I walked into Scott's room a week later and found him sitting on his bed looking nervous as hell.

"Hi," I said.

"Hey." He opened his arms and I crawled into his lap. "I have news, Charlie." He said it just like that. He had news. And he didn't even wait for me to respond before he continued. "I'm going to transfer to UNLV."

My jaw dropped. "You're leaving me?" I said, before I could think about how self-centered that sounded.

"No." He shook his head. "I'm not leaving you. I'm just going to move for a few years so I can be closer to my dad and Julia and the new baby. School is cheap there, and I can live in the dorms and still be less than a half hour from my dad's house, so I can really get to know her. But it's only until graduation, Charlie, I promise, and then I'll be back."

In retrospect, I think I was in shock and didn't truly snap out of it until after he'd gone. I remember promises of frequent phone calls and letters and visits. I remember the two of us being all over each other whenever we were alone, which, frankly, was no different than how we'd been from our first mutual orgasm. But I don't remember feeling sad, truly feeling sad, until about a week after Scott moved away.

I went straight from school to my job at the dance studio. He had an evening study group. Between those things and the time change and who knows what else, we missed our daily phone call. I'm pretty sure that's when it really hit me that he was gone and all the promises about things staying exactly the same between us weren't going to come to pass.

It took a little longer than that for things to unravel. We hung in there for close to a year. But Lauren and Dave went to Nevada for every holiday because Scott's dad had a giant house, and it made more sense than having the now-four-person Nevada contingent fly to New York and crowd together in a small apartment. It was too expensive for me to fly there, and even if it wasn't, I couldn't afford to take time off work. I was saving every penny to take more dance classes, working hard auditioning for whatever community theater had casting calls. That meant those frequent visits we'd planned to make didn't happen.

With everything we both had going on, the telephone calls eventually became less frequent. Then the letters died off all together. And at some point, one of us suggested that we call things off, at least until he moved back to town. But he loved being a big part of his sister's life, loved the slower pace out West, loved the warm weather, so I think we both knew by then that he wasn't ever coming back.

In retrospect, I realize that at twenty and twenty-one, it would have been damn hard to maintain a relationship even if we'd lived in the same city. Doing it long-distance was more than we could handle. But at the time, all I could do was ache bone deep and wonder what I'd done wrong, why I'd driven Scott away.

For another year or two, we called each other on birthdays, and I still spent a good bit of time with his mom and stepdad. But then I started feeling like just when I was getting a little better, something would remind me of Scott and I'd regress all over again. So I asked him to stop calling and I did the same.

I danced every minute I wasn't working and landed enough roles to be able to move out of my mom's place and into a dump in Queens. I cut my hair. I started going by Chase Rhodes, my childhood nickname, because my agent said it made me sound like a star. I even tried listening to country music. Basically, I did everything humanly possible to put Scott Boone in my rearview mirror and, eventually, I succeeded. Mostly.

Chapter 8

INTRODUCTION

Charlie ("Chase") Rhodes

I KNOW I should have warned you that breakup was coming, but, honestly, it hurts like a motherfucker either way and I didn't want to bring you down, so I figured tearing the Band-Aid off would be the least painful approach. As for me, well, about the only good thing I can say about the next few years in my life is that struggle and pain breed good art. So my heart was broken, my soul fractured, but I danced well. Totally worth it, right? Yeah, I never thought so either. Fucking sucked, but I survived. Bear with me here, and I'll tell you how.

I'm going to skip the gory, miserable shit because you don't want to know about how many nights I cried and how many assholes I dated. You don't want to hear about the times I walked along the street in the middle of the night and fucking screamed, or about how more than once, I fell to my knees and wondered if I was actually bleeding inside because it hurt so bad. And even if you do want to know about that time in my life, I honestly don't think I can dredge it up without getting depressed all over again, which is not something I'm willing to endure. So trust me when I tell you that my emotional state and my personal life were dreary and shitty and fucking pathetic for a long time.

But then one night, out of nowhere, a beam of light came in. Well, maybe that's not the best description because it makes him sound angelic, which is a piss-poor analogy for a man who rarely smiled, thought everyone on earth was annoying, and carried so much anger and pain inside him that he made my depressed soul seem joy-filled. But despite all that, there was something about him that drew me, something that made me feel an emotion other than misery and pain, something that gave me a glimmer of hope that maybe, just maybe my heart wasn't completely dead. His name was Adan Navarro, and the next picture in the album is one I took the night I met him.

My friend Selina and I walked into a bar—yes, I realize this sounds like the beginning of a bad joke, and there were times it felt that way. Anyway, we walked into the bar, and some girl neither of us had ever met came running over, waving one of those disposable cameras.

"You guys! You guys! Can you take our picture? Pleaaaase?"

Sister was drunk as a motherfuckin' skunk. Her shirt was stained with unidentifiable substances, and her skirt was twisted around and rucked up dangerously high. I mean, if she had sat on a barstool at that point, she'd have had to make sure her underwear was providing good coverage or else she'd have gotten *intimately* familiar with whatever shit was on there.

"Sure," Selina said. "No problem." Then she looked at me expectantly.

I chuckled and said, "Sure. Give me the camera."

"Thank you!" she squealed as she threw her arms around me and gave me a hug. "I totally owe you!" I had no idea what she owed or how I could collect, but I figured it didn't matter because by morning she'd forget all about me and be praying to the porcelain god. "Here." She handed me the camera and then hustled back to her friends.

"Want me to hold your bag?" Selina asked, gesturing to my dance bag. I had just left rehearsal and didn't have time to go home and change before meeting Selina for our biweekly catch-up session.

"Sure. Thanks." I gave her my bag and walked over to the group of people.

Judging by the way they were swaying and their bleary eyes, I gathered the whole lot of them was toasted. But they were happy drunks, laughing and smiling and wrapping their arms around each other affectionately.

"Okay, get a little closer together so I can fit you all in the frame." I gestured with my hand as I spoke. When I had them situated so that they all fit, I brought the camera up to my face. "Okay, on the count of three. One, two…." I tried to snap the picture. Tried being the operative word.

"Uh, I think you're out of film here." I held the camera out to Drunk Girl.

"Oh no!" She looked positively crestfallen. "We have to take a picture. We have to!" She turned to her friends and sounded frantic as she asked, "Does anybody have a camera? You guys! Do any of you have a camera?"

When nobody handed over a camera, her lip trembled, and I thought she was wasted enough to start crying, so I quickly said, "I have one. I can use mine, okay?" I flicked my gaze to Selina. "It's in my bag. Can you please grab it for me?"

"You do?" Drunk Girl looked awestruck, as if I'd said I had a time machine or a spaceship or Dolce & Gabbana's entire summer collection in my bag. "You guys, he has a camera!" she shouted gleefully as she threw herself back into her clustered group of friends. "The cute guy has a camera!"

Selina was cracking up and I was chuckling as I brought my camera up to my face.

"To the end of our second year!" Drunk Girl screamed, pumping her hand in the air.

"Only one more to go!" someone else threw in.

"I'm totally trashed!" a third person added.

I looked through viewfinder, gave them the countdown, and took the shot. Later, when I saw the picture, I noticed him at the edge of the group, standing as far as possible without being standoffish and smiling in a way that looked more like a grimace. His neatly combed black hair, ramrod straight posture, and dark-brown eyes, focused right on the camera, told me he hadn't been drinking as long or as much as the rest of his crew, which made sense to me once I got to know him and realized he was a complete control freak. He's a big guy and he tends to tower over everyone; that night was no exception. Plus, he has some pockmarks on his face, scars from acne in his youth, which give him an intimidating appearance. Though most people wouldn't have described Adan as handsome, his intensity, his strength, and that bit of rough in his voice made him sexy as hell in my book.

It isn't the most flattering photo I have of Adan, but it is the best reflection of the man I met that night. There were times later when I thought I snuck in under the cool exterior, times I thought the heat between us would melt all that ice away for good. But when I think of him back then, back when it all began, that rough, aloof guy is who I see in my head. So that picture of Adan clustered at a bar with his law school classmates is the next one I'm putting in the album.

Chapter *8*

Adan Navarro

THE second he walked into that bar, I knew he was gay. No straight guy would wear mint-green pants or a sleeveless white shirt, both tight enough to show *everything* underneath. And then there was his hair. Not the color, which was a rich, shiny brown. But the way he had it cut—long on the sides and even longer on top, and styled in a swirl thing. We were in a bar, so the lighting wasn't great, but when I peered at his lips, I was pretty sure he had something on them to make them look so shiny and soft. And maybe his eyelashes too, because they couldn't be that long naturally.

I was willing to bet the guy got his ass kicked on a regular basis, looking like that. Not that I condoned violence, but I figured he was asking for it. Otherwise he could have dialed down the whole "I'm here, I'm queer" look.

When I came out to my family, they were shocked. I was too strong, too big, too masculine to be gay. That's what they said. Two years and twenty-five hundred miles later, they still refused to accept the fact that I wouldn't someday walk into my parents' house with a woman on my arm. But I knew it wasn't going to happen, no matter how many times my mother cried or my father gave me the cold shoulder.

People like *him* were what my family thought of when they heard the word "gay"—the high laugh, the perfectly arched eyebrows, the slim, tight body on display in those flashy clothes. I hated being lumped in with those types of guys because I was nothing like them—I looked like a normal guy. The way I saw it, wanting to be with a man meant wanting to be with a *man*, and I couldn't relate to somebody like that—someone frilly who flounced and sashayed and might as well have had rainbows and glitter coming out of his ass. But for some inexplicable reason, I couldn't take my eyes off him.

When the flaming photographer finally finished dealing with the camera crisis and snapped the picture, Tracy, a woman from my con law class said, "Thank you so much!" She bounced over to him, stood really close, and put her hand on his chest. It should have been funny, watching her bark so hard up the wrong tree, but instead of laughing, I found myself frowning. And walking toward them.

"I'm Tracy Harrison," she said. "What's your name?" I couldn't be sure from my angle, but it looked like she was fluttering her lashes.

"I'm Chase Rhodes." His blue eyes twinkled as he gestured toward the woman who'd walked in with him. "And this is Selina Hernandez."

"I appreciate this, Chase," Tracy said dramatically. "I totally owe you."

"You're fine," Chase said with a chuckle. "Don't worry about it."

"No, seriously," Tracy insisted. "I'm a good baker. I can make you cookies or brownies and drop them off when I pick up the film. Where do you live?"

"Queens. But I work on—"

"I'll get the film from him," I said inexplicably. I marched over and grasped his bicep, knocking away Tracy's hand in the process. "With the way he looks, I seriously doubt he eats brownies." I tugged on his arm and said, "Let's go," as I started pulling us toward the door.

"Uh, where're we going?" Chase asked me, amusement clear in his tone.

Was he laughing at me? I glared down at him and snapped, "To get that film for Tracy."

"The film's in my camera." He jiggled the camera at me.

"Oh." I frowned and then wondered why I felt disappointed. "Ahem, right." Chase raised one thin eyebrow and looked at me expectantly. Those lashes looked even longer up close, and his eyes were amazing, a clear turquoise with flecks of navy. I felt my dick filling in response to his attention, which pissed me off. "So why'd you need his address, Tracy?" I growled.

"To get the film," she said slowly, looking at me like I was the one not making sense.

"You heard Chase," I said. "He has the film. You were just trying to get his address!"

"Uh," Tracy said slowly. Then she shifted her gaze from my face to my hand, which was still wrapped around Chase's surprisingly firm bicep. "Oh," she said, her expression indicating that she finally understood something, probably the fact that her come-on had been transparent. "I see. Okay, Adan, you get the film from him. Just make sure to get it to me, okay?" Then she giggled and said, "Selina, right? Want to get a drink and leave these two alone?"

I felt heat rise up my neck when her implication registered.

"Sure," Selina said. She kissed Chase on the cheek, handed him his bag, and said, "Call me later, honey."

The two of them walked away, arm in arm, and I was left alone with a guy who looked like he had just stepped away from a Pride parade.

"So," he said, his voice taking on a singsongy quality.

"What?"

"I think you just cost me some home-baked brownies."

"What're you talking about?" I asked.

"Your friend Tracy"—he flicked his eyes toward the bar, where Tracy and Selina had gone—"said she was going to bake for me. But now that you've taken on the responsibility to collect the film, I'm out the brownies."

I was pretty sure he was flirting with me, and I didn't like it. We were in public, a bunch of my classmates were nearby, he wasn't my type, and, worst of all, it was making my dick so hard I ached.

"Collect the... just give me the film," I snapped. "We already established you have it."

"No can do," he said patiently. "I'm only halfway through the role."

"Then finish it off," I said. "I'm sure you can take a couple of pictures here really fast and then give me the roll and leave."

His eyes widened in surprise, and he yanked his arm away from me, making me realize that I hadn't let go. "Look, I don't know what your problem is, but I just got here and I'm not leaving until I have a drink with my friend."

"My problem?" I asked incredulously, taking a step forward to close the distance he had put between us. "What's *your* problem? Is it the cost of the film?" I reached for my wallet. "How much is it? I'll pay you for it."

"The problem," Chase said, no longer sounding amused or happy, "is that I have some of my pictures at the beginning of this roll, so I can't just hand it to you. I need to develop the film and then I can give you the negatives of your friends."

That made sense, actually. I wasn't sure why I hadn't thought of it. "Oh."

"Yeah, oh." He rolled his eyes. "You know what? My friend Selina works at the copy shop across the street. I'll leave the negatives there when they're ready. See ya."

Before I could think of what to say, he was sauntering off toward his friend at the bar. Damn, but for a little guy, he sure had a nice ass. Firm and round, it filled out those ridiculous pants so well they actually looked good.

His friend looked surprised and maybe a little sad when he walked up. But Tracy was all smiles, scooting over on her barstool and patting the sliver of wood, like they could share it. To my surprise, that was exactly what happened. Chase sat down and flung one leg over Tracy's, half of his fine ass on the stool and the other half on her thigh.

Before I could stop myself, or even realized I was doing it, I was stomping over to Chase. Whether he heard me approach or whether he noticed the panicked look Tracy threw over his shoulder, I didn't know, but Chase turned his head back, took one look at me, and let out an annoyed breath.

"What?" he asked.

I had no idea what to say. I had been rude to him earlier. Well, maybe not rude, but I supposed I could have been more polite. So I said, "Sorry."

"Are you asking me or telling me?" he said, squinting in frustration. I wanted to see his eyes sparkle again, like they had when he had been smiling and laughing.

"What do you mean?" I asked.

"You said it like it was a question. *Sorry?* Like you were asking me."

For the life of me, I couldn't understand why I was still standing there, letting this little flamer scold me.

"Hey, cutie, what can I get you?" the bartender asked Chase.

We weren't in a gay bar, so it took me off guard. But Chase wasn't thrown in the least. He turned back around, giving the smile I'd wanted to the Gigantor tending bar and said, "A lemon drop, please."

71

"No problem, doll." One side of the bartender's lips curled up. "I get off in about twenty minutes." He picked up a glass with one hand and the rimming sugar with the other, and waggled his eyebrows. "Should I rim you?"

"Cute," Chase said with a chuckle. "I—"

"There's a diner down on the corner. They have a three-layer chocolate cake."

Chase looked at me over his shoulder, seeming surprised by my comment. He wasn't alone. I was flying totally blind.

"Chocolate cake?" he said.

"Yeah, uh—" I gulped. "You said I owe you for the brownies, so, uh—" I shifted my gaze over to the bartender, who was smirking at us, and then back to those captivating eyes. "They have fruit pies too. If you like lemon."

He stared at me, as if he was looking for something. After a few beats, I started feeling like he was trying to decide if I was worthy of his time, which pissed me off, but just when I opened my mouth to tell him to forget it, he slid off the barstool.

"I like lemon," he said. "That hint of sour mixed in with the sweet is great."

"Catch you next time, Chase," the bartender said with a wink.

Chase waved to him, said good-bye to his friend, and then slid his bag over his shoulder. "Does the offer come with coffee?" he asked good-naturedly as we made our way out of the bar.

I was fixating on that bartender and the familiar way he spoke to Chase, so I didn't grasp his question. "Coffee?" I repeated.

"Yeah. Do I get coffee with my pie?"

"Are you fucking that bartender?" I asked instead of answering his question.

He slid to a stop right outside of the bar. "Seriously?" he asked.

"No," I said, realizing my question was out of line. He dipped his chin and we started walking again. "So, are you?" I asked, apparently unable to stop myself.

Instead of getting pissed, like I'd expected, he scoffed and said, "No. I'm not fucking the bartender."

"Oh." I scooted a little closer to him as we kept walking. "You fucking anybody else?"

He glanced at me. "Not right now, no." I got even closer. "How about you?" he asked.

"Not right now, no," I said with a grin.

He gave me that smile I'd been wanting, and I nudged his shoulder. "So, do you want to be?" I asked.

"Let's start with coffee, okay?" The humor was back in his tone.

"Sure, sure." I bobbed my head. "Coffee, pie, and then...."

We'd reached the diner and I pulled the door open and held it for him. He stepped close to me and tilted his head up so our eyes could meet. "Coffee, pie, a little conversation, and then I'm going home."

He stepped inside and I followed him to a booth. "Works for me," I said as I scooted in across from him. "You live close or do we need to take the train?"

"Wow, you're something else," he said, leaning back and crossing his arms over his chest. "Alone. I'm going home alone."

"Oh." The answer took me off guard. "Why?"

"Because we just met!" Chase looked truly surprised. "You always hop into bed with guys you just met?"

The way he said it, I understood the answer was supposed to be "no," so I kept my mouth shut.

"I see," he said after the silence had drawn on too long. He reached for his bag and started climbing out of his seat.

"Where're you going?" I asked as I reached out and grasped his arm, keeping him in place.

"Look," he said with a sigh. "You're super hot in that rough and tumble way, and quirky in a funny way, but this"—he moved his hand back and forth between us—"isn't gonna work and I don't wanna waste your time."

I started preening inside when he called me hot but it was immediately tempered when he described me as quirky, which didn't sound so good.

"What do you mean?" I said. "We're getting pie, remember? Pie is never a waste of time." I smiled, trying to put him at ease. "Sit down." I gestured to the seat with my chin.

73

He lowered himself back to the seat and let go of his bag just as the waitress arrived.

"What can I get for you boys?" she asked.

"He'll have a slice of lemon pie and a coffee," I said. "And I'll have a piece of the chocolate cake and a glass of milk."

She nodded and hustled away.

"Milk?" Chase asked. His expression seemed to be teasing again, but his eyes were twinkling so I let it go.

"Milk goes with chocolate cake," I answered. "Everybody knows that."

"Is that right?" he asked with a laugh.

"Yup." I nodded firmly. "It's, like, a law or something. I'm pretty sure I learned it in my first year."

"You're in law school?"

"Uh-huh."

"And those people in the bar are your friends from school?" he asked.

"They're in school with me, yeah," I said, not responding to the friend question. I didn't consider anybody in that bar a friend, not really. But that was okay, because I hadn't moved to New York to make friends, I had moved because Columbia was the top law school I'd gotten into and I wanted to get a good education followed by a great job.

The waitress came over with our food, which was a good opportunity to change the topic.

"So is your name really Chase Rhodes?" I said after taking a bite of cake.

"It's Charles, actually," he said with a chuckle. "But everybody calls me Chase now."

"Makes sense," I said after looking him over carefully. "You don't look like a Charles."

"No?" he asked. "What does a Charles look like?"

"I don't know." I shrugged. "Stuffy and proper and tall...." When I noticed his shoulders shaking, I stopped talking and flicked a little piece of cake at him.

"Hey!" he said, trying to look affronted but failing. "Don't throw food at me!"

"Well, then, don't laugh at me," I countered.

"You do realize you were describing the prince of England, right?"

I paused and thought it over. "Was I?"

"Yes!" he huffed.

"Huh. Well, that makes sense too."

He furrowed his brow. "Why does that make sense?"

"Because—" I took another bite of cake and waggled my eyebrows at him. "The prince of England probably wouldn't let me fuck him either."

"Well, I'm not the prince of England," Chase said meaningfully.

"And yet...." I let the sentence trail off and raised both eyebrows.

"This is yummy." He pushed his plate toward me. "Do you want a bite of my pie?"

"Is that some sort of euphemism for fucking you?"

He chuckled and rolled his eyes. "No, it isn't. I'm literally offering to share my pie with you."

"Then no."

Chase shook his head, pointed his fork at my plate, and said, "Eat your cake."

The little lilt when he talked, the way he styled his hair, the clothes he wore, hell, even the way he swayed when he walked—Chase Rhodes was not my type. But my dick hadn't gotten the memo and my chest swelled every time he smiled and looked up at me from underneath his too-long lashes, so I did what he asked and ate my cake.

Chapter 9

INTRODUCTION

Charlie ("Chase") Rhodes

TO TEMPER the icy, harsh picture of Adan I added to the album, the next one is going to show a completely different, and rarely seen, side of him. I took it when he was asleep on my couch a few days after our first date. He looked young and vulnerable when he was at rest, and it was such a contrast to his normally rigid, tense demeanor that when I saw him sleeping, I knew I had to record it on film.

I bet you're wondering why Adan was sleeping on my couch. So was I. Here's what happened.

I had dated a few guys after Scott, but not for long and not seriously. I had come to terms with that after a few years, figuring I'd had my great love young and that was that. So it surprised me when I kept thinking about Adan after that first night and it surprised me even more when the sound of his voice on the other end of my phone two days later had my heart doing a long-since-forgotten flip.

"What're you doing?" he asked after we'd gotten the obligatory hellos out of the way.

"Right now?" I sprayed spot remover on my sofa and scrubbed at it with an old kitchen sponge. "I'm cleaning someone else's jizz off the back of my couch."

He coughed and said, "Uh, nice. So you're a top? Wouldn't have thought it."

"Right." I scoffed, rolled my eyes, and scrubbed harder. "Seriously, though, I think this shit is set in for life. The guy must have, like, super semen or something."

He chuckled and said, "So Tracy's been bugging me about the pictures. When can I pick up the negatives?"

"Oh, yeah. I was in the darkroom today. I have them ready for you." I sat back on my haunches and sighed in resignation as I looked at the white marks on the dark faux-suede fabric. "I'm never having houseguests again."

"Ah, that explains it," Adan said.

"What?"

"Someone else's cum on your couch. So is he gone?"

"Who?" I asked.

"Your houseguest."

"Oh. Yeah. He left yesterday, but he didn't mention the little present his trick left on my furniture." I took a breath and started scrubbing some more. "Why are guys in New York such self-involved, inconsiderate narcissists?"

"Are you talking about me?" Adan asked, deadpan.

I laughed at his joke. Or at what I'd thought was a joke until he said, "What? Why're you laughing?"

"Uh." I paused and then told myself he was kidding. He had to be. It was the only reason anybody would respond to a comment about self-involved narcissists by asking if the comment was about him. "I was laughing at your joke," I said.

"What joke?" he asked.

Okay, so maybe a joke wasn't the *only* reason for that type of response. I decided to change the topic. "So how're you doing? Anything exciting going on?"

"I'm good," Adan said. "Just packing a bag."

"Yeah? You going away for the weekend?" I gave up on the couch and stood up, staring at it in frustration before setting the cleaner and sponge on my kitchen counter, which was within arm's reach, and trying to figure out how I could rearrange my meager furniture to hide the evidence.

"Yup," Adan said.

"Where're you heading?" I combed my fingers through my hair in frustration when I realized the space was too small to accommodate the couch in any other location.

"Queens," Adan said.

"Queens?" He lived in Manhattan. Going to Queens wasn't exactly a weekend getaway. And I lived in Queens, so I should know.

"Yup." I heard a door slam and the unmistakable sound of locks turning. "I'm picking up some film from a cute guy and then making a weekend of it."

I shook my head in amusement. "Did you just invite yourself to spend the weekend at my place?" I asked.

"Yup."

"What if I have plans?"

After a short pause he said, "Do you?"

"No," I admitted. "But I'm not sleeping with you. The 'just met' thing still holds."

"We'll see," he said.

"Adan, I'm serious." Though I probably didn't sound serious through the chuckling.

"That's okay," he said. "We already established your couch is empty. So I can crash there if you kick me out of your bed."

And that's how Adan ended up asleep on my couch, unwittingly posing for the next picture in the album.

Chapter 9

Adan Navarro

I COULDN'T stop thinking about Chase Rhodes. It was ridiculous. I had half a foot and forty pounds on him. He put product in his hair and, I was pretty sure, on his face. When he talked, he flailed his hands around and the mannerisms were so obvious, it made me want to duck and hide my face.

But when I found myself beating off to a mental porno featuring captivating blue eyes framed by long lashes, I knew I'd have to take measures to stop the insanity. It seemed that my libido wanted the queen of Queens even though my brain knew he wasn't right for me in any way. So I decided the solution was to give my libido what it wanted and fuck the guy out of my system. Then I could stop thinking about him and move on with my life.

I took the train into Queens and, as a last-second move, picked up a six-pack of beer, thinking alcohol might make everything go more smoothly. It didn't take long to make it to his apartment, and three knocks later, I heard the locks turning.

"Hi!" he said brightly when he saw me leaning on his doorframe. "Come on in."

He stepped aside and let me walk into his apartment before closing and locking the door.

"Nice pla—" I stopped the automatic comment as soon as I actually looked at his place. It was maybe four hundred square feet with a tiny efficiency kitchen in one corner, a bed in another, and a couch and table occupying the rest of the space. There was a door on one wall, and I hoped it led to a bathroom. Other than that, the walls were covered in pictures.

"Oh, come on, it's not that bad," Chase said, apparently noticing my somewhat horrified expression.

"No, it's not bad," I said, trying to find a remnant of the manners my parents had tried to instill in me before they'd decided I was beyond redemption. "It's just small." Which was true. His place was clean, with shining wood floors, colorful tile counters, and striking photos on every wall.

"Five hundred square feet is plenty when you're living alone, and I'm a stone's throw from the F Line."

"You're right. Sorry." I shrugged. "I'm still not used New York. In Reno, we have lots of land, so the houses are much bigger."

Something passed over his face and the light in his eyes dimmed. "You're from Reno?" he asked.

"Uh-huh." I took a step toward him, wanting to smooth my hand over his face and bring back that smile.

"That's in Nevada, right?"

"Yeah. You been there?"

He shook his head. "No, but I…. No." He gestured toward my hand. "Here, let me get your bag."

I handed over my bag and tried to figure out what had gone wrong. Failing that, I held up the six-pack and said, "I brought beer."

He set my bag down next to the couch, not exactly what I had hoped for, and then flicked his gaze to my raised hand.

"Oh, uh, thanks." He walked into the kitchen. "Do you want a glass?"

"Nah." I set the beer on the counter and pulled one out. "Bottle's fine." I held it out to him. "Want one?"

"No, thanks. I'm not much on beer." He came over, picked up the rest of the bottles, and opened the door to a small refrigerator. "I'll put these in here so they stay cold." He pulled a bowl out of the fridge and then went over to a glass pan he had sitting on the counter.

"What's that?" I asked, nudging my chin toward the pan before twisting the cap off my bottle and tossing it into the trash can.

"It's going to be baked eggplant," he said as he reached for the bowl and scattered what looked to be shredded white cheese into the pan.

"Eggplant?" I furrowed my brow as I tilted the bottle against my lips and took a drink. "What do you mean? Eggs come from chickens."

He jerked his head up and stared at me. "You're not... are you serious?" he asked. When I didn't answer, he laughed so hard his face turned red. "It's a vegetable. It has nothing to do with eggs," he eventually said, sounding short of breath. "You've never heard of eggplant?"

Nothing pissed me off more than being laughed at, so I glared at him and probably spoke louder than I should have when I said, "Not everybody is a hippy foodie who eats all that organic shit!"

"It's not organic," he responded, still looking amused at my expense.

"You know what I mean," I barked as I waved at the food, sloshing a little beer over the lip of the bottle. "We don't all eat... lettuce and carrots and shit."

At that point, he bent over and held his stomach as he cackled. "Lettuce"—he gasped—"and carrots"—he gasped again—"and shit." When he finally managed to compose himself, he crossed the small space and threw his arms around me. My anger was immediately drowned out by the warmth that flooded me. "You're so funny," he said, blinking up at me, his smile back in full force and his eyes bright once again. "Thank you." He kissed the base of my neck, and I decided he could laugh at me whenever he wanted if it kept that expression on his face. "I needed that."

"Did you have a rough day, baby?" I asked him, wrapping an arm around his waist and combing my fingers through his hair.

He went rigid and I froze. Baby? Where that had come from, I couldn't say. It was out of character for me and out of line to say to a guy I barely knew, and who I planned to stop knowing after that night, or that weekend at the longest.

After a silence that was stretching into awkward, he extricated himself from my arms and walked back to the counter as he said, "Just the usual day. Gym. Work. Gym. But then I came home to the couch surprise." He opened the oven door and slid the pan inside. "Which, if I'm being honest, wasn't all that unusual either." He winked and grinned.

So we were ignoring my little slip. That was good. I wanted to thank him, but that would mean acknowledging it, which would bring the awkward right back, so I followed his tactic and engaged in the new conversation.

"You hit the gym twice a day?" I said as I dragged my gaze over his body. He was tiny but tight, all lean muscle and not an ounce of fat. I supposed the frequent workouts made sense. "I don't think you told me where you work," I added.

"That's because you didn't ask."

Though the words were snippy, his tone wasn't, so I didn't get offended. Plus, he was right. I hadn't asked him what he did for a living. Mostly because I didn't care. But it didn't look like he was getting naked anytime soon, so we needed to talk about something.

"Oh, uh, what do you do?" I asked.

He got a bottle of water out of the fridge along with some tomatoes, cucumbers, and lettuce. Then he dropped the produce into the sink and popped the top off the bottle, tilted it up, and took several long swallows.

The sight of him—ass leaning back against counter, shirt moving up just enough to expose a swath of golden skin and firm, flat stomach, and throat working to swallow down that water—was unexpectedly erotic. Jesus. I had to get him into bed. Had to.

"I'm a dancer." He wiped the back of his hand across his mouth and chucked the empty bottle into the trash can. "So the workouts are job related, but I'd probably go anyway." He shrugged and grinned. "Love the endorphins."

My brain stalled at "dancer" and a slideshow of erotic images immediately started flicking through my mind. My hand went straight to my groin and I gave myself a squeeze as I adjusted my hard-on.

"Not that kind of dancer!" Chase said with a laugh. "Does your head come out of your pants *ever*? You have one setting, seriously." He shook his head and smiled. "All horny, all day."

It was funny—not true, but funny. I mean, I liked sex as much as the next guy, but my head was usually focused on my schoolwork or my upcoming internship or my class rank. I was two years into a five-year life plan and everything I did, including networking with my drunken classmates the night I met Chase, was designed to advance that plan. At the five-year mark, I'd fine-tune the next five-year plan and roll it out.

Bottom line was, I knew the only way to live the kind of life I wanted was to set goals and meet them. Which meant my focus was usually unflappable. Sex was awesome. A six-figure salary by the time I turned thirty in three years? Even better.

But even the reminder of my five-year plan wasn't enough to eradicate the images of Chase wearing next to nothing and gyrating on a stage. "What kind of dancer?" I asked as I raised a shaky hand and brought my beer bottle back to my mouth.

"Ballet is my favorite, but I'm pretty versatile." He started washing the vegetables. "I'm in rehearsals for a cabaret off-Broadway right now. It's gonna be great."

Aaaand, now I was stalled on "versatile."

He looked back over his shoulder and said, "Are you going to be okay eating lettuce?" I could tell he was trying to look serious, but his grin broke through. It was the only reason I didn't scowl.

"Ha ha."

I tilted my hand back and forth, watching the remains of my beer splash against the bottle, and tried to think about how to approach the conversation I wanted to have without insulting him to the point where I'd have to work even harder to get him into bed. I was already past my normal limits.

He took out a cutting board, started dicing, and grinned up at me. "Tomatoes too. And cucumbers."

"All right, all right. You've made your point." I tossed my empty into the trash can, grabbed another beer out of the fridge, cracked it open, and took a swig. Then I had an idea. "I'm usually more of a beef or chicken guy, but salad is fine. I can be versatile." I paused and tried to make my meaning clear through my inflection when I added, "But I'm not *versatile* in all things."

He scrunched his nose, looking grossed out. "Good, because I'm not cooking dead animals for you."

Great. He was completely oblivious to my point. And he was some sort of animal rights activist. I ignored that because it wouldn't matter. I could go a weekend without eating meat, especially if he was eating mine.

With subtlety failing, I decided to just put it out there. "I'm a top." There. That was clear.

He slowly turned his head, looked me up and down, and went back to chopping. The lack of response was disconcerting.

"Aren't you going to say anything?" I asked when the silence became interminable.

"What do you expect me to say?" he asked. "It's not as if that's a shocker."

I furrowed my brow and said, "What is that supposed to mean?"

And, more to the point, why was I taking offense? I hadn't wanted to insult the guy by calling him a big 'ol bottom boy, even though, come on, let's be real. But coming across as a top wasn't shameful. I decided it was his inexplicable reaction that was getting to me.

Without so much as turning his head, he said, "You drink beer. You wear cargo pants. I don't even want to hazard a guess as to where you cut your hair, but I'm fearful it involves you in a mirrorless room with clippers." He scoffed. "Do you honestly believe anybody could think you're a bottom?"

I gaped at him and eventually said, "Are you listening to yourself?"

"What?" he glanced over, his expression completely guileless.

"I wear cargo pants? I drink beer? The way I cut my hair?"

He raised one eyebrow and cocked his hip. "Am I wrong?"

That stopped me in my tracks. "Well, uh, no."

"Okay, then." He went back to chopping. "As you lawyer types say, I rest my case."

I was pretty sure I'd just lost some sort of debate. I didn't like it.

"There's nothing wrong with my hair," I sputtered as I dragged my hand over my short locks.

He glanced at me, raised his eyebrow again, and then went back to chopping without a word. Neither of us said anything while he finished making the salad and tossed it together in a bowl. Then he donned some oven mitts and pulled the baked eggplant out of the oven.

"This needs to set for a little while," he said. "Then I'll make the salad dressing and we can eat." He waltzed over to the couch. "You coming?" he asked.

I was following him and thinking about whether I should grow my hair a little longer before I realized what I was doing and gave myself an internal smackdown. The goal was to get in, fuck him, and get out, not to change my appearance or anything else to accommodate him. How the man managed to, once again, get me all discombobulated, I didn't know, but I was going to stay strong and stay on task.

He settled in the corner of the couch and I plopped down next to him, leaving as little personal space as possible so I could make a move. I put my hand on his knee and squeezed as I worked it up his thigh. He twisted to the side, so he was looking right at me. Then he traced my jaw with one finger, moved it over to my temple and across my hairline, and started massaging my head.

I moaned and leaned into him. "Is it too short?" I asked, apparently unable to stop myself from going back to our conversation. "I used to have it longer on top, but it's easier this way."

"It looks good," he said, continuing his massage. "But a little longer on top would be nice. Longer sideburns would be super hot too." He put his other hand on my head, increasing the contact points of those magic fingers.

Before I knew it, I was lying across his lap with my eyes closed.

"You like that?" he asked quietly as he rubbed.

"Uh-huh." It was unexpectedly relaxing, having someone caress my head that way. I felt the tension about school and jobs and family seep from my body and my breathing slow. The last thing I remember was thinking how good he smelled and being too far gone to realize that type of sappy shit was not in my game plan.

Chapter 10

INTRODUCTION

Charlie ("Chase") Rhodes

SO, WHAT do you think of Adan so far? Yeah, at that point in our relationship, I wasn't so sure either. But I was undeniably drawn to him, which had been a rare to nonexistent reaction since Scott disappeared from my life. And—this is key—he was nothing like Scott. They didn't look alike—Scott was golden-skinned with blond hair and hazel eyes, Adan was a deep olive tan with chocolate eyes and black hair. Their voices were completely different—Scott's was a smooth, deep timbre, Adan's was a gravely, husky growl. And their personalities? Night and day.

Scott had been warmth and smiles, an easygoing "what you see is what you get" guy who everybody loved. Adan was cold, intense, and focused, a guy seemingly intent on keeping the world at a distance. But I had grown a lot in the decade since I'd met Scott. At twenty-five years old, I had a nice circle of friends, my career was on the right path, high school was over, and I no longer felt like I needed someone to protect me from the world or fill my otherwise empty time. More importantly, I didn't want to count on someone only to have him walk away without a backward glance.

Adan had a hard shell around him, sure enough, but I thought maybe I could be the one to crack it, which would make me special. And special people were held close, not thrown away. With those things in mind, I decided to let him spend the weekend, figuring we'd see how things played out.

I gotta tell you, neither of us would have accurately predicted where we'd end up, which leads me to the next picture in the album: dice. He wanted to play craps; I wanted to play cee-lo. We ended up drinking way too much, staying up way too late, and playing both.

The next morning, when I was bleary-eyed and willing to give my left nut for a cup of coffee, I noticed the three dice sitting in a small shot glass illuminated by the morning sun. At the risk of expiring from caffeine deprivation, I stumbled for my camera and took the shot. The gamble paid off—I lived and the resulting picture was gorgeous.

So, unexpected though it is, the next picture in the album is three gambling dice glowing together in the sun.

Chapter 10

Adan Navarro

MY GROWLING stomach woke me a couple of hours later. Even before I opened my eyes, I knew exactly where I was. Chase's thigh was pillowing my head, he was petting my hair, and the scent of his groin made mine tighten with need.

I blinked my eyes open and saw that he was holding a book with his free hand, the glow from a table lamp providing the only illumination in the apartment. With his focus elsewhere, I could look my fill without being noticed. The first place my gaze landed was on his eyes. That swirl of blues was breathtaking and served as the perfect jewel to highlight a face too pretty to be called masculine. I let myself examine every one of his delicate features.

It should have been off-putting—the long, dark lashes, the full red lips, the high, chiseled cheekbones, and the small, upturned nose. But once again, I had no control over my body's reactions. Desire pushed aside disgust when I looked at the beauty above me, and my breath hitched.

"Hey, you're awake," Chase said as he put the book down on the end table. "You must have been beat." He moved his hand from my head down to my cheek and rubbed his thumb back and forth over my skin in a caress. "Are you still recovering from all those exams?"

His sweet tone, the warmth in his eyes, and the tenderness in his touch, took me off guard. Or maybe it was the way my chest swelled in reaction to those things that was unexpected. Either way, I was too unnerved to speak, so I swallowed thickly and nodded.

"Poor thing. Well, a few good meals and a relaxing weekend should get you back on your feet. You had the right idea coming here." He traced my lips as he spoke, his expression fond as he looked at me.

I registered for the first time that he had cooked for me. And it sounded like he was planning to do it again. Other than my mother, nobody had ever wanted to take care of me, and she had resigned from the job when she realized there would be no woman in my life to take the baton.

"The eggplant is probably cold by now," he said. "But I can nuke it and it should be fine."

Realizing that was my cue to move, I sat up. Unfamiliar emotions still swirling inside me rendered me mute.

Chase climbed off the couch and ambled over to the kitchen, his easy gait indicating that he was unaware of my tension. "The bathroom's over there if you want to wash up," he said as he tipped his head toward the only interior door in his apartment.

I gave myself another few moments to watch his firm, high butt and lithe form. Then I took a deep breath and walked into the restroom, intending to splash some water on my face and smack some sense into my head. Being gay was one thing—I couldn't help that, couldn't stop it. But I sure as hell could choose what type of man I'd have by my side as I finished up my education and finally started to climb my way up the legal ladder. Chase was not someone who would help me make partner at a good firm or get appointed to a seat on an appellate court or start a political career.

The man was nice; I was willing to admit that. And my traitorous body found him attractive, something I couldn't deny with the proof throbbing between my thighs. But at the end of the day, Chase Rhodes was a joke, and if I brought him around, people would think I was like him; they'd be slammed with *his* image of what it meant to be gay and put it on me. No way could I earn anybody's respect being that kind of guy. Hell, I'd be lucky to have people wait until my back was turned before they started laughing.

With those reminders firmly in place, I felt ready to go out there and give Chase the only thing that made sense between us: a hot night and a firm good-bye.

"YOU'RE done for the year, right? That's what that girl Tracy said," Chase said while we were eating the delicious dinner he'd prepared.

"Yeah, I'm done with classes for the summer. I'm clerking at the district court, though, so I'll still be busy." I dragged my fork across my plate to scoop up the last bit of tomato sauce, cheese, and what I assumed was eggplant. It didn't taste like a vegetable or eggs, more like a lasagna or something.

"Here," he said as he pushed his plate over to me. "I'm done if you want some more."

I darted my gaze down to his plate and then looked at him as I lifted my fork, ready to dig in. "Are you sure? This is your first serving, and I ate the whole pan."

"Go ahead," he said. That was all the approval I needed to shovel a forkful into my mouth. "I don't usually eat a heavy dinner, which is why I made a small serving. Besides, I like salad better, and you were gracious enough to save all of that for me."

I paused midchew and looked at him appraisingly, trying to decide if he was making fun of me. The twinkle in his eyes and the slight curl of his lip told me the answer was yes.

"Next time I cook for you, I'll use a bigger pan. And I can make garlic bread too, if you don't mind the carbs."

I moaned in approval and forgot to be offended. Again.

Chase laughed. "Okay, that's a yes on the garlic bread. Got it. I can't do it tonight, though, because I don't have any bread, but I can make it up to you with dessert."

I paused with the last forkful a couple of inches from my lips and gulped down the food in my mouth. "Dessert?"

"Yes, dessert. Do you like chocolate?"

"I like sweet things in all their forms," I answered. And I included his sweet smile on that list, but I didn't say it out loud because then I'd have to kick my own ass.

"Good to know," he said with a chuckle. "How about we let dinner settle and then I'll get dessert going."

"Okay." I wiped my mouth off and tried to refocus on my seduction plan.

Finding that focus was surprisingly difficult. Not because I didn't want him; my still swollen shaft proved how much I wanted him. The issue was that I was enjoying spending time with him—chatting about school and work, sharing funny stories, getting to know each other—and I wasn't ready for that

90

to end. But once I fucked him out of my system, I wouldn't have any reason to stick around.

Of course, if I fucked him, then I'd get to fuck him. Not a particularly insightful or brilliant deduction, but one that made me groan.

"So," I said, my voice sounding huskier to my own ears. "What do you want to do?"

He pursed his lips in thought for a few seconds and then said, "Do you like to play cards? Dice?"

I wasn't a big gambler, my frugal nature wouldn't allow it, but I figured I could hold my own against Chase. Plus, he had unwittingly given me the perfect setup to get him naked.

"You're on," I said as I pushed my empty plate away. "How about strip craps?"

"Incorrigible." He shook his head. "My pants are staying on, hotshot. But, yeah, we can play craps."

Damn it. I wasn't going down without a fight. "Look, I'm in school and you have a… *career* in the arts, so neither of us is flush with cash right now. What's the point of playing if we can't gamble for something?"

"I'm doing just fine with my career in the arts," he said. "We can play for fun or bragging rights." I snorted derisively. He rolled his eyes and said, "All right, so how about the loser of each round has to take a drink."

Hold on, now, that had potential. "A drinking game?" I asked.

"Yup." He winked. "And you've already got a three-beer lead on me. Scared?"

"Please." I crossed my arms over my chest and smirked. "I'm going to kick your round little butt. And I'm warning you now, while you're good and sober, that my plan is to get your pants off. So when you wake up tomorrow with a sore ass, I don't want to hear any bullshit about how you were too drunk to know what you were doing."

Chase gaped at me in wide-eyed horror. "Okay, first, you're the lawyer, but I'm pretty sure that kind of philosophy could land you in jail. It definitely won't land you in my bed. And second, if you want any repeat customers, you need to work on your technique because unless you're packing a nightstick, there is no reason for anybody to wake up in the morning with a sore ass."

"I've never gotten any complaints," I said with a frown.

He looked me up and down, and said, "That's probably because you don't stick around long enough to get feedback."

"Hey!" I was actually feeling offended. "You don't know that. Maybe I just got out of a ten-year relationship."

He arched one eyebrow. "How old are you?"

"Twenty-seven," I mumbled.

"And you just got out of a ten-year relationship?" he asked.

The disbelief was clear from his tone and it pissed me off. I wanted to prove him wrong, but I had backed myself into a pretty tight corner.

"No." I ground my teeth. "But I could have."

"Riiiiight, you could have. And you also could have learned how to top someone without causing ongoing pain." He paused and curled one side of his lip up. "But you didn't do that either."

I was about to tell him to fuck off and storm out of his apartment, but then I noticed his shoulders shaking and realized I was being played.

"Are you trying to bait me?" I asked.

"Yup." He got up, cleared our dishes, and carried them to the sink. "And it was working." He waggled his eyebrows, looking inordinately pleased with himself.

My jaw dropped. "Why would you intentionally piss me off?"

"Because if you're all worked up, your concentration will be for shit," he said matter-of-factly as he washed the dishes.

"That's cheating!" My voice got embarrassingly high-pitched, so I slammed my mouth shut.

"It's not cheating," Chase responded. He turned off the water, dried his hands on a bright-purple towel, and got a bottle of vodka out of the freezer, a jug of cranberry juice out of the fridge, and a couple of small glasses off the shelf. "It's strategy." He sauntered past me and over to the couch. "You coming or do you wanna forfeit right now?"

For the first time since I'd met him, I had an inkling that maybe playing Chase Rhodes and walking away unscathed wouldn't be as easy as I'd first anticipated.

THE cranberry juice was gone, the vodka was perilously low, and the room was spinning.

92

"What's with all the plants?" I asked as I waved my arms around, promptly smacking myself in the forehead. "Ouch!"

Chase snorted, looking amused. When he didn't answer my question, I asked again.

"Seriously," I said. The word sounded strange rolling off my tongue so I swallowed and tried it again. "Seriously." I decided the problem was that my tongue had mysteriously grown and it no longer fit my mouth. "Seriously." I said the word slowly, trying to enunciate despite my teeth getting in the way. "Ser-i-ous-ly," I said each syllable individually.

"Stop," Chase said as he slapped his hand over my mouth. "No more."

"What?" The word was muffled against his palm, and my tongue, happy to be released from its too small cage, decided to take a taste.

"Are you licking me?" Chase asked.

"No," I said. Well, I tried to say it, anyway. I was having a hard time getting the word out because I was busy licking him.

"Yes, you are. You're licking me."

I kept licking.

He yanked his hand away, said, "Eww," and then he wiped it on my shirt.

"Seriously," I said.

"Oh, for fuck's sake!"

I blinked in surprise at his sudden outburst. It was loud.

He looked at me as if he was waiting for me to say something.

I looked back and opened my jaw, trying to get hearing back in my left ear.

He sighed in relief.

My ear popped. I licked my lips and said, "Seriously."

"If you say 'seriously' again, I'm going to kick your ass," Chase warned.

"Please," I scoffed and waved my hand at him, somehow smacking my own shoulder. "Like you'd stand a chance. You're itty-bitty." I held my hand up with my thumb and pointer finger a few inches apart. Looking at them made my eyes cross.

"Seeing as how you can't even sit up straight, I think I like my chances," he said with a smile.

He sounded way too sober.

"You sound way too sober."

Why was that?

"Why is that?"

"Because you lost every single round of craps and then cee-lo, so I've been sticking to juice and you're drunk as fuck."

"Huh." I furrowed my brow and considered his comment. "That makes sense." I leaned back. "You want to fuck now?"

He chuckled. "No, I really don't. And even if I did, I doubt you'd be able to get it up in your current condition."

"I'm fine, baby," I said with a leer. Well, I was going for a leer. I ended up drooling a little, so I wiped the back of my hand across my mouth. "I got what you need right here." I grasped my cock and balls and squeezed. More harshly than I intended. "Fuck!"

"Hey, take it easy." Chase uncurled my fingers from my dick and patted it gently. "Just because I'm not interested tonight doesn't mean I don't want him in working order."

That sounded hopeful. I raised my head and met his gaze. "Yeah?"

He shrugged. "Maybe."

"When?"

He laughed at me. Again. "I don't know."

"Now?"

"No."

I paused for a few beats and then said, "How about now?"

"You're cute when you're drunk, you know that?" he said.

"So is that a yes?"

"It's still a no." He climbed to his feet and held his hand out to me. "Come on, let's get you to the bathroom before you pass out and embarrass yourself."

It took me three tries to land my hand in his. "What do you mean?" I staggered to my feet and swayed.

"Never mind. Let's go." He wrapped his arm around my waist and led me to the bathroom.

"You never answered my question," I said.

94

"I answered your question a hundred times. With the amount of liquor in your system, the only thing I want from your dick is for it to not piss on my couch during the night."

"Not that question."

"Oh," he sounded surprised. "What question?"

It took me a moment to remember. "What's with all the plants on your windowsill?"

"I like hydrangeas," he said.

We'd reached the bathroom. He pushed the door open and waited for me to step inside.

"They're nice," I said. I tried to lean on the doorway and look suave, but I misjudged my proximity to it and slipped, hitting the sink.

"Are you okay?" Chase leaned in and helped me right myself.

"No." I shook my head vehemently. It made the room spin. "I think I hurt my dick again." I reached for his hand. "You better check."

"You're ridiculous," he said, stepping away.

"I'm horny," I corrected him.

"And you're gonna stay that way." He pointed at the toilet. "Go do your business. It's late, I'm tired, and you're drunk."

I wove my way to the toilet, took several tries to unzip my pants, and finally fished my cock out. The room started spinning so I reached out with my free hand to grab the wall. It was farther away than I realized.

"Shit!" Chase said. Before I could turn to look at him, he was standing right next to me and reaching for my dick.

"See?" I said with a smirk. "I knew you wanted it."

"What I want is for you to piss in the toilet and not my wall or my floor." He aimed my dick into the bowl. "I hope to God you remember this tomorrow, because it's gonna be hella more fun to tease you that way."

I turned my head and looked down at his face. He was right there. Close enough to kiss.

"I want to kiss you," I slurred.

"You're oddly charming," he said. Then he tilted his chin toward my dick and said, "Piss."

"No, seriously." The word seemed to come out better that time. "I don't usually go for kissing all that much, but you have pretty lips."

"Lucky me. Piss."

"Your eyes are pretty too. Did you know that? They're all big and blue, and you have lashes like a girl."

"I take it back. You're an ass and I'm odd for finding you charming." He squeezed my dick. "Drain the lizard, Adan. Let's go."

I closed my eyes to concentrate and then heard the stream splashing into the bowl. "I did it," I said as I opened my eyes.

He shook his head. "Good for you. Keep going."

"'Kay." When I was done, he shook me off, tucked me into my pants, and zipped me up. "You going to kiss me now?" I asked while he was washing his hands.

"You smell like a brewery," he said.

"I can brush my teeth," I offered.

He wiped his hands on his pants and walked out of the bathroom. "Toothbrush and toothpaste are on the counter. Brush your teeth. I'm gonna make up the couch for you."

"Then will you kiss me?" I called out after him as I squeezed way too much paste onto his toothbrush.

"I wish I had a video camera," he muttered. "I'd have blackmail material on you for the rest of your life."

"I can get a video camera," I shouted excitedly, drooling foamy paste over my chin. "Then we can make a sex tape like Pam Anderson and Tommy Lee."

"Are you hung like Tommy Lee?" Chase asked as he walked back to the couch with sheets in his arms.

I spit into the sink and frowned. I was eight inches hard. Did that mean I'd blown my chance with him? I'd never been ashamed of my size, because no matter what bullshit guys spew, eight inches is a good-sized dick. Besides, it wasn't exactly something I could hide.

"No," I reluctantly admitted.

"Good," Chase said. "'Cause that shit would be painful."

Relieved, I rinsed my mouth, splashed some water on my face, and went back to the couch. Chase was fluffing a pillow. I reached for him. Well,

I tried to reach for him. Mostly I fell on him. He grabbed my hips and lowered me onto the couch.

"So we're seriously not going to fuck?" I asked him.

"Hard as it is to resist you in your drunken, messy, somewhat smelly state, yeah, 'fraid not." He grasped the bottom of my shirt and tugged it up my chest. "Raise your arms," he said. I did and he pulled my shirt off. "You're on your own for your pants, Romeo."

My eyelids were feeling heavy anyway, so I didn't bother arguing anymore. "But I get a kiss, right?" I asked. I really wanted that kiss.

Chase smiled at me fondly, hunched down, and cupped my cheek. He pressed his lips to mine in a soft, gentle, perfect kiss. Then he walked over to the bathroom. I admired his ass as I toppled across the sofa and shoved my pants down over my hips.

"Good night, Adan," he said, looking at me over his shoulder.

"Good night, Chase."

I was out like a light before he left the bathroom.

Chapter 11

INTRODUCTION

Charlie ("Chase") Rhodes

I'M NOT a complete idiot.

Okay, I feel better having gotten that off my chest. Because I suspect it's what you'll think when you hear that the next picture in the album relates to Adan. And it isn't one of a curb. (Kick his ass to the curb, get it? No? Fine. Whatever.)

Now, here's the thing: I knew Adan wanted to get into my pants. I mean, with the way the guy was working it like the rent was due tomorrow, I'd have had to be comatose to miss that. But despite all of his come-ons and more than slightly horrifying warnings about what he wanted to do to me, the look in his eyes and expression on his face when he gazed at me made me certain he had more than sex on his mind.

Not that there's anything wrong with sex. I don't want to give you the impression I'd committed myself to celibacy during the five years between when Scott walked out of my life and Adan walked into it. I had flirted with guys over the years, dated guys over years, and slept with guys over the years. But what I hadn't done was *connect* with any of them. Until Adan.

From the first moment he approached me in the bar, I felt a twinge of interest that had been missing from my emotional Rolodex. And the more time I spent with him, the stronger that interest got. He was sexy, sure, but that wasn't the draw. Okay, fine, it was part of the draw. But he was also smart and unintentionally funny, and he made me feel wanted.

So when he made no move to leave my apartment Saturday morning, I followed his lead and forged ahead with the assumption that he'd be hanging out the rest of the weekend. We went to the store on the corner for groceries, but other than that, we spent two days holed up in my apartment. We laughed a lot, drank some, and managed to get to know each other along the way.

By Sunday evening when we were saying good-bye, I wanted to get naked with Adan as much as he wanted to get naked with me. But strangely enough, I felt like we knew each other too well for that. And yet didn't know each other enough. Bear with me here; it actually makes more sense than it seems at first glance.

When I met a guy at a club or anywhere else and decided I was going to take him home, I generally didn't know anything about him except how he looked and the few tidbits of information I picked up between the meeting point and the bed. And that was more than fine; it was a plus because it eliminated all awkwardness and expectations. To be clear, I don't just mean his expectations, I mean mine too. A hookup was a hookup; my brain and heart knew that, so they didn't get involved and left the heavy lifting to my dick.

After the time we had spent together at dinner the first night, followed by the weekend, Adan and I knew each other too well to categorize any sex as a hookup. And yet, whatever we were forging together was so new, so fragile, that I didn't know what to call it or how long it'd last. So I didn't want to introduce sex into the relationship, because it wasn't at all clear we were in a relationship. Basically, we were in some sort of sexual dead zone until I knew rolling into the bed wouldn't destroy what I hoped we could become.

Because the truth was, no matter how easy it was to find willing and attractive bed partners and no matter how busy my life was with work and friends, I missed the comfort and connection that came with being part of a couple. I missed having someone to call about mundane things and important things. I missed feeling like I mattered, really mattered, to somebody. I guess what it came down to was that I'm one of those people who feels happier being in a relationship than living the single life, and for the first time since my relationship with Scott ended, I had finally met someone who intrigued me enough to want to try coupledom again. But first I had to navigate the dangerous field of dating when there was more on the line than a couple of orgasms.

And that brings me to the next picture in the album. I was getting into bed on Monday night when I noticed something on the floor, next to the end of my bed. I squatted down, snagged it, and held it up next to the lamp on my nightstand. Adan's driver's license.

My first instinct was to call him to tell him he'd lost it at my place, but I dismissed that right away as the wrong choice. Adan hadn't been in my bed that weekend, and anyway, he had no reason to be digging in his wallet and misplacing his driver's license. Once I thought about it, I became convinced he had left the license there on purpose so he'd have an excuse to see me again.

A part of me wished he hadn't felt like he had to manufacture a reason to see me. But another part of me was too happy about the fact that he wanted to spend time with me to worry about how he was expressing that want. It was that second part that grabbed the camera and took a picture of Adan's driver's license.

Because it's a symbol of what I saw as Adan reaching out to me, my snapshot of his driver's license is the next picture going into the album.

Chapter 11

Adan Navarro

CHASE RHODES was fruity and flamey and flamboyant. He didn't try to look more like a man and less like someone who would turn heads and cause people to whisper and laugh. Instead Chase seemed to intentionally ham it up. I was certain he had been wearing makeup the first time we'd met. He chose clothes that were too tight, too loud, and too feminine to be appropriate for men. Hell, even the roll of his hips when he walked and the cadence of his speech screamed out what he was. All of which should have driven me right off.

But though it made no sense, I found myself genuinely liking him. He was confident, sarcastic in a biting, funny way, deceptively intuitive, and strikingly beautiful. From the first moment I saw him, I wanted to fuck him. After spending time with him, I wanted to see him smile and hear him laugh, even if it was at me. I wanted to learn about what he did in his free time and watch him putter around in his kitchen, hopefully while he was making me more tasty meals. And I still wanted to fuck him.

Artist types were supposed to be messy and disorganized, or so I'd always thought. But Chase's tiny apartment was neat and orderly, so I was sure he'd call me to let me know he'd found my missing driver's license. Not that I knew I had lost it at his apartment. It could have been anywhere: the subway, the street, any number of diners where I'd grabbed food. All I knew was that when I opened my wallet on Monday morning, my license was missing. And the last time I'd seen it was when I was in Chase's apartment on Sunday. As I set the license down next to his bed.

Anyway, when he hadn't called by Tuesday, I was second-guessing the whole neat thing. Maybe he had cleaned up to impress me but he was normally a total pig and as soon as I'd left his place, the license had gotten covered by clothes and pizza boxes and beer bottles. Not that he drank beer. And a body as fine as his couldn't indulge in all that much pizza. And with as meticulous as he was about his frou-frou clothes, I doubted he'd leave them crumpled on the floor.

It took until Thursday before I admitted to myself that maybe he wasn't calling because I'd put him off. It was possible I had been a little overly aggressive. But that was only because he kept turning me down, so he was half responsible and he had no business holding it against me. The more I thought about it, the more pissed off I got, because I was thinking about it, which meant I was thinking about him. I wasn't some teenage girl who was going to pine, especially not after some fem aspiring dancer. I was on my way to becoming a successful attorney with a big house and a BMW convertible and Chase twirled around for a living. Come on.

By Saturday morning, I decided I had no choice but to call him. Not because of the recurring sex dreams I had about him. Not because I walked by a bodega that sold those hydrangea flowers he liked so much and stopped to think about whether there was room on his windowsill for another plant. Not because I saw some guys playing street dice and laughed at the memory of some of the funny things he'd said when we played at his apartment. But solely because I needed my license so I could go out that night and pick up another guy. That was it.

I refused to think about why I chose to go to his apartment instead of calling him and asking him to leave the license somewhere for me. I got showered and dressed in my most flattering jeans and a shirt that pulled across my chest and arms in a way that showed off the muscles I worked hard to maintain. Then I went to Chase's apartment.

"Adan?" he asked through the door when I knocked.

It took me off guard, because I hadn't told him I was coming. Eventually, I said, "Uh, yeah. Ahem, it's me."

The locks turned and then he pulled the door open. My confusion took a backseat and lust moved front and center as soon as I saw him. He was wearing skintight white pants and a white tank top that showed his sculpted arms and defined pecs. It looked like he had painted under his eyes with some dark pencil, which made the blue pop even more, and his lips shimmered, looking kissable.

"Come in. Everything is ready except the garlic bread, but that just needs to broil for five minutes."

He stepped to the side and I walked in, trying to catch up to what was happening. The apartment was as clean as when I'd left. There was a salad and a pan of something cheesy on the counter. It looked like lasagna. And next to it sat my driver's license.

"I picked up some beer for you," he said as he walked to the fridge. I dropped my gaze to his ass and moaned out loud. Fuck me. Those white pants left nothing to the imagination, and I didn't know guys could wear thong underwear. "Do you want one or do you want to start with water?"

"Beer," I rasped.

He retrieved a bottle from the fridge, twisted off the cap, and handed it to me. I gulped half of it down, wiped the back of my hand across my mouth, and focused on what was happening. Still had no clue.

"Chase?"

"Uh-huh." He was slipping a cookie tray with bread on it into the oven.

"What's going on?"

"I waited to put the bread in so it'd be warm for dinner."

Nope. Still lost.

"But how did you know I was coming over? We didn't talk about it." I had a moment of fear where I thought I'd lost my mind. "Did we?"

He looked at me, moved his gaze over to my license, and then looked at me again, raising one eyebrow.

"Oh." So my mind was intact, but my subtlety was lacking in subtlety. I opened my mouth to deny his implication, to say I had misplaced my license, to explain I had no intention of seeing him again. But he had worked so hard on dinner, and I didn't want to be rude. Also, he was spot-on. But that had nothing to do with it.

"I made a tres leches cake for dessert." He reached up and picked a couple of plates off the shelf, and I snagged my license and stuffed it into my wallet as quickly as possible. "I know tiramisu would go better with Italian, but I want to impress you, and my tres leches is the best."

"Baby, if you want to impress me, all you have to do is drop your pants and bend over. There's no reason to spend all day in the kitchen."

He snorted and shook his head. "I can't believe you say shit like that."

"Is it working?" I asked with a waggle of my eyebrows.

"Depends on your goal." He dished a large serving of lasagna onto a plate and added a couple of salad leaves. "If it's to make me laugh, then, yeah."

The time for subtlety was long gone. I had to get rid of my hard-on, and taking care of it myself, again, wasn't doing much to satisfy me. "The goal is getting you into bed," I said.

Meeting my gaze, he quietly said, "Surprisingly enough, yeah, I think it's working on that front too." He handed me the plate. "Lord knows why."

"Because I'm suave," I explained.

"You're cheesy," he responded as he scooped a lot of salad and a bit of lasagna onto his plate. "Go ahead and sit. The bread should be ready."

I was about to remind him that he'd just agreed to go to bed with me, but the food looked delicious, so I decided I could eat first and fuck after. We chit-chatted a little, but mostly I ate my body weight in lasagna and Chase smiled.

When we were almost done, I dragged the last piece of bread through the tomato sauce on my otherwise empty plate—except for those damn salad leaves, but that didn't count—and asked, "So what made you change your mind?"

Chase swallowed the food in his mouth, took a sip of water, and then said, "Change my mind?"

"Yeah. Last weekend you were like a Victorian maiden protecting her virtue, and today you offered me your ass seconds after I walked in the door. What gives?"

His jaw dropped and he stared at me. "I don't know. I guess I thought your whole driver's license thing was cute." Hearing that made me give myself a mental pat on the back for not spewing any bullshit denials about why I'd left my license at his place. "But after that comment you just made, I can honestly say I have no idea. Truly, none." He shook his head in disbelief. "Maybe I have a brain tumor like that guy in the Woody Allen movie."

"The brain tumor turned Lukas Haas into a radical Republican, not a raging slut," I corrected.

Chase tilted the sides of lips up and his eyes twinkled. "I'm going to ignore the fact that you just called me a slut for agreeing to do what you've been trying to get me to do since the second we met and focus on the part of that sentence where you know details about a Woody Allen movie."

I ducked my head, moved my fork around my empty plate, and hoped the warmth on my face wasn't visible. I hadn't intended to let that cat out of the bag. Those types of movies were my guilty pleasure and I'd always managed to keep that on the down-low.

"I would have figured you more for an action-adventure type," Chase continued unperturbed. "You know, explosions and car chases and shit. Not dry humor about New Yorkers done to song."

"I like action movies," I said.

"Of course." He nodded seriously. "But what's your favorite Woody Allen?" he asked.

"*Hannah and Her Sisters*," I answered automatically and then flinched at having confirmed his suspicion.

But instead of making fun of my movie taste, he said, "Shit. If that's your favorite movie, I'm glad I have a sister and not a brother. Otherwise, I'd worry you'd try to get into his pants."

Desperate to change the topic, I accidentally asked him about his family, something I normally considered too personal to bring up with my tricks. "You have a sister? Does she live nearby? Is she a dancer too? What about your parents?" A wave of sadness washed over Chase's face, and I kicked myself for breaking my own rules and getting personal. "Never mind," I said. "It's none of my business."

"No, it's okay." He took a deep breath and squared his shoulders, seeming anything but okay as he stared at a spot behind me. "My dad took off when I was kid and I never hear from him, but I don't remember him having any sort of rhythm. My mom's a nurse and she lives in Florida with her new husband. My sister's a nanny right now. She used to be a waitress and she worked at a makeup counter at the mall and a bunch of other things too, but she's never danced. We used to be really close, but she moved to—" He gulped. " —the other side of the country and she spends a lot of time with my ex, so it's hard."

My stomach rolled over when Chase mentioned another man. I cracked my knuckles, and before I could stop myself, asked, "How ex?"

"Huh?" He blinked and refocused on me.

That conversation was the worst foreplay ever. I knew I should let it go, say never mind and take his clothes off. What did I care about his family and his ex-boyfriend and really anything except his gag reflex and how long I could keep his ankles pinned to his ears before he raised a fuss?

105

"Your ex-boyfriend, the one your sister likes, how long ago did you break up?" I asked, seemingly incapable of exhibiting good judgment. And then, because that wasn't pathetic enough, I added, "Are you still hung up on him? Is that why you keep turning me down?"

"Keep turning you down? We've known each other for just over a week, Adan. Where I come from, that isn't a very long courtship." He held his hand out in a stop motion and said, "Wait, don't tell me. This isn't a courtship; it's a booty call, right?" He laughed, but it wasn't the happy, lighthearted sound I'd gotten used to hearing. I hated it. "In answer to your question, he was my first love. I'm not sure you ever get over that, right? But we broke up years ago and we don't keep in touch, don't have mutual friends, won't run into each other, et cetera, et cetera, et cetera."

I wasn't thrilled about the implication that he'd never get over his ex and I wanted to ask more questions about it, but that would leave the door open for him to ask me about my past relationships, of which I had none. Needless to say, I wasn't interested in telling Chase that I managed to make it all the way through college and a year into a job working for a consulting firm in San Francisco before I had come out and that I'd spent the four years since then fucking my way through a slew of nameless, faceless men in my limited free time. And talking about his family put me at risk of fielding questions about my family, something I didn't want to do until, at a minimum, my mother managed to look up the word "gay" in the dictionary and stop asking me if I'd met a nice girl yet.

So I kept my mouth shut, because telling Chase about my background could make him change his mind about being the next notch on my belt. My silence had nothing to do with the jolt of worry about what he would think of me and whether I'd blow my chances with him. I gave myself an internal reminder that the only chance I wanted was to feel him blowing me.

"All right," I said as I got up from my chair and yanked my shirt off. "This conversation got too serious. Let's get naked and promise never to talk about shit that matters again." I toed my shoes off, unbuttoned my jeans, hooked my thumbs in the waistband, and pushed my jeans and briefs down together, making my already hard dick bob. "Deal?"

Chase dragged his gaze over my chest and down my happy trail to my rigid shaft. He dropped to his knees, wrapped his fingers around my dick, and nuzzled my balls before looking up at me through heavy-lidded eyes and saying, "Deal."

I liked to pride myself on my stamina, but I was only one beer in and Chase looked unbelievably sexy down on his knees with his mouth stretched over my cockhead. He sucked hard and then twirled his tongue around my glans, letting saliva drizzle down. The reason for that became clear when he wrapped his fingers around my shaft and jacked me while he continued sucking and licking.

Getting head was one of my favorite activities, and I wasn't one to deny myself pleasure, so I'd received a lot of blowjobs. When Chase moved his hand down to my balls and sucked my entire dick into this mouth, I decided none of the other guys I'd been with had a clue what they were doing, because nothing and nobody had ever made me feel that good.

He cupped and rolled my balls, sucked his way up and down my dick, and somehow managed to lap his tongue against my heated skin at the same time. There was no way for me to hold back for long, not with the way he was touching me, not with those amazing blue eyes filled with lust and staring right at me, not with a symphony of his whimpers and moans mixing with crude slurping sounds filling the small space. I tangled my fingers in his soft hair and thrust my hips, slowly at first and then more quickly as my belly tightened and my orgasm approached.

"Chase!" I shouted. He increased the suction and moved his mouth faster. "Jesus fuck. You're an amazing cocksucker. A fucking natural."

I shoved my hips forward and stiffened just as he popped his mouth off and pumped me with his slick hand. I might have cried out his name again or I might have just grunted. The only thing I knew for certain was that my vision went black from the power of that orgasm.

By the time I was done emptying my balls, my knees were weak and my lungs hurt. The chair caught me when I stumbled back. I sat, catching my breath, and looked at Chase as he raised himself up and walked over to the sink. Though my brain was fuzzy from the force of the pleasure he'd wrung from me, I could tell from the set of his shoulders that something was wrong.

Not knowing what to say, I went with, "Thanks. That was great."

He turned on the water, lathered and rinsed his hands, and then dried them off, all without saying a word and without looking at me. Then he took a deep breath, straightened his posture, turned around, and leaned against the counter.

"I'm glad you enjoyed yourself and I get that you're lacking in the sensitivity department, but you call me a cocksucker again and I'm kicking your ass out no matter how hard your dick is." He paused and glared at me. "We clear?"

I opened and closed my mouth several times, trying to figure out what to say. "I didn't mean anything by it. It's just dirty talk. No big deal."

"This isn't a porno or an alley behind a seedy bar, and I'm not a fucking hustler, Adan!" He screwed his eyes shut, took a calming breath, and wiped his hands on his pants. "All right," he said quietly when he opened his eyes. "You got what you came for. Door's that way."

Somehow I'd gone from him being pissed but talking about a next time to him kicking me out right then. That probably meant I'd said the wrong thing.

"I'm sorry," I said.

"Apology accepted." He walked to his front door and started turning the locks.

Right, so that didn't fix whatever I'd broken.

"I don't want to go," I said.

He stopped moving, his back to me and his hand on the lock. "Why not?" he asked.

I racked my brain trying to figure out what to say to keep him from throwing me out. It was early still for a Saturday, and I'd been looking forward to talking and laughing late into the night, to waking up with him on Sunday morning and watching him move gracefully around his kitchen, to spending more time together. He was right—I was lacking in the sensitivity department, which meant I had no idea what I could do to make those things happen.

I slumped in defeat and said, "I don't know, Chase. I didn't mean to piss you off, okay? I have fun with you. I didn't just come over for a blowjob. I've been looking forward to hanging out with you all week."

Saying the words made me realize they were true, which was a little scary because I'd never been much for socialization. My friendships had been acquaintances and professional contacts. My relationships had been hookups. Even the time I spent with my family was due to obligation, not desire. But it was different with Chase.

"I like you," I whispered as I got up and walked over to him.

He turned around, pressed his back against the door, looked me over, and warily said, "You trying to get into my pants?"

"No." I shook my head, paused, and then nodded. Whatever shortcomings I had, lying wasn't among them. "Well, yeah." I reached him and raised my hand to caress his cheek and pet his hair. "But that's not why I want to stay." I dipped my face until our eyes were at the same level and our mouths were almost touching. "I want to be with you, Chase, even if you keep your pants on."

He made a soft whimper sound in the back of his throat, and it spurred me into action. I held on to his waist with one hand and his nape with the other and pulled him close as I slanted my mouth over his. As soon as our lips connected, he went soft and pliant in my arms. He draped his forearms over my shoulders and darted his tongue out to flick mine before sucking on it. Though I'd just shot my load, I felt my dick filling again, so I shoved my knee between his thighs and ground against him.

"Adan!" he cried out, riding my thigh.

"Right here, baby," I said, smirking in satisfaction as I looked at his glazed eyes and swollen lips. I moved my hand and turned the locks, securing us inside. Both of us. "And just because I'll stay even if you keep your pants on, doesn't mean we wouldn't have a hell of a lot more fun if you took them off."

Chapter 12

INTRODUCTION

Charlie ("Chase") Rhodes

I HAD a boyfriend.

Some people might describe him as prickly, but I knew his demeanor was a defensive strategy to keep anyone from getting close enough to hurt him. Six months into our relationship, Adan and I had kept up our "no serious conversations" pact. That meant he didn't talk much about his family, but I gathered they weren't close. And I couldn't help but notice that though we spent every weekend together, he hadn't ever said we needed to make an appearance at a friend's birthday or a celebration dinner or whatever, indicating to me that after more than two years living in New York, he hadn't made any friends. So it wasn't hard to figure out that he held himself apart from everyone around him.

I understood that outlook. I'd had to force myself not to hide away from the world for a long time after Scott left. If it hadn't been for my mother telling me the pain would pass, my sister calling and saying the best way to get over a man was to get under another one, and Selina dragging my ass out to interact with our friends, I could have ended up just as walled off as Adan.

So because I understood, I didn't mind being patient while he learned to trust me and navigated his way around being in what I was sure was his first relationship. I don't want you to think it was all a huge sacrifice for me. The reality was that I was amused by his lewd come-ons, I was in awe of his intelligence and drive, he was great in bed, and he was fun to be around.

Which brings me to the next picture in the album: me and Adan in bed. No, it's not a sex picture. He's helping me fly. Adan is lying on his back with his legs and arms up at ninety degree angles and his feet and hands facing the ceiling; I'm stretched out with my legs and arms straight out, my hips resting on the bottoms of his feet, and my fingers twined with his for support. He said all I needed was the cape to look like Superman. And I thought the way he made me feel was more amazing than any superpower.

Chapter 12

Adan Navarro

I DIDN'T know how it happened—mostly because I refused to think about it—but somehow summer passed, fall was almost over, and I was still spending time with Chase Rhodes. Lots of time.

I'd gotten into a routine where I spent weekends at his apartment and also went there on days that I had a light class load. His schedule was different from mine because his evenings were usually spent working, whereas I had class during the day. But he gave me a key and I hung out at his place because his refrigerator was always stocked, his couch was comfortable, he had good lighting... and also because I knew he'd walk through the door at the end of the night, usually with a big smile and a funny story.

One night in early November, I fell asleep studying on the couch. The sound of the locks turning woke me up, so by the time Chase walked in, I was sitting and rubbing my palms over my eyes.

"Sorry," he said as he hung up his coat. "I didn't mean to wake you up."

I expected him to walk over, sit on my lap, and kiss me. That's what he usually liked to do, and I didn't mind, so I let him. But that night, he dropped his bag by the bed and shuffled into the bathroom, barely looking at me, let alone touching me.

With a frown, I set my book down and approached him. "What's going on?"

He had his shoes and shirt off and was working on his pants. "Nothing." He kept his gaze lowered, not making eye contact with me. "Just gonna grab a shower."

"Chase," I said gently as I grasped his arm. "What's wrong, baby?"

With another shake of his head, he managed to cover his eyes with his hair. A sniffle and a gulp told me what he was trying to hide.

"Are you crying?" I asked worriedly as I pushed his hair back and tilted his chin up. His eyes were wet. "You are. What happened?"

"It's nothing," he insisted. "Give me a few minutes in the shower and I'll be fine."

"No." I dragged him close and wrapped my arms around him. "Something's wrong. Talk to me."

"Don't we have that rule where we can't talk about family or shit that matters?" he asked with a sniffle, but he circled his hands around my waist and held on tightly, so I suspected he wanted to talk.

"What can I say? You've turned me soft."

He chuckled and reached between us, groping for my dick. Being close to him had caused the predictable response. "You don't feel soft," he said as he rubbed the heel of his hand up my shaft. "But I know how to get you there."

"And I'm going to take you up on that." I twined my fingers with his, brought his hand up to my mouth, and kissed the back of it. "Right after we talk about what has you down."

He sighed deeply and looked up at me from under his lashes. "You really wanna know?"

Surprisingly, I did. "Yes."

"My director Jared had his kid at work today. I went into his office after the show, and he was holding his son up and flying him around the room like an airplane and making whoosh noises. The kid was giggling like crazy."

"That sounds, uh, cute."

"It was." Chase nodded. "But then it reminded me of this girl who lived down the hall from me when I was little. Her dad used to do that too, and I always wanted my dad to give me an airplane but he was barely there and when he was he was usually fighting with my mom, and then he took off." Chase took a deep breath and I tried to process his quickly spoken ramble. "See?" he said. "It's stupid. Lots of people don't see their fathers and it's not like it's new for me." He shrugged. "Maybe I'm being extra sensitive because this is gonna be my first Thanksgiving since my mom moved away. We have a show on Friday and Saturday, so I can't go to Florida." He rubbed his lips together and dragged his fingers through his hair. "But, again, that's not a big deal. A bunch of my friends are getting together, or I can have dinner with Selina and her family or I can fly solo or… whatever. See? No big deal. I'm fine."

But he wasn't fine. I only had to look at the set of his shoulders, the red rims around his eyes, and the grimace he was trying to pass off as a smile to know he was down. Even though I often rolled my eyes at his exuberant personality, the truth was, I liked how happy and bouncy he was all the time and I hated seeing him down.

"Come on," I said as I tugged his hand and led him out of the bathroom.

"Where're we going?" he said, but he followed me without hesitation. "I'm not dressed."

"You don't need to be dressed for this."

"Oh." He pressed his chest up against my back and rubbed on me. "Well, in that case, I'm too dressed. Let me take my underwear off."

"I'm giving you an airplane." I lay down on the bed and held my hands out to him. "You can take them off or keep them on. Your call."

"What?" He stood at the end of the bed with his hands on the waistband of one of his many sexy-as-hell briefs.

"An airplane, like you said. I can't do it while we're standing, but you're small enough that I can hold you above me." I scooted until my entire body was on the bed. "C'mere."

"You're serious?" Chase asked, looking equal parts surprised and thrilled.

"Yup." I was proud of myself for having come up with a way to cheer him up.

"Hold on. I gotta get a picture." He rushed over to retrieve his camera and set it up on the dresser. "Okay. Timer's set." He hopped on the bed, smiling like a little kid. "Where do you want me?"

It was hard not to answer with my usual thinly veiled innuendos like, "I want you on your hands and knees with your ass in the air." Okay, maybe that wasn't so much an innuendo or thinly veiled. Anyway, I kept it PG and said, "Right over here."

He climbed over me. I tucked the bottoms of my feet under his hips and wove my fingers with his; then I stretched my legs and arms up so he was hovering above me, his body flat as a board. He looked like he was flying.

"Whoosh!" I shouted while I moved my legs from side to side and back and forth, giving him as much motion as possible.

"You're nuts!" he said through joy-filled laughter.

"All you need is the cape and you'd look like Superman."

He gazed at me and beamed, looking so damn happy. "Thanks, Adan."

My chest constricted and an unfamiliar feeling washed over me, leaving me petrified. "You can thank me later by getting on your hands and knees and sticking your ass in the air." There. I hadn't changed. I was still me. My fear ebbed leaving me with warmth in my belly.

"You can count on it. But can we do this for a little longer?"

"Sure thing, baby. Anything you want." I clasped his hands tightly and shifted my legs down. "Whoosh!"

Well, maybe I'd changed a little.

THANKSGIVING sucks. There, I said it. The whole day is spent rushing from one relative's house to the next—my grandparents on my father's side, my aunt on my mother's side, my mother's best friend's parents—eating more than any person should and then chewing Tums in the car while my parents talk about who was rude and who dressed slutty and who looked like maybe she was pregnant again.

My sister was usually good for a laugh or at least moral support, but that year she left after round one because, and I quote from my mother's oft-repeated explanation, "Lucia is spending the rest of the holiday with her future in-laws." Seems reasonable until you realize Lucia wasn't engaged, as of Halloween she hadn't had a boyfriend, and whatever boyfriend she had drummed up in the interim hadn't joined her for the first Thanksgiving meal of the day with our family. It sucked being left to deal with the parental units solo, but I couldn't blame her for escaping if she could get away with it. No reason for all of us to go down on the sinking ship of boredom and annoyance; it was every man for himself, real or imaginary.

By Friday afternoon, I was ready to jump off the roof to get away from family time, but my parents lived in a ranch house, so the most I could hope for was a sprained ankle, which wouldn't have saved me from the mental torture and boredom.

"Are you going to spend time with your friends tonight?" my mother asked excitedly.

"My friends?"

"Loretta said Cynthia gets together with a bunch of kids from your school each year on the Friday after Thanksgiving. I know she'd be *very* happy if you went with them."

Loretta was my mother's best friend, Cynthia was her daughter, and nobody would be happy if she was forced to drag me around with her friends. What both of our mothers failed to realize was that: (A) none of us was a child any longer; (B) my high school stopped being my school when I went to college and then law school; (C) Cynthia and I hadn't run in the same high school social circle, mostly because she was this übcroutgoing cheerleader type and I could barely tolerate my classmates over the lunch hour, let alone in my free time; and (D) despite their dreams of uniting our families by marriage, I wasn't interested in Cynthia for a lot of reasons, one of which was that she wasn't a guy, and Cynthia wasn't interested in me for a lot of reasons, one of which was that I was interested in guys.

But rather than explaining all that to my mother yet again, I said, "Oh, I wish I could, but I need to get to the airport on time for my flight."

"Your flight?" my father said. "You're not leaving until Sunday."

"Did I forget to tell you that I have to leave early this year? Sorry. There's an important study group I can't miss."

It was not only a lie, but a terrible lie, because my chances of getting a flight out at the last minute were slim to none and in addition to not running in Cynthia's social circle in high school, I didn't run in any social circle and I hadn't kept in touch with a single classmate, which meant I had nowhere to crash. Nevertheless, I stuck to my story, because an airport motel had to be better than any more quality time with my family.

"Actually"—I looked down at my wrist where a watch would go if I wore one, which I didn't—"I better go pack."

Not only did I escape getting struck down dead for lying to my parents, but the gods of air travel were smiling down on me, because with a minimal fee, I changed my flight to a standby ticket and then got the last seat on a redeye to New York. Airplanes aren't the most comfortable places for a guy my size—my shoulders are broad enough to bump the people next to me—

but it didn't matter because I slept most of the flight. Even though I wasn't need-to-sleep tired by the time I landed, I was emotionally drained and all I wanted to do was go home and relax.

It wasn't until after I told the cabby Chase's address that I realized what my mind equated with home. I gave myself leave to freak out about that later, because at that moment, I wanted nothing more than to crawl into bed with Chase and not get out for the rest of the weekend. And I didn't care what that meant.

The bodega next to his apartment was selling potted hydrangeas, so I picked some up, knowing how much he liked those damn flowers. Then I used my key to let myself into his apartment. As I expected, he was asleep in his bed. What I hadn't expected was to find two men sharing the bed with him and another two on his couch.

The logical part of my brain registered that everyone was, at a minimum, wearing underwear. I also took note of the various wine bottles and liquor bottles on the counter and table and guessed that a night drinking with friends had turned into friends crashing at his place because they were too drunk to go home. Again, logical brain said that was completely normal behavior for a twenty-five-year-old guy. Well, completely normal behavior for one with friends, anyway. It wasn't something I'd ever done.

So logical brain was all good. Unfortunately, irrational hothead brain shoved his ass aside and screamed, "What the fuck is going on here?"

One guy rolled off the couch onto the floor, another guy shot up in bed, two guys stayed fast asleep, and Chase rubbed his palms over his eyes and then blinked them open in confusion. "Adan?" he said when he spotted me standing in his doorway. "What's going on? I thought you weren't getting in until Sunday night." His sleepy gaze moved from my face to my hand and he smiled sweetly. "You brought me flowers?"

I decided not to kill everyone in the room.

Chase slowly crawled off the bed, apparently nudging still-sleeping-bed-guy, because he muttered something and shoved a pillow over his head. Awake-bed-guy said, "Who the fuck is that? Man, it's too early for visitors."

Maybe I'd jumped the gun on the no-murder decision. I had a key. Couldn't asswipe tell that meant I was more than a visitor?

"You're here," Chase said dreamily as he walked toward me. "I missed you."

I forgot about asswipe, dropped my bag on the floor, and kicked the door closed.

"What the fuck?" previously-sleeping-couch-guy yelled when the door slammed.

Already-awake-and-on-the-floor-couch-guy said, "Tell me about it."

I considered beating them over the head with the flowers.

"These are so pretty," Chase said. He wrapped his hand over mine, brought the flowers to his nose, and inhaled their scent. "I love hydrangeas."

"I know." I puffed up a little, feeling proud of the fact that I knew how to please him. I'd need to find something else to use as a weapon against the annoying shits who were making no move to get dressed and get out of our... his apartment.

"Thanks, Adan. I can't believe you found hydrangeas in November." He cupped the back of my head, got on his tiptoes, and drew me down for a kiss. "This was sweet of you, but is everything okay? I know I didn't forget your flight time."

I wrapped my free arm around his waist and dragged him forward until we were pressed together tight enough to give my groin the pressure I'd been craving since the moment I last saw him. "Everything's fine." I nuzzled his neck. "I just missed you, baby."

"Oh, for fuck's sake, get a room already, you two. We're trying to sleep."

I wasn't sure which of the small-brained freaks had said that last one, but it didn't matter. "We have a room but you're in it," I yelled. "Get the fuck out."

"Chase," one of them whined. "'M tired."

"Yeah? Well I'm horny." I scowled at everyone, not that they were looking. "Leave."

It might have been a rude thing to say, but Chase knew me well enough by then to understand that I meant it. He chuckled, grasped my hand, and said, "C'mere."

"Where're we going?" I followed him through the apartment, stepping over clothes and limbs as I went.

"Bathroom," he said. "So we can have some privacy and take care of your, uh, needs."

"Why do we have to hide away like a couple of kids?" I whined, sounding very much like a kid. "They should leave."

"Yes, I know. But they're hungover and tired and it's mean to kick them out."

"I don't care." Chase was nice but I wasn't. At least not when it came to something standing between me and the orgasm I'd been craving since I skulked out of my parents' house.

"Getting rid of them will take forever," he said as he walked us into the bathroom. He set the flowers on the counter and closed the door behind me. "You can think of this as an 'I missed you' appetizer and we can have the main course after they're gone."

"There are four guys in there," I grumbled. "Seems to me you should be too full for appetizers after playing with them all night."

"Aww, are you jealous?" He smiled as he pushed my coat off and kissed my neck.

"No."

"No?" He grazed his lips up to my jaw and groped my dick through my jeans. "'Cause you sound a little jealous and you looked like you wanted to hurt someone back there."

I grunted, leaned back against the door, and widened my stance, giving him better access to my package.

"You don't need to worry." He flicked his tongue over my earlobe and unbuttoned my jeans. "You know how into you I am." He sucked on my lobe and pushed my boxers and jeans down to my thighs, exposing my semierect dick and full balls to cool air. "I don't want anybody else."

Yeah, I knew that. It was obvious Chase was totally into me. I relaxed and traced his lips with my thumb. "Show me, baby."

"Gladly."

He had just dropped to his knees when someone pushed the door open, slamming the knob into my back and catching me off guard. I bucked forward, knocked Chase's nose with my hip, and sent him sprawling across the floor.

"What the hell?" I shouted, turning to face the door.

One of Chase's buddies tried to squeeze into the room. "I need to take a piss," he said.

I cracked my knuckles and got ready to break his nose.

"Come on, Trev," Chase said as he scrambled up from the floor. "You knew we were in here."

"Yeah, yeah," the guy said, completely undeterred. "You were trying to get a little dick. Got it. But nature calls."

"It sure as fuck isn't little," Chase said with a wink. "Quit screwing around and give us some privacy."

The guy looked from Chase to me and then dragged his gaze down to my exposed and, by that point, flaccid dick. He didn't utter a word, just raised his eyebrows meaningfully and smirked.

"Hey! I'm a grow-er not a show-er," I said defensively. The asshole scoffed disbelievingly. "No, really, I am." I looked at Chase imploringly. "Tell him."

The asshole laughed and Chase's expression went from amused to pissed. He squeezed past me and shoved his friend out of the bathroom. "You're out of line, Trev. And, by the way, I've seen your dick and guys in four-inch glass houses shouldn't throw stones at other guys who are over eight inches and thick. Get out of here."

I stared at Chase as he forced his friend out of the room and closed the door. "You need a lock for this door."

"I need to get new friends." He was vibrating with anger.

"Maybe he was jealous," I said magnanimously, expecting Chase to tell me I was wrong, that he was just friends with that *Trev* person, that there had never been anything between them.

"Maybe," he admitted. "But that doesn't give him an excuse to be an asshole to you." Chase dropped his forehead against my chest. "Sorry."

I caressed his hair and tried to stay calm when I asked, "Did you used to date him?"

"Not really." He shrugged. "I don't know. Maybe he saw it that way because we fooled around a couple of times, but it wasn't any good, so we stuck with the friendship. I wouldn't call it dating."

"I don't understand the difference," I admitted, hoping he couldn't feel my muscles tightening. It wasn't like either of us had been a virgin when we'd met. I had no reason to be upset. But I was. "Spending time with someone, being friends with them, and having sex with them. That sounds like dating to me."

120

He looked up at me, chewed on his lower lip, and furrowed his brow in concentration.

"Yeah, that's true. I guess what I mean is that we weren't in a relationship, you know? It wasn't like how things are between us." He rested his cheek against my chest again and sighed contentedly when I hugged him to me. "I didn't love him."

It was the perfect thing to say to stem my rapidly rising jealousy. And also the thing sure to open the floodgates on a whole other kind of panic.

Chapter 13

INTRODUCTION

Charlie ("Chase") Rhodes

HAVE you ever known someone who looks at life through a completely different lens? Like, for example, you could be at dinner with ten people and someone can say something. Then later, if you ask all ten people what happened, nine will tell you one story and the tenth will say something totally different, something tainted by that person's faulty life-view lens. If you know a person like this, then you've probably figured out that they don't realize they have a faulty lens. They honestly believe that what they think happened is what actually happened.

Well, at age twenty-six, I was forced to admit that maybe I had been looking at life through a faulty lens. Going on eight months into what I'd thought was a great relationship with a lonely guy who cared about me as much as I cared about him, I was slapped in the face with an alternative reality: the reason I hadn't met any of Adan's friends or coworkers or classmates or family members wasn't because he wasn't close to anybody except me, it was because he was ashamed to introduce me to the people who mattered in his life.

If you've ever had your world tilt on its axis that way, you know that the pain of your discovery is equal to the insecurity you carry into every other interaction in your life. After you realize you missed all the signs of something you should have seen all along, you can never trust yourself to see even the most obvious things clearly.

The next picture in the album isn't a happy one, even if it looked that way through the camera lens. Because that picture was taken on the day that my entire world stopped and reshaped itself, the day I stopped trusting Adan Navarro, and, what's worse, the day I stopped trusting myself.

We're sitting side by side on a bench inside a temporary restaurant. He's holding a drink in one hand and a piece of bread in the other. I have one hand on his knee and my arm stretched in front of us, holding the camera and snapping the self-portrait. We're both smiling in the picture. But my smile, at least, didn't last for long.

Chapter 13

Adan Navarro

FINALS sucked, and not just because they were hard and I had to study every single second I wasn't sleeping, but also because all that studying and focus meant I couldn't see Chase. It was the longest dry spell I'd had since we'd met, and I hated it.

I didn't bother going back to my apartment after my last final; I went straight to Chase's place. I'd barely gotten my key in the lock when I heard him racing toward the door and the locks being flipped from the inside.

"Adan!" he said as he yanked the door open. He dragged his gaze from my face down my body and then back up again. "Adan," he rasped, the need in his voice clear.

"Did you miss me?" I pulled my key out, tossed it onto his counter, and pressed my chest to his, moving him into the apartment as I kicked the door closed. He trembled and whimpered. Seeing the way I affected him, how much he wanted me, made me feel like the most powerful man around.

"God, yeah," he said. He shoved my coat off, threw his arms around my neck, and tried to climb up my body.

I loved his eagerness, loved how open he was with his emotions. I chuckled, grabbed his butt, and yanked him up so he could wrap his legs around my waist.

"Better?" I asked when he sighed happily and started sucking on my neck.

"Yeah." He nibbled on my earlobe. "It'd be even better if we were in bed."

I walked us over to his bed, squeezing his ass along the way.

"'S so hot how strong you are," he mumbled as he kissed his way up my chin.

We reached the bed and he slowly slid down my body, rubbing against my dick and making me groan. Foreplay was nice but I was so damn hard I ached.

"Get your clothes off, Chase." I yanked my shirt over my head. "This first time's going to be fast."

In the time it took me to get my button open and my zipper down, Chase shimmied out of his pants and stripped his shirt off, leaving himself completely naked.

"Fuck, you're hot," I said, my voice sounding rough to my own ears. I let go of my pants, grabbed his shoulders, and turned him around. "Can you reach the lube?"

He shook his head. "No, it's in the nightstand."

I kissed the back of his neck and then I planted my hand in the middle of his back and shoved him face-first onto the mattress. He was bent over, feet on the floor, chest on the bed, ass in the air.

"Then you're going to take me on spit." I dragged my finger down Chase's crease, pressed my mouth to his ear, and whispered, "Don't worry, baby. This'll hurt you more than it'll hurt me."

After a two-second silence when I assumed he was processing what I said, his shoulders started shaking with laughter. "You are such an ass," he said as he reached back and smacked my hip.

I smiled and nuzzled the spot where his shoulder met his neck. "Seriously, you okay with this?" With a whimper, he spread his legs and tilted his ass up, giving me his answer. "Oh yeah," I said as I dropped to my knees and circled my finger over his pucker. "You want this, don't you?"

He answered with actions instead of words: he reached back with both hands and spread his cheeks apart.

"That's it, baby." I licked long swipes up his channel. "Show me everything."

Rimming was something new to both of us, but ever since the first time we tried it, I'd become addicted. I loved listening to Chase moan and gasp and knowing I was the cause of his pleasure. After a few more passes over his crease, I flicked my tongue against his hole.

"Ungh!" he groaned.

I smiled and rubbed my whiskered face over his sensitive skin, making him shudder and gasp in surprise. When I had him shaking and begging, I gathered saliva on my tongue and pressed it into his body.

"Yeeees," he whispered, sounding completely blissed out.

I slowly fucked him with my tongue, going as deep as I could and moving it inside his silky heat. My mouth was pressed up against his hole, my face cradled between his muscular butt cheeks, and my tongue was buried in his tight body. Add to that his near constant moans and cries and his flexing ass, and I was ready to pop.

"Can't wait," I gasped. I climbed to my feet, shoved my boxers under my balls, and grasped my rigid shaft. "Jesus, Chase." I absorbed the sight of him lying prone before me, giving me total control over his perfect body, trusting me completely. "I'm going in."

I spit onto my hand, rubbed my saliva over my shaft, and pressed my slick glans against his entrance. Chase raised his fine ass higher, spread his muscular legs wider, and moaned with pleasure when I pressed inside him.

He turned his head to the side, looked up at me, and said, "Feels so good," his voice rough and strained.

"Always does." I didn't stop my slow slide inside him until my balls were pressed snuggly against his heated skin; then I closed my eyes and took a deep breath, trying to keep my orgasm at bay. But Chase whimpered, making my eyes open reflexively. I took in his golden skin, flushed cheeks, and erotic expression, and knew it was a losing battle. "Like Henry the Eighth said to all six wives, 'This won't last long.' Hold on, baby."

I held on to his hips, pulled out until my crown was spreading his ring of muscle wide open, and then shoved back in hard. He turned me on too much for slow and gentle. In and out I moved, faster and faster, until I could feel the wave of my pleasure reaching its peak.

"Chase!" I cried out, thrust as deep as I could, and arched my back, shooting so hard my knees almost buckled.

My mind was still foggy when I heard Chase shout out my name and saw him drop his hand to his side, his fingers coated in ejaculate. I collapsed on top of him, pressed my chest to his back, and grabbed his wrist.

"Give me that." I helped him raise his hand to my mouth and licked his semen off his fingers.

"Fuck, Adan," he groaned. "I can't get hard again so fast."

I twirled my tongue around his finger and slurped it into my mouth. When his breath hitched, I pulled my lips back and asked, "Are you sure?" before sucking the next digit in and fellating it.

"Oh, damn," he moaned. "Okay, but let's get your pants off this time, okay?" I had been in such a rush to taste him and fuck him that I hadn't bothered taking my pants off, just opened them up and shoved the front of my boxers down. "And let's get in bed. If we go at it like that again, I might pass out."

"Mmm—" I licked the back of his neck. "I sure do like having goals."

"I'M HUNGRY," I said later that evening when we were tangled together in bed.

"Oh, is hunger the source of that noise?" Chase asked, his head resting on my chest. "I thought maybe an alien was about to burst out of your stomach."

I reached down and pinched his ass.

"Ow!" he squealed.

"Don't mess with the bull, baby, you'll get the—"

"Even you don't have the stamina to give me your horn again this quickly."

"Oh, that's bad," I said with a chuckle. "But you're right. I need to refuel so I can fuck you into unconsciousness. What're you feeding me?"

"Umm," he said thoughtfully. "My fridge is pretty bare. It was a crazy week with the show running its last performance, and I didn't have time to shop. Oh!" He shot up. "I heard of a fun new place I want to try."

"Uh, I don't know, Chase. I'm not big on going out."

"It'll be my treat to celebrate the end of your semester." He curled his fingers around mine. "This concept sounds neat. They call it Guerilla Gourmet and their shtick is that they open at a new location every week, just, like, random places that are vacant, so they rush in, set up for food service, and then a week later, they're out."

The restaurant sounded intriguing and my stomach was growling, but I had some trepidation.

"Come on, please?" Chase pleaded.

He was bouncy and excited and begging, and it was impossible to refuse him. So I agreed to go out to dinner, not realizing that would put us smack dab into the defining moment of our relationship: I was faced with the prospect of admitting to someone in my world that we were in a relationship.

It sounds so simple. It *was* so simple. But at the time, I was twenty-eight going on eight and I blew it. Totally and completely blew it.

The beginning of the meal was great. The restaurant was in a closed-down bookstore, making the atmosphere unusual but fun. The bookstore's genre signs were still hanging from the ceiling: Nonfiction, Cooking, Self-Help, and the rest of them. The walls were covered in dark wood paneling. And in the middle of the space, the Guerilla Gourmet people had set up a bunch of picnic tables.

We sat down and ordered our food. The salad course was delicious. And then everything went to shit.

"I want to get a picture of us," Chase said as he got up from his bench, which was across the table from mine, and came over to my side. I moved to the end of my bench. "Scootch closer," he said. I moved an imperceptible amount. "Closer, Adan, otherwise I can't get both of us in the shot." He fiddled with his ever-present camera, completely unaware of my turmoil.

Chase was wearing pink pants, a patent leather belt, and a light-yellow shirt. If he had tattooed "I'm a giant fairy" on his forehead, it would have been less obvious. I'd gotten used to his unique wardrobe by then and when we were at his place or with his friends, it didn't bother me. But we were in a crowded restaurant in an upscale part of town. "Come on, Adan, I don't have many pictures of us together," he said imploringly, still trying to get me to sit closer.

"You have plenty of pictures of us together," I replied in a lowered voice.

Red heat crawled up his neck. "Fine. I don't have many pictures of us together while we're dressed."

"I fail to see the problem here."

I waggled my eyebrows, making Chase laugh. Of course, his laughter was infectious, so I was chuckling along with him. The next thing I knew,

Chase had moved so we were shoulder to shoulder and he was holding the camera in front of us and snapping a picture.

"Adan Navarro, right?" a voice boomed from behind me.

I jumped away from Chase and spun around to see the source of the voice. It was the managing partner of one of the top paying firms in New York. Actually, they were one of the top paying firms in every one of their many international locations. They had made me a job offer to start after graduation, and I was trying to decide whether I should take it or clerk for a judge first.

"I thought it was you," he said, slapping my back. "Have you made a decision about next year?"

"Oh, uh, hi, Mark. It's great to see you." I reached out to shake his hand. After that greeting was out of the way, he turned his focus to Chase, clearly expecting an introduction. "Uh, Mark this is my friend Chase Rhodes. Chase, Mark is one of the most skilled litigators in the tri-state area." And one of the highest earners, but I figured that was implied.

"It's nice to meet you, Chase. Maybe you can convince Adan to join our firm."

"He's just a friend," I snapped out, feeling panicked at the prospect of the man who had control over my career options associating me with someone who carried himself like Chase. "He doesn't have anything to do with my decisions." I felt Chase stiffen beside me, but he stayed silent.

Mark walked away a couple of seconds later with a promise to call me the following week to check in. I waited a beat, excused myself to go use the bathroom, and then sat on the bench across from Chase when I returned.

I should have realized something was wrong when Chase didn't say more than two words the rest of the meal. Or when he barely ate his meal. Or when he stared down at his plate and didn't look at me. But I was too busy replaying the conversation with Mark in my mind and jerking my head around the room to see if I saw anyone else who'd recognize me. So it wasn't until we were walking away from the restaurant that I realized Chase was upset.

"What was that in there?" Chase had been silent for so long, the sound of his voice took me off guard.

"What do you mean?"

We walked a little farther and then he said, "With that guy. Mark or whatever. What was the deal?"

I shrugged. "He wants me to come work for his firm after graduation, and I haven't decided if I should cash in and do that right away or clerk for a year first."

"That's not what I meant." He came to a halt and sighed, "Adan, are you out?"

I got closer to him so we could talk quietly, then took note of our proximity, darted my gaze around, and stepped back. "Of course I'm out."

"Okay, don't be mad, it's just...." He bit his bottom lip. "It didn't seem that way in there." He took in a deep breath. "You told him we were friends."

I had an inkling of where the conversation was going, but not the sense to take it in a different direction. "We *are* friends."

Chase rolled his eyes. "Come on. You know what I mean. You didn't want him to know that I'm your boyfriend. If you're in the closet at work, you can tell—"

"I don't hide who I am!" I shouted, feeling offended at the accusation and frustrated by the conversation. Especially because it was Chase's fault. Those clothes didn't just appear in his closet. "But having the balls to be honest about that doesn't mean I have to shove it in everyone's faces all the time, and it really, really doesn't mean I have to play to every ridiculous gay stereotype!"

His jaw dropped and his eyes widened. "Uh, I think I missed something here. Rewind." He made a rolling gesture with his hand. "Why are you pissed?"

"See!" I shouted accusingly and pointed at his hand. "Why do you move your hands that way? And look at how you're standing!" He looked down at his hand, then at his body—his hip was hitched to the side and his leg stretched out—and furrowed his brow in confusion. "And don't even get me started on those clothes. I am going to be a professional attorney, Chase, do you honestly think anybody is going to pay four hundred dollars an hour for my time and trust my judgment if they think I'm like *you*?"

"Think you're like me?" he repeated slowly.

"You know what I mean!"

For the first time since I'd met him, Chase looked truly sad. It was different from the few times he had been upset about his family or something at work. His posture slumped, his face fell, and his eyes glistened with tears.

"Yeah," he said thickly and then swallowed hard. "I think I do. I need to go home."

"Right, good." I was disarmed by his expression; I hated to see him upset. "Let's go."

"No." He shook his head. "I need to go home alone tonight and think about all of this and maybe—" He gulped. "You need to do some thinking too, because if you actually believe all those things about me, I'm not sure why we're together."

"Come on, Chase, don't be such a drama queen."

It wasn't a fair accusation, because despite having a career in the theater, Chase was an easygoing, drama-free guy.

"Drama queen?" His voice took on a hardened edge. "Tell me something, Adan: Why haven't I met your friends?"

"What?"

"Do you have friends?"

"Of course I have friends." They weren't the kinds of friends that he had, not people I'd known for years or I could call in a crisis or who I wanted to spend time with outside of class.

"Why haven't I met them?" he demanded.

"There's no reason for—"

"Is it because you're ashamed to tell them you're dating a guy *like me?*" Hearing my words thrown back at me was like a slap to the face. I reeled back. "What about your family?"

"What about them?" My blood pressure was rising, defenses up, temper flaring.

"Am I ever going to meet them?"

Just the thought of my father and mother seeing Chase in all his flamboyant glory made me wince.

"I see," he said. "I'm going home."

"They're on the other side of the country. What's the point in you meeting them?"

"The point.... Adan, I love you," he said. I almost choked on thin air. "Yeah, it's scary for you to hear, I know, which is why I haven't said the words but—call me stupid—I thought you knew."

I did know, because whether he remembered doing it or not, he had said he loved me once. I'd ignored it then and I planned to do the same thing now. But this time, Chase wasn't going to let it go.

131

When I didn't respond, he took in a deep breath, and said, "I thought you felt the same way about me."

"I never said—"

"I know. From the first day, you made it clear that all you wanted was some fun in bed, but I thought you were joking." That sadness had enveloped him, taking away the light in his eyes, making him look pale. "I guess the joke's on me."

He turned on his heel and started stomping away from me.

"Chase, wait!" I jumped forward and grabbed his shoulder. "Don't be like that!"

His chin dropped and he didn't look back at me. "I am *like that*, Adan, and I'm not going to change. Not for you, not for anybody. There's nothing wrong with how I am, and like you said about yourself, I'm not going to hide it!" He rubbed his shaky hand over his styled hair. "If you decide there's more than just a good time between us, call me." He sucked in a deep breath. "Otherwise, lose my number."

IF I had to name the five biggest regrets of my life, that moment would have taken the top four spots. And the fifth would have been occupied by my failure to fix it.

Oh, I sort of tried. I went home for Christmas and New Year's, came back to New York in the middle of January, and finally broke down a month later. I called him, but his number had been disconnected. I went to his place, but my key didn't work, and when I knocked, a stranger answered and told me she'd just moved in. I even called his friend Selina, but all she did was shout out creative ways she hoped I'd be dismembered and castrated; then she told me Chase was gone. She said he'd left New York, taken a job somewhere else, and wanted nothing to do with me.

Instead of insisting she give me his contact information or trying another way to reach him, I told myself it was for the best, that there wasn't room in my life plan for someone like him, that I'd gotten what I wanted out of him and I'd have no problem finding someone to fill his space. None of that was true and I knew it, but it didn't stop me from stupidly walking away.

I've heard people say they wouldn't change anything in their past, not even the bad stuff, because it got them to where they are in the present. I'm not one of those people.

It took longer than it should have, but eventually, I grew up enough to realize I'd been an ass to a man I should have cherished. I realized that getting to relish in the joys of a relationship meant having to work through the challenges. I realized that strength of self and strength of character come in different forms and I hadn't been exhibiting any of them.

All those realizations made me a better man, a better boyfriend, and eventually a better partner, but that didn't mean I wouldn't have changed the past. I would have given up all of that personal growth and self-realization if it had kept Chase Rhodes by my side. Unfortunately, life doesn't grant do-overs.

Chapter 14

INTRODUCTION

Charlie ("Chase") Rhodes

IF THIS was a movie, we'd be at the part where the guy is doing meaningless tasks while the seasons change around him and he grows a beard or cuts his hair or does something else to show time moving forward. But I don't have facial hair or stimulating visual effects, so I'll just tell you that the years kept coming and the years kept going.

I left New York, toured with a well-regarded company, and danced for large audiences. I worked on cruise ships and saw parts of the world I never thought I'd encounter outside of books. My twenties passed, my thirties were half over, and I started working on breaking into choreography because dancing into my forties wasn't going to be easy. I made new friends, fell out of touch with some friends, and kept in touch with others. I met men who made me laugh, men who made me think, men who made me cum. But I never met another man who made my heart leap and had me hoping for forever. Two chances at love in one lifetime, it seemed, were the maximum any one person got.

During my bitter moments, it made me mad because I'd lost both Scott and Adan before I turned thirty, which left me with a long life alone. But in my positive moments, I told myself that some people aren't even lucky enough to find one person who makes them feel warm and right and good, and I'd had two. Of course, they'd shattered my trust and my spirit, but it's better to have loved and lost than never to have loved at all, right? At least that's what *they* say. If you ever meet "they," kick him in the shin for me, would you?

All right, that's enough naval gazing. Are you ready to hear about the next picture? Okay, well, to understand this one, I have to tell you about the worst thing that ever happened to me.

My sister died.

She was living in Nevada with her two kids from two different unnamed fathers. She had been working late. There was a drunk driver. The roads were slick with September rain. And I got a call in the middle of the night from her friend-slash-nanny telling me that Rachel was gone and my six-year-old niece and seven-year-old nephew needed me.

My mother and I flew down there, got Bobby and Stephanie into counseling, and agreed that more changes wouldn't be good for them, so they should stay in Las Vegas, at least to finish out the school year. My mom was in her late sixties, not in the greatest health, and married to a man who owned a business in Florida. So once things were settled, she went back to her home at the other end of the country. That left me in Nevada as the legal guardian— on the way to becoming the adopted father—of two small children.

None of it was what I'd expected or wanted, but life throws shit at you and you have to deal. At age thirty-five, I'd long since figured that out. So I called a buddy who worked at one of the Vegas shows, got a gig dancing and training under the lead choreographer, and moved my life to Nevada.

As you might recall, Scott's father and stepmother lived there and, last I'd heard, so did he. When my sister broke up with the guy who moved her to Vegas, she was looking for work. As luck would have it, Scott's parents were looking for a nanny right then. My decision to cut off all contact with his family didn't apply to my mother and sister, so Rachel had ended up nannying for Lloyd and Julia. Thankfully, she had respected my request not to talk about Scott, understanding how painful that breakup had been for me.

The downside to that courtesy was that I didn't realize she had kept in touch with Scott long after the nannying gig for his father ended. And that lack of knowledge left me completely unprepared for what happened next. Are you ready? Don't worry, the bad shit's over, I promise.

Daniel, a guy I'd sort of dated and who had remained one of my closest friends was in town for the weekend, and I'd promised I'd meet him for dinner and dancing one night. I hadn't done anything but work and bond with

Stephi and Bobby in the month since I'd moved into town, so I was looking forward to it. I called Stacia, my sister's friend and the kids' former nanny, and asked her to babysit.

So far so good. But then, minutes before I was expecting her, my phone rang.

"Hi, Charlie, listen, I'm sooooo sorry to have to do this, but I feel like shit and I just threw up, so I can't watch the kids tonight." Before I could buck up and tell her it was okay and to feel better, she added, "But I didn't want to leave you hanging, so I asked someone else to fill in."

Other than people from work, I didn't know anybody in town, not even any of Rachel's other old friends, so I wasn't inclined to let someone else watch my kids.

"Thanks for the offer, Stacia, but don't worry about it. I don't feel right leaving the kids with a stranger."

"Oh! He's not a stranger. Don't worry. The kids love him. He's—"

The doorbell rang and both kids screeched, "Let's hide! Let's hide!"

It was a favorite game whenever anybody came into the house, including me. I can't for the life of me explain why it was entertaining, but there you have it.

"I think he's here, Stacia, I'll take care of it. Thanks again and feel better."

I hung up the phone and walked over to the door, trying to decide whether I should trust this person on Stacia's word or send him away. I was so lost in thought, I had the door open before I looked up. I raised my head when I saw two sets of feet walk in.

And there, standing in my apartment, were Scott Boone and Adan Navarro. I gasped and leaped back from the physical embodiments of the ghosts who had never stopped haunting me.

"Charlie!" Scott shouted happily, and at the same moment Adan excitedly cried out, "Chase!"

It was like a fucking nightmare.

"Fuck," I muttered and turned my head quickly from my first love to the only other man I'd trusted with my heart. They'd each eviscerated me once upon a time, and though I'd healed, mostly, being faced with both of them at the same moment was still too much... way too much. I suddenly felt as nauseous as Stacia.

Adan slowly turned his head to Scott, whose mouth was gaping open. "Charlie?" Adan asked weakly.

Scott closed his mouth and gulped. "Chase?" he said.

"Fuck," I groaned, as my brain started catching up to the comedy of horrors unfolding in front of me. It wasn't just that they were both there at the same time. They had been standing close together when I'd opened the door. Really close. And was Scott's arm around Adan's back?

They both looked over at me and stared.

"Charlie?" Scott asked, his voice hesitant, the question clear from his tone.

"Chase?" Adan asked, sounding equal parts incredulous and horrified.

Their tones and body language had already clued me in to what I was seeing, but when I shifted my gaze from Scott's eyes to Adan's and then back again, my suspicion was confirmed. I knew them well enough to recognize what I was seeing.

I'd loved two men during my thirty-five years on this planet. Only two. And I'd lost them both. Wouldn't it just figure that they'd found in each other what they had both deemed missing in me?

I dropped my face into my hands and whispered, "Fuck."

And that's when Bobby ran over and said, "I found your camera, Uncle Charlie! Can I take a picture?"

Adan looks green. Scott looks pale. I look like I'm going to pass out. And not a single one of us is looking at the camera. That's the next picture in the album.

137

$$Chapter\ 14$$

Scott Boone

FIFTEEN years. That's how long it had been since I'd talked to *him*. The first boy I'd ever loved. The one who had made me realize without a doubt that I was gay because there could be no other explanation for the way my heart raced every time I saw him. The person who had looked at me like I held all the answers to all the questions in the universe and who had never stopped glowing when I walked in the room. The guy who had never judged me, never found me lacking, and always put me first.

Charlie Rhodes: the person I had been too young to appreciate, too distracted to hold on to, but too in love with to ever forget.

Being with him had been both the best and the worst first relationship imaginable. Best because it was, in most ways, idyllic and happy and generous. Worst because measuring any adult relationships against it had left them lacking.

Which wasn't to say I hadn't had any other good relationships. I am a relationship kind of guy; hookups and flings have never been my cup of tea, so there had been other boyfriends in my life since Charlie and I broke up. But really, none of them had ever captured me like he had, made me feel what he did; none of them had found a place in my head and in my heart and never let go.

Well, none except for the man who shared my bed, my mortgage, my law practice, and, at that moment, my shock—Adan Navarro.

"What the fuck just happened here?" Adan asked, his gaze fixed on the door that had just closed.

"I don't—" I gulped, listened to the rapid footsteps fade away, and shook my head. "I don't know."

Seven-year-old Bobby jumped in with the oh so helpful summary: "Uncle Charlie said he'd be back by midnight, and your friend said a bad word." He planted his hands on his hips and glared at Adan. "Mr. Scott, tell your friend he isn't allowed to say bad words. It's my mother's rule."

Great. We'd violated his dead mother's rule. Never mind that I had heard Rachel cuss more than a drunken sailor. If people could see those they left behind from the afterlife, I had no doubt Rachel was, at that moment, laughing her butt off at me being scolded by her son.

"I'm sorry, Bobby," I said as I hunkered down so we were at eye level. "We'll be more careful from now on." I smacked Adan's shin. "Won't we?"

"Oh, uh, yes. More careful," Adan said.

"Who is he?" Bobby asked as he looked at Adan warily.

"This is Mr. Adan. He's my boyfriend and he's going to hang out with us tonight, okay?"

"Does he play Legos too?"

I smiled. Bobby had become obsessed with Legos a couple of years earlier, so whenever I went to Rachel's for dinner, our agenda included a good bit of time with me sprawled on Bobby's bedroom floor building animals out of Legos. Of course, Adan didn't know that because he had never met Rachel or her kids.

Part of that was because Rachel had never had any interest in meeting him or any of my previous boyfriends. I figured her reason was a self-imposed loyalty to her brother, so I'd never given her a hard time about it. Plus, the truth of the matter was, she looked enough like Charlie that I would have felt strange touching anybody else in front of her.

So, by unspoken agreement, whenever I spent time with her, I did it solo. I'd go over for dinner when Adan had late meetings or spend an afternoon with them when he traveled for business. It was easier that way. But now Rachel was gone, I'd been needed for last-minute babysitting, and bringing Adan with me had seemed like a good idea.

"Sure he can. Right, Adan?"

"Uh-huh, sure." Adan looked at Bobby and said, "Do you know where Chase... I mean, Uncle Charlie went tonight?"

Okay, so maybe bringing him hadn't been a great idea. Though I had been expecting Charlie's mom to be with the kids, not Charlie, so it wasn't like I could have anticipated how it would play out. That... and the fact that I had no idea Adan knew Charlie.

"Is he going out on a date with his boyfriend? Does he have a boyfriend? Does he date?" Adan fired out the questions in rapid succession.

I was still squatting, so I smacked him in the shin again and said, "Come on! Get a grip. Not in front of the K-I-D-S."

"I can spell, you know. I'm seven," Bobby notified us.

"Shi... I mean da... I mean, uh." I blinked rapidly, tried to get my brain in order, and toppled backward, landing on my ass.

Adan started laughing hysterically.

Bobby snorted, rolled his eyes, and said, "You guys are weird. I'm going to play with Stephi." Then he vacated the room almost as quickly as Charlie had bolted from the apartment.

"So," Adan said.

"Yup," I answered.

"That's the Charlie you talk about?"

I furrowed my brow and looked up at him. "I don't remember us ever discussing exes, Adan. In fact, I think that was something we both agreed to from the beginning. Leave the past in the past, isn't that what we said?"

"You talk in your sleep sometimes, hon."

"Shit." I stood up, feeling horrible and needing to apologize for the pain that must have caused him.

He held his hand out and helped me up. "No cussing in the house," he said, waggling his eyebrows.

"God, I'm sorry. Are you mad?"

"No, I'm not," he assured me. "I'm not going to say I liked it, but it's not like I didn't understand."

I wrapped my arms around his waist and looked into his eyes, trying to read his expression. He looked tired and sad, but not angry. "Why didn't you ever say anything?"

He sighed deeply and then said, "Because it would have made me a hypocrite."

"A hypocrite?"

"I have my own one-that-got-away, Scott. The only difference is, I kept my mouth shut about him when I was awake *and* when I was asleep." He paused, looking deeply pained, shuddered, and then added in a whisper, "But that doesn't mean I stopped thinking about him."

"Charlie?" I asked.

He nodded. "I know him as Chase, but yes."

We stood in silence for a couple of minutes, both of us thinking, and then I said, "We should probably talk, huh?"

The corners of Adan's mouth curled up. "You want to have a conversation? What, like about feelings and shit? Do people even do that anymore?"

I chuckled, but I felt too weighed down with emotions to find the humor in the situation. "I love you. I want you to know that. Whatever I said in my sleep and whatever I felt—" I paused and took a deep breath, forcing myself to be honest with the man who shared every facet of my life. "—or feel about Charlie, doesn't impact what you mean to me. It doesn't change how much I love you."

When he didn't respond and stood there, looking as melancholy as I felt, I started to worry. "Adan." I kissed him gently. "We agreed to build a life together and share our future, and I've never regretted that, not once. Please believe me."

"I do believe you, hon." He circled his arms around my hips, and we held each other. "And I feel the same way. I've never regretted it, even when things haven't been easy and even though everything isn't always perfect."

I understood what he meant. We loved each other, liked each other, and respected each other. But life in the bedroom could be a challenge. It wasn't an issue of attraction—I found him sexy as hell and I could tell from the way he looked at me and the way he touched me that he felt the same way about me. But before we'd gotten together, I had dated guys who liked to bottom with only an occasional desire to change it up, and he had topped exclusively. We'd found a middle ground over the years, both of us learning to bend, learning to move outside of our comfort zones to find happiness together. But we had always known that was one area where compatibility was a bit of a challenge.

And then there were the ways in which we were sometimes too compatible. We were partners in our own two-person law firm. We worked out together at the same gym. We lived under one roof. So there were nights when we'd look at each other and without saying a word, know it was time to go out, time to catch up with friends, time to find someplace loud and full of energy to break up our routine.

"Scott?"

"Yes?"

"You said you don't regret our life, don't regret our decision to build our future together."

"I don't," I said vehemently.

"I know. But—" He took a deep breath. "Do you regret losing him?"

Honesty was one thing, hurting a man I loved was another. "Adan, let me explain. I—"

"Do you regret not having a future with him?" he added.

"I—"

Thankfully he cut me off, because I wasn't sure what I was going to say. "Because I do."

"Shit." I took in a deep breath and dragged my fingers through my hair. "I guess we do need to talk, huh?"

"Hey, don't look so down about it." Adan grinned at me. "We've managed to hold off what some might consider a basic conversation for five years. That's pretty good, right?"

I shrugged. "I guess. Think after this one we can avoid it for another five?"

All the humor left his face. "Not if the conversation ends up where I think it should."

That comment could have meant a couple of different things, one of them being that we wouldn't be together for another five years. But I knew that wasn't what he meant, not only because I knew Adan almost as well as I knew myself, but also because I understood without him saying a word how he thought things should end up. It was easy to know, because, crazy though it was, I felt the same way.

Thankfully, the conversation had to wait, because right then, Stephi raced up holding a huge book. "Mr. Scott, can you read this to me?"

Bobby was on her heels. "No! It's Lego time."

"I was first, Bobby!" Stephi shouted as she squeezed herself between me and Adan and thrust her book up.

"No, you weren't." Bobby tried to shove her out of the way. "Scott already promised he'd play Legos with me!"

I had some experience with kids because my sister was twenty years younger than me and I spent a lot of time with her. But because of our age difference, we were both essentially only children, so sibling rivalry was a completely foreign concept.

"I have an idea," Adan said unexpectedly. "How about I read to Stephi while Scott builds with Bobby?" The kids stopped pushing each other and looked at him, seemingly trying to weigh this new offer. "And then we can trade spots and you can vote on who was the best builder and who was the best reader. Won't that be fun?"

I would have rolled my eyes at how my übercompetitive boyfriend had managed to turn an evening with children into a game of winners and losers, but Stephi was already walking over to the couch, holding her book with one hand and two of Adan's thick fingers with the other, and Bobby was tugging me to his bedroom, whispering about how I had the advantage because I had already played with his Legos.

"Who knew you had such a way with kids?" I said to Adan as I followed Bobby.

"I never have," he said to me. "But they're Chase's, um, Charlie's right? So *we* need to learn how."

My heart tripped and my breath hitched. "You're right. *We* do."

And with those words, we had come to an agreement. No conversation needed.

UNFORTUNATELY, the conversation respite didn't last long. By the time the kids were bathed and put in bed, and then given another glass of water and put in bed, and then read another book and put in bed, and then taken to the bathroom again and put in bed, and then mercifully fell asleep, Charlie walked in the front door.

He had looked horrified and shocked during the sixty seconds we'd spent together in his apartment before he said his good-byes to the kids and ran away. When he shuffled in the door at the end of the night, he looked just as horrified, just as shell-shocked, but also bone tired, and so miserable I wanted to scoop him up in my arms and promise I'd make everything okay.

Adan and I had just collapsed on the couch, but we both jumped to our feet when the door opened.

"Charlie," I said happily.

At the same time, Adan, his voice filled with longing, said, "Chase."

"Haven't we already done this part?" Charlie asked. He tried to smile, but his voice was weak and his eyes were sad, so it didn't come off as happy.

"What do you want to be called, baby?" Adan asked. "You tell us, and we'll keep it straight."

Charlie jerked his gaze over to me the second Adan called him baby. It was strange to hear, both because my boyfriend was using the term to refer to another man and also because someone else was calling Charlie "baby." But the other man was Charlie, and the someone else was Adan, and somehow that made it all right.

"I go by both," he said. "It doesn't matter."

Adan took a couple of steps toward him. "It matters to us." He took another step. "You matter to us."

The expression that took over Charlie's face right then was completely foreign. It was a horrible combination of bitterness, anger, and resignation. "Cut the shit, Adan. I haven't mattered to you in a long time." He coughed out a brittle laugh. "Hell, I probably never mattered to you."

Adan winced, and I could see pain flash in his eyes.

"Charlie, that's not true." I started walking over to him. "He cares about—"

"Scott, don't." Charlie threw his hand up. "I get that you're with him now, and I have no idea what he told you about our relationship and, really, it's none of my business, but you weren't there, so don't assume he cared." He glared at Adan. "He didn't care about anything but getting his rocks off." Charlie hadn't moved far from the door, so it took no time for him to turn the handle and swing it open. "Thanks for watching the kids tonight. I know it was awkward. Don't worry, it won't happen again. Vegas is a big city, and I promise to stay out of your way."

Adan still hadn't said a word or moved an inch since Charlie's angry remark, but he looked devastated. It was completely unlike Adan, who was normally unflappable and not particularly sensitive or emotional, so I found the reaction very disconcerting.

Knowing it was up to me to make inroads with Charlie, I said, "You're right, seeing each other after all these years caught us off guard, but, Charlie, please, we don't want you to stay away from us. We still care about you. Both of us. We—"

"Get out." His expression was icy.

"Don't do this," I begged.

"You're good at that, remember?" he said snidely. "You're good at walking away from someone like they don't even matter, good at walking away from all your promises. Get out of here, Scott, and take your boyfriend with you."

I didn't recognize this vicious, rabid version of the happy, loving boy I'd known. Had I done that? Had I hurt him so badly that this was what he'd become? I wanted to cry, wanted to beg for forgiveness, wanted to punch myself in the face.

"Charlie, please, we—"

"Leave!" he shouted, and then he darted his gaze toward the hallway leading to the children's bedrooms, took a deep breath, and in a calmer, lower voice, said, "Get out of my house. Get out of my life. Both of you. Get. Out."

Chapter 15

INTRODUCTION

Charlie ("Chase") Rhodes

THAT reunion wasn't exactly sunshine and roses, I know, but, really, can you blame me? I was still neck-deep in pain over my sister's death, still trying to learn how to be a parent, still adjusting to living in a new city and starting a new job, and, let's be honest, I was still in love with both Scott and Adan, even though I knew it was weak and stupid and pointless.

Holding myself together after seeing either of them would have been hard. Managing to keep the tears at bay when I was faced with both of them at the same time was a small miracle. Keeping myself upright when I realized they were a couple should have qualified me for some sort of lifetime achievement award. But keeping calm while Adan "All I Ever Wanted Was a Fuck" Navarro spewed lies and Scott "Now You See Him, Now You Don't" Boone claimed he wanted to be part of my life was more than I could handle.

So I lost my temper, raised my voice, and played the part of the bitter ex who can't move on with his life. It wasn't my proudest moment. It would have been much more fulfilling to look great, have a super hot, super smart, super nice boyfriend to throw in their faces, and come across as blasé over their unexpected and unwelcome appearance. But you know what? Fuck it. One out of three isn't bad, and no matter what they did to fuck with my heart and my head and my spirit, I still looked damn good.

It's better to look good than to feel good, right? I was pretty sure I'd seen that on a mug or a bumper sticker or a T-shirt at some point, so it must be true.

And even if it isn't true, I was in the best shape of my life and my tight pants and sleeveless shirt weren't doing anything to hide it. Adan, on the other hand, looked like maybe he had put on some weight. Of course, it just served to make him look more masculine, just made me think about how much I enjoyed being covered by that wide, strong body. And that made me want to strangle myself because it was insane to still be lusting after a man I hated. Well, loved and hated. Hated that I loved.

Back to how great I looked. My hair was still as thick and healthy as it had been in high school. Scott, on the other hand, was sporting a receding hairline. But somehow the short hairstyle he wore made even thinning hair work. When I had last seen him, he had been barely into his twenties, still a tad round-faced, with hair long enough to fall into his eyes more often than not. There was nothing round about his face anymore; it was strong-jawed, sculpted-angle perfection. Even the little lines next to his hazel eyes looked sexy.

Okay, fine, I looked hot, but so did they. Damn them for having aged so well! And damn me for noticing. I wanted them out of my sight. I wanted them out of my head. I wanted them out of my heart.

But, thankfully, I didn't get any of those things.

Which brings me to the next picture in the album: Adan is sitting on the grass, surrounded by geese, and looking paler than I would have thought possible for a Latino man. Scott is a couple of feet away, balancing Stephi on his hip, holding Bobby's hand, and laughing fondly at Adan. And even though you can't see me, when I look at that picture, I distinctly remember hiding behind the camera and wondering whether I was in a waking dream or a living nightmare.

Chapter 15

Scott Boone

IN ALL the years I had known Charlie, he had never yelled at me and I had never refused him anything. But there he was, shaking with anger, glaring daggers, and shouting at me to leave. And there I was, not budging an inch and refusing to give him what he wanted. It was horrible. Every single part of that exchange was horrible. So I did what came naturally and looked to Adan for help.

"I'm afraid of geese!" Adan yelled.

My jaw dropped. We were losing Charlie and he was talking about poultry? I swung around to face Charlie, ready to jump back into the driver's seat of the regain-his-trust train, and saw that he was looking at Adan in a way that seemed interested rather than angry. That was a hopeful development, so I kept my mouth shut.

"Geese?" Charlie said curiously.

"Yes." Adan licked his lips nervously. "When I was a kid, my parents took my sister and me to the park. It was big with walking trails and hills and a lake, and the lake had lots of ducks and swans and geese. Well, one time we were there and I had a bag of old bread to feed the ducks. I couldn't have been more than four or five, and the geese surrounded me, trying to get the bread. I was pretty short and they're surprisingly big and very aggressive and they have those eyes on the sides of their heads, which is scary as hell and—"

"Why are you telling me this?" Charlie whispered. "I don't think you said word one about your family the whole time we were together. Why now?"

"Because I want you to know that I've changed." Adan sounded so earnest, so hopeful.

But apparently Charlie didn't see it that way, because he scoffed and in a disbelieving tone said, "You've changed?"

"Yes. You said it yourself, I never told you anything before, and now I confessed—"

"Great. You confessed your deep dark geese-fearing secret." Charlie rolled his eyes. "Do you actually expect that to make a difference? Do you actually think I give a shit about ducks that freaked you out thirty years ago? Do you—"

"Remember when we went to get pie that night and I wouldn't share with you?" Adan asked.

Charlie stilled and furrowed his brow. "Which time?"

"Every time," Adan rasped.

"I remember." Charlie closed the door and leaned back against it. "At first I thought you didn't like pie, but when I baked them at home, you always ate them, so I figured you had a germ phobia or something about sharing food."

"I used your toothbrush the first month we were together," Adan reminded him. "I never had any phobias where your mouth was concerned, baby."

"Jesus." Charlie flicked his eyes toward me and then back to Adan. "You're exactly the same. Still running on that same track, even with your boyfriend standing a couple of feet away."

"No, I'm not." Adan walked to the couch and slumped down.

"Are you saying that wasn't a come-on? Because that'd make you a slut *and* a liar. At least before you had the decency to be honest about your motives."

"I'm not denying the come-on." Adan looked at me, the question clear from his expression. I nodded, and he turned back to Charlie. "From the first moment I saw you, I was attracted to you and that never stopped. Not while we were together. Not while we were apart. And not now." He glanced at me again, and I could see how nervous he was, so I walked to the couch and sat next to him, resting my hand on his knee to give him support. With his gaze fixed on Charlie, he said, "I want you, baby. I never stopped wanting you. I was honest with you about that then and I'm being honest about it now." He covered my hand with his. "But I wasn't always honest about everything."

Charlie came closer. "What—" He swallowed thickly. "What weren't you honest about?"

Adan squeezed my hand and squared his shoulders. "The reason I didn't share your pie wasn't because of germs. It was because we were in public and I didn't want anybody to think we were together."

I gasped, but Charlie didn't even flinch. Instead, he took yet another step forward. "Together as in—"

"It's stupid, right?" Adan said, his voice sounding thick. "I figured if I didn't dip my fork in your food, nobody would think we were fucking."

"Yeah, that's stupid." Charlie took another step. "If sharing food meant sharing a bed, I'd have been sleeping with Selina for years."

Adan smiled at Charlie, but rather than coming across as happy, the expression made him look even more downtrodden. "I was a real idiot. I thought the way you dressed and the way you acted made you weak and silly, and I was terrified anybody would think I was like you."

My jaw dropped and I jerked away from my boyfriend. I loved him, I did. But I loved Charlie too, I always had, and hearing Adan talk to him that way made me sick.

Amazingly, Charlie seemed completely unfazed. "I still dress the same way, Adan." Charlie motioned to his tight sleeveless shirt and form-fitting skinny pants. God, he was gorgeous. So gorgeous. Even more so as an adult than he'd been as a teenager. "And I'm still as queeny as ever."

"Yes, you are. But I'm not the same, baby. I know you weren't the weak one back then, it was me. I know how much braver you were, how much more self-confident. I know you were the one strong enough to be yourself no matter what anybody else said and no matter what it cost you. And I know I was the idiot who was too scared to admit how much I wanted you."

Charlie moved closer; his gaze was fixed on Adan. "You never had any trouble saying you wanted me."

"I never had any trouble saying I wanted you on your knees. I never had any trouble saying I wanted to fuck you. I never had any trouble asking you to suck me off."

"Adan!" I hissed. "Stop it. Are you listening to yourself? How could you—"

"It's the truth," Charlie said. He sat down at the edge of the coffee table, close enough to touch.

"But what I didn't say," Adan continued, his voice shaking, "was that I wanted to hear you laugh. I wanted to hear stories about your day and listen to the way you saw the world. I wanted to watch you cook dinner and read a magazine and practice for your shows. I never admitted to you or even to myself, that those clothes you wear, the way you stand, the things I complained about? I never admitted that they turned me on, that I got hard just looking at you, and that I was ashamed of myself for feeling that way." He reached for Charlie's hand and, to my surprise, Charlie didn't pull away. "I was ashamed of *myself*, baby. I blamed you, I said it was you, but it was me. It was always me." He took in a deep breath. "I'm sorry. So sorry. Please believe me. Please forgive me."

I didn't know what to do. The conversation was surreal. Well, the whole situation was like the Twilight Zone, really, but that moment had to be the apex of bizarre. There I sat with my boyfriend and his ex-boyfriend... who was also my ex-boyfriend.

Charlie, who I remembered as happy and upbeat, looked exhausted and devastated. I wanted to tell him that he should never let anyone run him down the way Adan had, that it was unforgiveable. But I also wanted to beg him to forgive Adan; I wanted to point out how hard it must have been for Adan to expose so much, how sorry he was.

Adan, who was usually about as emotional as a statue, had unshed tears in his eyes. I wanted to comfort him and tell him everything would be okay. But I also wanted to kick his ass after hearing him talk about the way he'd treated Charlie.

"I forgive you." Charlie sniffled and cupped Adan's cheek with his free hand; the other was still twined with Adan's. "Don't cry, okay? I forgive you."

With a choked cry, Adan lunged for Charlie, wrapped his arms around Charlie's tiny waist, and jerked him into his lap. He buried his face in Charlie's neck and mumbled, "Thank you." He moved his mouth up Charlie's throat. "Thank you." He dragged his lips across Charlie's chin. "Thank you." Then he gazed into Charlie's eyes and slanted their mouths together.

As soon as their lips connected, Adan moaned and Charlie whimpered. The kiss was tender and emotional, and it made my chest ache. I couldn't pull my gaze away, couldn't stop my heart from racing, couldn't contain my own sounds of need.

"Shit," Charlie said breathlessly as he tore his mouth from Adan's. "I'm sorry, Scotty. I don't... shit." He tried to scoot off Adan's lap, but Adan was twice his size and he wasn't letting go.

"It's okay," I assured him. "You didn't do anything wrong."

"I am making out with your boyfriend!" Charlie reminded me. Then, after a pause, he asked, "Wait, he is your boyfriend, right? You guys are together?"

I scooted closer to them, pressed my thigh to Adan's, and draped my left arm over his shoulders. "Yes, we've been together for five years now."

He darted his gaze back and forth between me and Adan. "I don't understand what's going on."

I heard his question, but at that moment, I couldn't focus on anything except how much I wanted to touch him, to make sure he was okay, to know he wasn't angry with me anymore.

"Charlie, can I...." I circled my right arm around Charlie's waist, clutched him tightly, and blinked rapidly to keep my tears at bay. "Do you hate me?"

"Ah, Scotty, no." He twisted in Adan's lap until he was facing me. "I could never hate you. You know that."

I nodded, feeling relieved. "I didn't mean to break my promises. You were my first love, Charlie. But I was so young, *we* were so young. Do you remember? I never thought I was running away from you, and I didn't realize you saw it that way."

"I know," he said. "I understand. I've always understood. But it still hurt." His voice broke on the last word, and my restraint snapped.

Within seconds, I was kneeling on the sofa, cupping his face between both of my palms, and taking his mouth in a smoldering kiss. We were both panting by the time we pulled our lips apart. I rested my forehead against his and rubbed my thumbs over his soft skin.

"That was so hot," Adan said hoarsely.

I chuckled. "Yes, it was."

Charlie shook his head and said, "This is deeply, deeply fucked up." He tried once again to move away, but both of us held on to him.

"No, it's not," Adan disagreed. "It's perfect."

"Stay," I said. "We want you to stay with us."

"You have each other," he reminded us.

Adan and I looked at one another and sighed in unison. I tilted my head toward him, indicating he should take the lead.

"We want you too," he said.

"No way." Charlie shook his head vehemently. "Look, it's cool if you guys have an open relationship or you like to pick up guys to share your bed, but I'm not interested."

"That's not how things are between us," I grumbled. "Neither of us has been with anybody else since we got together. We're in it for the long haul. We own a house and a business together. We share a checking account. We're not playing around; this isn't a game to us."

"Fine. Good." Charlie managed to wiggle free. He stood up. "I'm glad you have each other," he said, looking pained. "And I don't want to get in the middle of that."

"What if we want you in the middle?" Adan asked as he climbed to his feet.

"No." He shook his head. "I know I haven't seen either of you in years, but it could never be casual for me"—he looked back and forth between us—"not with either of you."

I got up and stood on the other side of him. "Who said we're looking for casual?"

I had forgotten how small Charlie was. He measured in at barely five and a half feet, so at six foot two and six foot three respectively, Adan and I both towered over him. I found the difference in our sizes sexy as hell, and because those tight pants Charlie wore allowed for no secrets, I could see that he was turned on too.

"This isn't just about sex," Adan added.

"Who are you and what have you done with Adan Navarro?" Charlie asked with a smile.

"I'm serious," Adan responded.

Charlie raised his hand and traced Adan's jaw. "I know you are, but come on, what else could it ever be?" He turned to me and rubbed his thumb over my lips. "Like you said, you guys have the house, the car, the business." He sighed and folded in on himself. "You don't need me. You already have everything."

"We have a good life," I admitted and reached for Adan's hand at the same time he reached for mine.

Adan raised my hand to his mouth, kissed my wrist, and said, "We're happy."

I smiled at him and then focused on Charlie. "I guess you're right. We do have everything."

Charlie slumped in reaction to my comment.

"But as it turns out," Adan said quietly, "everything isn't enough."

"What does that mean?" Charlie asked. "You want more than everything?"

Both of us nodded. "We want you," we said in unison.

THOUGH we had been in Charlie's apartment for only a matter of hours, so much had changed that it felt like days. Adan and I stayed quiet during the drive home. I was processing everything that had happened and I assumed he was doing the same. The silence stretched through our arrival home. We each got ready for bed, crawled underneath the cool sheets, and hit the lights.

I was exhausted. It had been a busy week, and Fridays always seemed like the days when multiple clients had urgent matters pop up. By the time Stacia had called to ask us to babysit, we barely had time to wolf down a sandwich at the deli outside our office before we had to go to Rachel's... Charlie's apartment. After that, well, I think "unexpected" is an understated way of describing the rest of our day. Yet, despite being tired, both physically and mentally, I couldn't sleep.

"Adan?"

"Uh-huh."

"You sleeping?"

He rolled over and faced me. There was enough light in the room for me to see his expression. He looked tired, which was expected, but he also looked petrified.

"So, I'm guessing you want to talk about tonight," he said.

"Right now, I want to talk about what happened between you and Charlie." I tried to keep my tone and expression even, but I couldn't fool Adan.

"You're pissed, right?" he said.

We always prided ourselves on having an honest-to-a-fault relationship. That was critical professionally, and it ensured any problem in our personal lives didn't fester. It was safe to say we had just experienced the biggest obstacle we'd faced as a couple, and I decided sugar-coating things at that point wouldn't serve us well.

"Well, I guess it depends. Did I get an accurate picture of how things were between you two?"

"From what we said tonight, you mean?" He shrugged. "It probably wasn't *completely* accurate."

I breathed out a sigh of relief. Nobody would accuse Adan of being particularly sensitive or demonstrative or affectionate outside of the bedroom, but the way Charlie had described him, the way he had described himself, was like hearing about a stranger. A piece-of-shit stranger I wanted to deck.

"I was actually much worse," Adan said. "But you know Chase. He's very forgiving." At first, I thought he was kidding. Then I hoped he was kidding. Then he said, "I'm not kidding, hon. I was a real dick to Chase."

"Charlie," I growled.

"What?"

"His name is Charlie! Chase Rhodes is a stage name or something." It felt good to yell, to be mad. Even if it wasn't about what was actually upsetting me. "We're not fans, we're family! That means we call him Charlie."

"Okay," he said gently. "I was a real dick to *Charlie*."

"Don't push me, Adan. Not tonight. I'm not too happy with you right now as it is."

"That makes two of us." He rolled onto his back and took in a deep breath. "I've always wished I would have done things differently with him, always hated myself a little for the way I treated him. I know you're pissed, Scott, but I doubt you could be any more upset with me than I've been with myself for a lot of years now."

It was hard to hold on to my anger when he sounded so remorseful, and it was impossible to beat him up when he was already doing a fine job of it himself.

"Why did you do it?" I asked, a hint of anger creeping into my tone.

"Why did you leave him?" he said to me.

"I didn't leave him! I moved to be close to my sister and my dad."

"Did you ask him to come with you?"

I scoffed and rolled my eyes. "Adan, I was twenty-one years old. Come on. But it wasn't like I broke up with him. We were too young to do the long-distance thing, so we drifted apart."

"Well, it sounds like neither of us was mature enough to make things work with him back then."

My jaw dropped. "How can you compare me moving away to you making him feel like you were embarrassed by him and like he wasn't good for anything but sex?"

"I'm not trying to keep score here, Scott. But you asked me a question. You want to know why I did it, and I'm telling you. I was twenty-seven when I met him. I'd only been out to my family for a couple of years, and they were even worse back then than they are now, if you can imagine that. All I could focus on was proving that I was as macho as my dad, that I could outearn every one of my straight cousins, and that all the shit they said about gay people wasn't true. At the time, Charlie seemed like an impediment to every one of those goals, but I wanted him too much to walk away."

"So you dated him but treated him like shit?" I asked incredulously. "That was your compromise?"

"It wasn't like I set out to do that, it wasn't a conscious decision, but, yeah, that's what happened." When I didn't respond, he said, "I know it might be asking too much to be forgiven for what I did to him, but I hope you know me well enough to realize I learned from those mistakes and I would never, ever treat him that way again."

"He already said he forgives you," I reminded him.

"That's one out of two." He turned his head to the side and looked at me. "How about you, Scott? Do you think you can forgive me?"

I loved him unconditionally. That included the ugly parts of his past. So I rolled on top of him and nuzzled his neck. "I do know you're not that same guy anymore." I thought about everything he'd said and added, "And you know what? I'm not the same kid who didn't know enough to appreciate what he had." I dragged in a deep breath. "So I guess the hard part is going to be convincing Charlie to give us another chance?"

Adan kissed my forehead and chuckled. "We already did that, hon."

I flattened my hands on the bed and straightened my arms so my face was above his. "What are you talking about? We made up from all the shit in the past, but he turned us down flat when we said we wanted to get back together."

Adan shook his head and said, "He didn't turn us down."

"Uh, yes, he did," I argued. "Were you and I listening to the same conversation back there?"

"If you were getting hung up on his words, then no."

"I have no clue what you're saying," I grumbled in frustration.

He chuckled. "The thing about our Charlie is, you can't just listen to his words. If you want to hear what he's saying, you have to look at his expressions, you have to look in his eyes, you have to listen to how fast he's breathing, you have to pay attention to the way he's holding himself." Adan shrugged. "We're lawyers. We make a living using words and logic. But Charlie's a dancer. He'll tell us a lot more with his body than he will with his mouth, and he'll follow his heart even when his head tells him to do the opposite."

I furrowed my brow and chewed my bottom lip. "I can't decide whether that's incredibly insightful or incredibly condescending."

"It's incredibly accurate. I saw the way he looked at you tonight, Scott. You haven't talked in fifteen years, and he still looked at you like you were the second coming. And the fact that he didn't kick me in the nuts means he still loves me." He stretched up and bussed his lips over mine. "The hard part is already done: he still loves us. Now we need to make him realize it and to show him that this time, we're going to hold on to him."

There was a crazy sort of logic to Adan's patronizing analysis. "How do we do that?" I asked.

"Well, first things first. Tomorrow morning, we're picking up lunch and taking him and the kids to the park for a picnic."

Adan Navarro had suggested we spend our Saturday afternoon having a picnic. My life was no longer recognizable. Strangely enough, I was okay with that. But I doubted Charlie would feel the same way.

"What makes you think he'll agree to meet us?"

"Meet us?" Adan raised his eyebrows in shock. "We are not asking him to *meet us*. We're going to show up at his apartment, knock on his door, and park our asses on his couch until he agrees to spend the day with us. Then we're going to have the best damn picnic in the history of picnics and he'll see we're serious about him."

Loath though I was to admit it out loud, it wasn't a bad plan.

"Then what?"

Adan pursed his lips and squinted. "Umm, I don't know yet, but we'll figure it out. Don't worry. Charlie wasn't able to resist either of us alone; he doesn't stand a chance against a dual seduction."

I couldn't hold back a laugh at the return of my confident boyfriend. "Nice to see you back, Mr. Cocky."

"Mr. Cocky is too tired to make an appearance tonight," he drawled. "Hit me up in the morning and I'll see if he's up for some fun."

I grimaced and moaned, "Oh, that was bad."

He smacked my butt. "You know it was funny."

I rolled off him and rubbed my backside. "I know I love you, but that's all you're getting me to admit."

"Fine," he sighed dramatically.

"Go to sleep, Adan, you're punch-drunk."

He gripped my waist, tugged me closer, and tossed his leg over my hip. I burrowed against him, rested my head on his shoulder, and closed my eyes.

"We're okay, right, hon?" he asked.

I combed my fingers through the hair on his chest and kissed his nipple. "We're solid, Adan. You don't need to worry about us. We need you to focus all your Machiavellian brilliance on getting Charlie home."

Chapter 16

INTRODUCTION

Charlie ("Chase") Rhodes

SO HOW'RE you holding up? Doing okay so far?

Me? I'm great now, but back then I was living on the corner of Emotional Whirlwind and Mental Breakdown. Thanks for asking.

All right, now that the niceties are out of the way, let's get back to the album.

After a month spending every waking weekend nonworking moment with Scott and Adan, along with phone calls every day and dinners a couple of times a week, I decided I hadn't been a complete fool in falling for them. Whatever bad stuff had gone down in our past, they were good guys, and I genuinely liked both of them.

Scott was as earnest as ever. He was generous with his laughter, his compliments, and his sweet touches. When we chatted, even if it was about the most mundane things, he seemed fascinated by every word I said. He had endless patience for Bobby and Stephi, laughing when they crawled all over him even if it left him coated in ice cream or pasta sauce or any number of other unidentifiable stain-causers.

Adan was as intense as the day I'd met him. He was laser-focused on Scott and, it seemed, on me, and though he didn't talk as much as either of us, he was always paying attention, watching what we did and listening to what we said. Oh, and the way he looked at me. Jesus, his heated gaze was enough to make my breath catch, and there were many occasions when I had to excuse myself to splash water on my face or stick my head in the refrigerator so I could cool off. Bobby and Stephi didn't jump all over him like they did Scott, but they instinctively respected him, going to him with questions about their homework or something they heard at school. On the nights Adan and Scott came over for dinner, it was Adan they ran to with their bedtime books in hand.

As time passed, I became less able to explain our relationship to myself. We were friends; that much I knew. But I wasn't used to my friends looking at me like they wanted to eat me alive. My friends didn't call me "baby" and hold me close at the end of every night. And none of my friends resented the time we spent apart and acted like the evenings we spent together were the highlights of their week.

Those descriptions matched how a boyfriend would act, but Scott and Adan already had each other to fill that role. When we said our good-byes, sometimes so late it was already morning, they went home together and had the pleasure of sharing a bed and sleeping in each other's arms. I would have been jealous to the point of madness if the fantasies of what they did in that bed hadn't turned me on to the point of distraction.

The next picture in the album is a funny memory of a typical evening we spent together. Scott is sitting at the kitchen table with Bobby and Stephi, eating hot dogs and spaghetti and chatting. Adan is in the background, leaning against the counter, holding a beer and smiling at them. Thinking of that night always makes me laugh, and after the wringer I've put you through, I think you're due a little laughter.

Chapter 16

Scott Boone

"WHAT'RE we having for dinner?" Adan asked Charlie.

"You can offer to help, you know," I reminded Adan, who was reclined on the couch, watching TV. I was sitting next to him, brushing Stephi's hair, Bobby was taking a shower, and Charlie was in the kitchen. "He's not your wife."

"What is that supposed to mean?" Adan said as he reached for the remote and turned off the TV.

"It means what I said. Charlie isn't your wife, so quit acting like it's his job to make you dinner."

"Stephi, sweetie, will you go pick out your jammies and books for tonight?" Adan said to Stephi. As soon as she was gone, he glared at me, crossed his arms over his chest, and said, "What's wrong with being the wife?"

I could see Charlie from the corner of my eye. He was moving toward the edge of the kitchen and watching us.

"He's a man, Adan, that's what's wrong with it."

"So if he was a woman, it'd be okay for him to make us dinner but because he's a man it's not? Am I following your reasoning here?"

Before I could see it coming, he had flipped his insulting comment around and made me look like a misogynist. It was that kind of quick thinking that made Adan so damn good at his job, which was fine when we were on the same side, but I didn't appreciate having it turned on me.

"You know damn well that's not what I'm saying!" I snapped.

He arched his eyebrows. "Other than being a guy, why can't Charlie be the wife?" he asked. "He likes to take care of everyone, he likes to cook, he likes taking the kids to school. What's wrong with being the wife?"

I had a mental image of both my mother and my stepmother kicking my ass. "Not all wives do those things. It's not 1950, households have equal divisions of labor, and—"

"I asked what he was making for dinner. You're the one who said that was treating him like a wife."

Being on the losing end of the argument had me scrambling. "I meant a housewife."

Adan rolled his eyes. "Fine. Whatever. So what's wrong with being a housewife?"

"Nothing! There's nothing wrong with being a housewife. I never said—"

"Great. So why can't Charlie be the wife, er, housewife?" He paused and then waved his hand dismissively. "Other than the guy thing, I mean."

"I don't, uh, Charlie has a job!" Finally grasping on to some sort of logic helped clear my mind. "He's worked hard to get where he is in his field, and—"

"Please," Adan scoffed. "He's got a bit part in a Vegas show; this isn't the apex of his career. And you saw his paycheck—you know he's barely making enough money to cover his bills."

I wanted to crawl under the couch but instead, I jerked my gaze over to Charlie. He hadn't moved from his spot, he was still watching us, but he hadn't said a word about the fact that we'd snuck a peek at his paycheck or about the way Adan was insulting his career.

"He'd make more if he had a bigger role in a bigger show, but then he'd be working every night, and he can't because he has to be here for the kids, Adan, you know that."

"Yes, I know. I've seen him dance, Scott. Don't act like I'm insulting his talent. He's amazing. But on the days he has evening shows, he's miserable about leaving Stephi and Bobby with a sitter. Plus, he's bone tired every day because he's running around like a chicken with his head cut off to get to work and drive the kids everywhere they need to be. It seems to me his job is a hindrance to what he actually wants to be doing."

162

"Care to enlighten me as to what that is?" Charlie asked, finally joining the conversation.

Adan leaned back in the sofa and relaxed his stance. "You already know."

Their gazes locked.

"You think I want to be a housewife." It sounded like a statement, not a question.

"I think you want to quit that silly job. I think you want to sign Stephi up for ballet class instead of having to say no because you're working at four and she has to be in aftercare and you can't afford to buy the costume for the recital. I think you want to be here every night when they go to sleep. I think you want to make them dinner, but some nights you feel like you're going to pass out if you don't get at least a few minutes off your feet, so you stop at the drive-through. I think being a single working dad sucks and you hate that there's no end in sight."

At the beginning of Adan's rant, I thought he was being an ass and I was gearing up to drag him out of the room before he ruined our plans and pushed Charlie further away. But somewhere along the way, his description of Charlie's life and struggles began sounding familiar. They reminded me of Charlie, but not in the way he meant.

"Charlie," I said quietly. He looked at me, his eyes shining and his cheeks flushed. "It doesn't have to be like it was for your mom."

When he gulped and trembled, I knew I'd hit the nail on the head. I remembered how hard his mother had worked the whole time I'd known him. I remembered how alone Charlie had felt and how exhausted his mother had been.

"How could it not?" he asked hoarsely.

"You know how," Adan said gently.

"No... I can't." He shook his head. "It's not...."

Adan moved over and patted the spot between us. "C'mere, baby."

After a brief hesitation, Charlie hurried over and sat down between us. I wrapped my arm around his shoulders and Adan caressed his knee.

"Let us take care of you, Charlie," I whispered.

"I can't do that. It's not right." His words were a definite no, but I was getting better at listening to those other forms of communication. I heard the yearning in his voice; I saw the way his shoulders were shaking, like he was barely holding it together, and I couldn't miss the hopeful look in his eyes when he gazed at me.

"Of course it's right. Adan and I both do very well. We don't have any debt or anybody to spend our money on." I dipped my face and kissed his neck. "Let us take care of you."

He clenched and released his fists nervously. "But I'm not even sleeping with you."

"Is that the holdup?" Adan said with a chuckle. "Because I'm more than happy to put a stop to that impediment tonight. We can get naked, get busy, and clear that problem right up. Done and done."

Charlie shook his head and snorted. "Not gonna happen."

"Famous last words, baby," Adan said. "Remember what happened last time you made that claim?"

"That was a long time ago." Charlie's cheeks reddened. "It won't happen again." His breath hitched. "I'm not going to bed with you guys."

"We're not asking you for sex in exchange for letting us take care of you," I assured him.

"Then what do you want?" Charlie asked.

I cupped his cheek. "We want you to let us in."

Adan dropped to his knees and grasped Charlie's hands. "We want you to rely on us. We want you to trust us to be here for you and for Stephi and Bobby."

After several long moments, Charlie let out a shaky breath and said, "I do trust you." He shook his head. "That might make me the biggest fool around after everything that's happened, but I trust both of you."

"Thank you, baby," Adan said.

"You're sure about this?" Charlie said, flicking his eyes from Adan to me. "I can quit my job and you'll support me and the kids?"

I nodded. "We're sure."

"Okay." Charlie dragged in a deep breath and wiped his palms on his jeans. "Okay. I'll give my notice tomorrow."

He sounded nervous, but also relieved, and his body looked less tense, like a weight had been lifted from his shoulders. I glanced at Adan and dipped my chin in acknowledgement of his part in making that happen. His words had been horrifyingly offensive, but his heart, as always, had been in the right place. He knew exactly what Charlie wanted, what Charlie needed, and he'd found a way to make it happen.

A timer went off in the kitchen, and Charlie jumped up. "Pasta's ready."

He was halfway to the stove when Adan said, "Oh, and Charlie?"

"Yeah?"

"If you change your mind about the no-sex clause of our agreement, just let us know. I think you can probably convince us to amend that term."

"I'll be sure to do that just as soon as pigs start flying," he said sarcastically. "Go wash up for dinner."

"YOU said we were having pasta dogs," Bobby whined as he pushed his fork around his bowl seemingly searching for something that wasn't in it.

"That is pasta dogs," Charlie said.

"No, it's not," Stephi argued.

"It's sliced up hot dogs with spaghetti," Charlie insisted.

"Ten bucks says those aren't real hot dogs," Adan muttered under his breath.

I threw Adan an elbow.

Charlie glared at him and said, "They're tofu dogs and they taste exactly the same."

"When was the last time you ate a hot dog?" Adan challenged Charlie.

"In 1999. But I'm sure they taste the same."

"Says the man who hasn't put a real beef wiener in his mouth this century." He waggled his eyebrows. "I think you should let me and Scott put an end to that dry spell, baby."

I started laughing and coughed to cover it up.

Charlie rolled his eyes.

"Uncle Charlie!" Bobby shouted. "The spaghetti is supposed to go *through* the hot dogs."

"Like beads on a necklace," Stephi added helpfully.

"*Through* the hot dogs?" Charlie said disbelievingly. He walked over to the bowls on the counter and picked up a slice of hot dog with one hand and a cooked noodle with the other. "You guys have any ideas?" he asked me and Adan.

"I'm sure we can figure it out," I said as I joined him at the counter and picked up my own sliced dog and cooked noodle. "Maybe we need to poke a hole in it."

"That's a good idea," Adan said. "I'll get a fork."

He grabbed a fork and came to stand on the other side of Charlie. "Give me your wiener," he demanded.

"You're incorrigible," Charlie said as he handed over a piece of hot dog.

Adan lined up the endmost prong of the fork and pushed it through the sliced hot dog, then set the fork down on the counter and held his palm out. "Noodle."

I handed the noodle to Charlie, who handed it to Adan, who tried to thread it through the hot dog.

"The hole closed up," Adan said in frustration.

"Here, let me try it," I said.

Adan handed me the dog. I picked up a fresh noodle and gave it a try, but all I succeeded in doing was squishing the pasta against the hot dog before dropping the whole thing onto the floor. "Damn it!"

"That's a bad word!" Stephi yelled.

"Sorry," I said. "Are you sure the noodles go through the hot dogs?"

"Yes!" both kids insisted.

"Maybe if we make the hole bigger," Charlie said as he picked up the fork. He shoved the prong through the hot dog and wiggled it roughly.

"Damn, baby," Adan said. "I know you don't have a lot of experiencing being on the prong end of a good forking, but don't be so rough."

Charlie snorted as he picked up a noodle and tried to push it through the hole. He managed to get the tip inside but nothing else. "It's too soft," he lamented, turning to me.

Adan leered and said, "It's got to be hard to go in, baby."

All three of us froze, looked at each other, and died laughing.

"I think I have an uncooked box of spaghetti and more hot dogs," Charlie said breathlessly as he opened a cabinet.

"I'll boil the water," I offered.

"And I'll carefully poke those hard noodles all the way through the soft beef, er, tofu," Adan said in a sultry tone.

Charlie scooped up some of the cooked noodles and tossed them at Adan, who peeled one off his face and slowly sucked it between his lips. "Mmm," he groaned.

"Can't you make him stop?" Charlie asked me as he sliced up an uncooked hot dog.

"You've known him longer," I responded. "Can you?"

Charlie pushed a raw stick of spaghetti through a sliced hot dog and then flicked his eyes toward Adan, who had started fellating yet another noodle. "I'm not sure if I want to," he whispered.

Adan caught my gaze and arched his eyebrows meaningfully. I swallowed my smile as I walked up to Charlie, made sure our sides were touching, said, "I'll help," and then I reached around his back to get the box of pasta, grazing his ass with my palm.

He shivered and moaned, and for the first time in a month, I felt like we were making real progress.

Chapter 17

INTRODUCTION

Charlie ("Chase") Rhodes

SLEEPING in was a foreign concept to children, especially on a Saturday, because they didn't have school. Yes, I know, that makes no sense. To me, not having to be up for something meant I didn't get up. But to them, not having to get up for something meant getting up earlier. Thankfully, Saturday morning kids' shows kept them occupied for a little bit, so even though I couldn't sleep through the laugh tracks, at least I had the luxury of lounging in bed.

Six months into my nonrelationship with Scott and Adan, which felt more committed than any of my previous actual relationships, including the ones I'd had with them, their Saturday morning arrival to my apartment came earlier than usual. I was lying in bed, trying to muster the brain cells needed to get upright, when I heard the doorbell.

"I can get it," Bobby yelled.

I leaped out of bed and shouted, "We don't open the door to strangers!" as I hustled out of the bedroom.

"Who is it?" Bobby asked.

The walls and doors and windows in that apartment weren't all that well insulated, so even from my spot in the hallway I could hear Adan's muffled, "It's us."

Bobby turned the lock and pulled the door open. "You're early! Usually you don't get here until *Full House* is over."

"Wasn't *Full House* over twenty years ago?" Scott asked as he strolled in with Adan right behind him.

I shuffled into the front room and rubbed my palms over my eyes as I said, "Thanks to the magic of reruns, it'll never be over." I yawned. "Never."

I heard Scott gasp, "Jesus," followed by a bumping shuffling sound, and then Adan saying, "Scott, what the he—Oh Christ."

"What?" I dropped my hands and looked around frantically. "What happened?"

"Adan bumped into Scott," Bobby reported. Then he went back to his spot on the couch and focused on the TV.

"Are you guys okay?" I walked over to them.

"Damn it, Charlie, you're killing us," Scott said. He moved his gaze across my bare chest and down to my groin. "You're not wearing anything underneath those little shorts, are you?" He groaned and stared at my dick, which plumped up in response to his attention.

"Let's get you dressed," Adan rasped.

He marched over to me, grasped my arm, and yanked me over to the bedroom. Scott followed us. As soon as we got inside, Scott shut the door and locked it.

"What're you... mph!" I moaned when Adan shoved me against Scott. "Adan?" I gasped.

"No more, baby." He ground his hips against mine. "You can't parade around like that and expect us to resist you."

"You have the best body," Scott said from behind me as he circled his arm around my chest and started tweaking my nipple. I arched, hitting my head against his shoulder. "Do you have any idea how much we want you?"

Two sets of hands clutched my hips and waist, and then Scott thrust forward, rubbing his hard length against my backside.

"What...," I said. Scott's hot breath ghosted over my neck right before he started licking and sucking my skin. "Oh God, Scotty." I pushed back against his erection. "Scotty, what're you—"

Adan slammed his mouth on mine, cutting off my words with a knee-buckling kiss. I clung to his shoulders and rocked back and forth between Adan's erection rubbing against mine and Scott's dick sliding against my ass. All the while, Scott kept nibbling, licking, and sucking on my neck and shoulder.

It had been so long since I'd had any kind of sex other than by my own hand, and I had been yearning for both of them for so long, that within minutes I was practically screaming into Adan's mouth, stretching up on my tiptoes, and shaking as I came in my shorts.

When my balls were finally drained, my muscles relaxed. I dropped my forehead against Adan's chest and gasped for air.

"Oh God." I shook so much my teeth chattered. "Oh God."

"Shhhh." Scott gently kissed his way up my neck and petted my back. As if by instinct, he scooted closer to me, leaving me pressed tightly between their large, muscular bodies.

I was surrounded by their strength and scent and safety on all sides, and to my complete and utter horror, I started crying.

"We have you, baby," Adan whispered in my ear and combed his fingers through my hair. "You can let it out. We're here."

"I don't want you to leave me again." My voice sounded weak and shaky, which was exactly how I felt. "I need you both so much."

"We need you too," Scott said, squeezing me tighter.

"We aren't going anywhere, baby, not now, not ever. You're ours and we're keeping you."

I had no right to ask, but I did anyway. "Promise me. Promise you won't get bored or frustrated or decide it's too hard or—"

Adan gripped my chin and raised it until our gazes met. "I love you." He had never said those words to me before, so hearing them made my world spin.

Before I could get my bearings, Scott turned me around and said, "I never stopped loving you, Charlie, not ever, and these past several months getting to know you again made me fall harder."

I gulped and nodded, filing away the moment and their promises so I could think on them later that night, when the kids were in bed.

Speaking of the kids, Stephi chose that moment to shout, "I'm hungry! Uncle Charlie! I'm hungry!"

Adan stepped back. "We're taking you to breakfast and then swimming. Go get dressed."

"We'll get the kids ready," Scott said as he opened the door.

"Isn't it too cold to swim?"

"The pool's heated."

In New York, people don't have swimming pools at home; or at least not regular people. But in Vegas, pools are almost common. My sister's apartment complex, which had turned into my apartment complex when I'd moved there to pick up where her life left off, didn't have a pool. Yet, somehow, Stephi and Bobby were little fishes. They both swam better than I did, apparently due to lessons at the local YMCA, and if ever an opportunity arose to take a dip at a friend's house or anywhere else, they'd bounce and beg and plead until I had no choice but to grab some towels and hustle us over to the promised land. Or, in this case, the promised water.

Which (finally) brings me to the next picture in the album: Scott, Adan, Bobby, and Stephi, all leaping off the side of the deck and into our pool in unison. Yes, I said *our* pool.

Chapter 17

Scott Boone

"I HAVE no idea how you guys can eat like that and then go swimming," Charlie said as we drove away from the restaurant.

"Eat like what?" I asked.

"You ate an entire dead pig's worth of bacon in there." He snorted. "Are you kidding me with that question?"

"You're exaggerating," I said with a chuckle.

"Pig killer," Adan hissed.

"Says the man who inhaled his sausage," I replied.

"I do love to suck down some good sausage," Adan admitted. "And I believe you've both begged me to do it. Repeatedly."

"Adan," Charlie warned.

"What?" He was trying to sound innocent but that would never happen because he had irrevocably parted ways with innocent and then gotten a restraining order forbidding it from coming within one hundred feet of him.

"You're being a pig," I answered.

"Oink, oink."

"Charming," Charlie said sarcastically. "Hey, you guys never told me where we're going swimming."

I had wondered how long it was going to take him to ask that question. Apparently, the answer was thirty seconds from our destination.

"Here," I said as we pulled up to a huge stucco home with flagstone covering the lower half.

"Whose house is this?" Charlie asked.

"Stephi, Bobby, are you ready to go swimming?" Adan asked.

The car had barely stopped before the kids were scrambling for their seat belts and jumping out. The adult contingent exited the vehicle at a more leisurely pace.

"I'll get their stuff and help them get changed," Adan said as he picked up the bag we'd packed with the kids' swimsuits, goggles, towels, and pool toys. Then he turned to me and asked, "You got this?"

I nodded, said, "Yup," and I wrapped my arm around Charlie's shoulder.

"What's going on?" he asked.

"We want to show you something." From the corner of my eye, I saw Adan open the gate to the backyard.

"You're freaking me out, Scotty."

I moved in front of him and rubbed my hands up and down his arms. "It's a good thing, baby." I gazed into his eyes. "But first, I want to make sure you're okay about what happened earlier."

He blushed and dipped his chin. "It felt good, if that's what you're asking."

"Oh, I know you felt good. Watching you feel good was even hotter than I remembered." I kissed the top of his head. "And believe me, I spent *a lot* of time remembering how you looked when you felt like that."

"Is that true?" Charlie looked up at me from underneath his lashes.

"What? That I fantasized about you?"

He shrugged.

"Yes, it's true. And it wasn't just sexual." I cupped his cheek and rubbed my thumb over his jaw. "For years, I'd see something and it'd remind me of you. Clothes. A photograph. Certain food."

"Me too," he whispered. "I missed you so much, Scotty." He raised his face and looked into my eyes. "So so much." I pulled him into a hug and he clutched my shirt, clinging to me. "It hurt."

I nodded and hoarsely said, "I know. For me too." I cleared my throat. "But that's all in the past. We're all grown up now. No more being apart." I took in a deep breath and gathered my nerves. "Which is why we brought you here."

Charlie had always been intuitive, and he knew me and Adan better than anyone, so I wasn't surprised when he darted his gaze toward the house and then back to me and said, "Did you two buy this place?"

"Yup." I nodded. "We signed the contract yesterday, which means we have ten days to back out, no questions asked. If you don't like it for any reason, tell us and we'll find a different one."

"What does it matter if I like it? It's your house," he said, sounding weak and shaky.

We both knew that wasn't true and we both knew that was why he was nervous.

"It's going to be *our* house. All five of us. That's why we're buying it. If you want to go house hunting to pick something else, great."

"I don't know anything about that stuff, and you know how much I hate making decisions." He paused, shook his head, and said, "Besides, who said I'm moving?"

Knowing he didn't actually expect an answer, I took his hand in mine, led him up the sidewalk to the house, and started the tour. "It has a two-car garage on the left and a one-car garage on the right, so all three of us have room to park." I unlocked the door with the key the Realtor had given us and walked Charlie through the entryway, formal living room, formal dining room, open concept family room off the huge kitchen, two and a half bathrooms, master bedroom, and den downstairs, and the three bedrooms, three bathrooms, and loft upstairs. He didn't say anything, but he listened carefully to my descriptions and examined every room, sometimes quickly and sometimes for longer. He ran his hand over countertops, touched molding, and sighed happily in front of the many huge windows.

We ended the tour in the family room, standing in front of the french doors overlooking the backyard. Charlie quietly watched Adan and the kids laughing and playing in the pool. I pressed my chest to his back, circled my arms around his waist, and nuzzled his neck.

"They're having a great time," I whispered. He nodded. "Want to tell me what you're thinking?"

Charlie took in a deep breath and then said, "I'm thinking this house is amazing. It has everything we could ever want. The kids would love it. I'd love it. And we could be together all the time."

"But?" I asked, because Charlie's ramrod-straight posture and clenched fists told me there was more on his mind and that I probably wouldn't like it.

"Do you know that I've never met Adan's family?"

"I'm not surprised. We've been together going on six years now, and other than his sister, I've been around the rest of his family maybe a handful of times."

"His parents live here, right?" Charlie asked.

"Uh-huh, in Reno. But they're not close." My response didn't loosen Charlie's tense muscles, so I kept talking. "Not every family is like our families. We got lucky."

"My mother lives on the other side of the country, and I haven't heard from my father in so long I have no idea if he's alive or dead."

Okay, so perhaps *lucky* was the wrong word choice.

"What I meant was that your mom loves you and supports you like you are. Same with my parents. Adan's family isn't like that, Charlie. They're cold almost to the point of mean. They know we live together and they know why, but they'll only refer to me as his roommate. They've never once come over to our place, and they tell him not to bring me around. The few times he has, they won't even look at me, let alone talk to me, which isn't as big a deal as it might seem because they're distant with him too." I moved my hand under his shirt and rubbed his belly. "Not introducing you to his family doesn't mean anything except that they're assholes and he doesn't want to subject you or himself to them unless it's absolutely necessary."

"What do you think his family will say if we all move in together? If they can't deal with him having a boyfriend, how do you think they'll feel about me and the kids being added to the mix?"

I chuckled at the visual of Adan's family hearing that information. "I think they'll lose their minds."

"See?" Charlie yelled.

"See what? That his parents'll be pissed? Who gives a damn, Charlie? You're not moving in with them. You're moving in with Adan and me."

"I bet Adan doesn't see it that way," he mumbled.

I flipped him around, looked straight at him, and said, "You'll lose that bet. Adan loves you." Charlie's eyes glistened. "He barely tolerates his parents, but he *loves* you."

At first, I thought I'd gotten through to him—his lips had started curling up in a smile and his posture lightened—but then he dipped his chin and rubbed his toe back and forth in front of him.

"Charlie," I sighed and tried to come up with the right words to reassure him about Adan's feelings. "I know things were tough between the two of you, but he isn't the same guy. You have to have seen how he looks at you. I never see his eyes that warm. And the way he talks to you? Not when he's making his silly sex cracks; the rest of the time? With his voice so soft? How can you not see how he feels?"

"I see it," he said quietly without looking up.

"Oh." I furrowed my brow. "Then what's the problem?" I paused. "Is it me? Are you still worried about how I feel? Because I thought you knew how much I lo—"

"It's not that." He put his hand on my chest and finally raised his gaze to meet mine. "I know you love me, Scotty. That's one thing I never forgot. It's just…."

"What?"

"Does it bother you?" he whispered.

I tried to understand what he was asking, but I was lost.

"Does what bother me?"

"You're standing here telling me how much your boyfriend loves me." He arched his eyebrows. "You gotta know how weird that is."

I crooked my lips up. "Yeah, it's a little outside the norm. I'll give you that."

"A *little* outside the norm?" he asked incredulously.

"Okay, fine, more than a little." I chuckled. "But this isn't a normal situation. If Adan thought I wanted another guy, he'd probably take a shot at him. And if he told me he had feelings for anybody else on earth, I'd lose my mind and key his car or hem all of his pants two inches higher or—"

"Wait." Charlie waved his hand in front of me. "What?"

"You know how much he loves that stupid BMW."

"Not that. I know he's got a hard-on for his car. I mean the pants. Why would you hem his pants?"

"Because can you imagine how annoying that would be? He'd put them on and they'd be a little off but he wouldn't know why and then he'd think they shrunk, so he'd try another pair, but they'd be too short too, but not like totally too short, just a little, and then—"

"You know what? Forget I asked. I get your point. You're not only the jealous type, but also the vindictive type. Who knew? And yet here you are telling me to give him a chance, to move in with you, telling me how much he loves me and how he looks at me and talks to me and—"

"But that's because it's *you*, Charlie, and *I* love you as much as he does. Do you get that? It's not him loving you or me loving you or you loving him or you loving me! We all love each other—all three of us. We have for years. Do you get how amazing that is? I mean, what are the odds? So it's unusual and a little complicated. Fine. Whatever." I took a deep, calming breath and lowered my voice. "We found a gift of tremendous happiness sitting on our doorstep. We can have everything we ever wanted, all of us. We'd be idiots to toss it away."

For a long time, Charlie didn't say anything, but he didn't look away from me either. Then he sighed and glanced around the huge room. "More than everything," he mumbled.

"What?"

He looked into my eyes. "You're serious about us moving in together?"

"Of course we are." I sighed in relief. "We want you and the kids with us all the time. We want to be a family."

Charlie took my hand in his and traced the lines on my palm with one finger. "It feels like we already are," he whispered.

CHARLIE said he wanted a little bit more time to think about moving in together, but we knew he loved the house and, more importantly, we knew he loved us, so we barreled ahead with inspections and financing and figured he'd commit by the time the moving company came to pack him up.

Work was crazy that week, but we managed to make it to Charlie's early enough to eat dinner with him and the kids on Monday and Wednesday. By Friday, we'd been apart from him less than forty-eight hours and already I was getting itchy.

"Adan," I said as I knocked on his open office door. "How busy are you?"

CARDENO C.

He looked up from his monitor. "I have time. Why? Do you need me to jump in on a matter?"

When we didn't have client meetings, we tended to push business casual to its breaking point. That day, Adan was wearing a gray button-down shirt with the sleeves rolled up past his elbows, exposing his muscular forearms, and the top few buttons undone, exposing his bronze chest. I closed his office door.

"You're sexy. You know that?" I said as I dragged my gaze down his chest and walked around his desk. He was wearing jeans that hugged him in all the right places, and I enjoyed the view as I got closer.

"What were you working on that has you ready to bust out of those chinos?" he said breathlessly.

When I got within arm's reach, he grabbed my ass with one hand and cupped my bulge with the other, giving me a squeeze.

"Ungh," I moaned and rocked into his touch. "I'm so hard."

He climbed to his feet and rubbed his hand up and down my shaft and balls. "Seriously, hon, were you watching porn at your desk?"

I reached for him and returned the favor, making him gasp and then groan. "No. I was looking at those pictures Charlie sent."

"I haven't had a chance to open his e-mail yet. I thought it was his usual updates of kid pictures." Adan pushed against my hand even harder. "Did he finally buckle and send us nudie pics?"

My breath was coming out faster, balls drawing tighter. I rested my forehead against Adan's and said, "No. It's the usual stuff. But there are pictures in there from last weekend, including some we took of him at the pool."

Just the mention of Charlie wet and almost naked had Adan's breath hitching. "He looked so fucking hot," he said.

"I know. There's one you must have taken when he wasn't looking. It's a back shot. His suit is clinging to his ass." I thrust forward against Adan's hand and bit his neck. "I want in there so bad, Adan."

"Me too." He gulped and arched his neck. "Oh Christ. Me too. It's so good, hon."

I hadn't ever had the pleasure of fucking Charlie; we were too young when we were together. But I'd wanted it, thought about it, even dreamed about it.

"He gets off on it, right?" I asked, already knowing the answer from stories Adan had told me.

Neither of us truly enjoyed bottoming. We tolerated it occasionally for each other, liked giving each other pleasure, but it had never been what got either of us going. Two tops don't make a bottom, that's what one of our friends said when we first started dating. He was right, but we'd made it work anyway, and we'd found a good rhythm, inside and outside the bedroom. But that didn't mean we'd lost the desire to push inside a hot body and let go completely.

"Fuck yes." Adan was breathing harder, rocking faster. "He loves it, Scott. Wait until you see his face when you push inside." He shuddered. "His eyes get wide, like he can't believe how good it feels, and he makes these noises like he's going to die if you don't go deeper and harder. And he's the only guy I've ever been with who can cum just from getting fucked."

I gasped and shoved his shirt collar to the side so I could suck on his shoulder.

"Tell me," I said.

"You have to do it from behind, standing up. The angle hits him just right. I used to bend him over his bed, tell him to hold on, and then I'd grab his hips and go to town." Adan gulped. "He'd fucking scream his head off when he came like that." He closed his eyes and licked his lips. "Jesus, I want to see you do him. Want to see your face when you feel how good it is with him. Want to hear him beg for you."

Making out in the office was hot. Getting off in the office with our receptionist and secretary in the other room and no change of clothes was not a good idea. We moved our hands off each other's dicks and held each other for a few minutes, letting our heart rates go back to normal.

"I don't know how much longer I can wait," I whispered.

"Me either."

"I know it's only noon, but if you don't have anything that has to be done today, let's take off early and go over there, okay? I need to touch him, even if it's just holding him while we watch TV. I just—" I gulped and took in a shaky breath. "I need him."

Adan nodded. "Let me save this document and I can shut down and go." He sat down, reached for his mouse, and started clicking. "Hey, is that plant nursery around the corner still open?"

"Um, I think so." I shrugged. "I never paid much attention, but didn't we drive by there the other day and see cars out front?"

"Probably. Let's stop there and get him that plant he likes." He finished up on the computer, pulled his drawer open, and got his wallet and phone.

"What plant?"

Adan furrowed his brow. "Uh, hydrangeas. I think that's what they're called." He stood up and put his wallet in his back pocket and his phone in the front one. "I'll recognize them when I see them."

"Okay. We can stop by there on the—" A memory slammed into my head. Prom, senior year of high school. Charlie helping me with my cummerbund. And the corsage I'd gotten for my date, whose name I'd long since forgotten. "Do the flowers look like pom-poms?" I asked quietly.

He peered at me and understanding dawned. "Tell me."

I hoped my eyes didn't look as wet as they felt. "The corsage I got for my prom date was a blue hydrangea. I remember Charlie saying he liked it." I sighed. "That's the first night I kissed him."

Adan threaded his fingers with mine. "We're almost there," he reminded me. "We've almost got our boy completely back."

Chapter 18

INTRODUCTION

Charlie ("Chase") Rhodes

ON THURSDAY night, or more accurately, Friday morning, instead of sleeping, I was lying in bed trying to decide if I should ask Scott and Adan to spend the weekend or if I should see if Stacia was available to stay over with the kids for a night so I could go to their place. Yes, you heard me right. I was done keeping them at a distance, done worrying about whether it was all too good to be true or whether one or both of them would get sick of me, and done keeping my damn pants on when the two sexiest guys I'd ever known had some great fucking plans they wanted to try out naked.

Unfortunately, my apartment was tiny and inhabited by two young children. In the new house, our bedrooms would be on two different floors, so I'd be able to moan and beg and scream without waking them up. But in that apartment, any sex would have to be careful and quiet. I didn't hold out a lot of hope that the three of us would be able to keep it down when we finally *got* down.

That was the dilemma I was trying to solve when I heard a noise outside. Seconds later, my phone vibrated. I shot up, scrambled for the phone, and answered the call without checking who it was.

"Hello?"

"Hey, Chase, it's me."

It took only a second for me to place the voice. It was my old friend Daniel. I'd danced on board cruise ships for a couple of years, and we'd roomed, and slept, together for some of that time. The sex had been mediocre, but the friendship we'd formed was strong. He didn't live in Vegas, so the last time I'd seen him was when he was visiting on the night Adan and Scott had unexpectedly shown up at my door. But we'd kept in touch through texts and e-mails and even the occasional phone call.

"Daniel? What's wrong? Why're you calling in the middle of the night?"

"Sorry." He sounded horrible. "I'm at your door. Can you let me in?"

I was out of bed and through the apartment before he finished his sentence.

"What happened?" I asked as I frantically yanked the door open. "Are you hurt?'

He shook his head, dropped his bag, and practically collapsed into my arms.

"I don't want to talk about it," he muttered into my shoulder. "Can I crash with you for a little while?"

"Yeah, of course." I rubbed his back. "Your choices are the couch or my bed. I'll grab your bag."

"Thanks." He shuffled away, rubbing his eyes. "I feel like I could sleep for days."

With his bag in my hand, I closed and locked the door. "Then the bed will be better. Otherwise my kids will wake you up in about three hours."

"Your kids." He shook his head. "Crazy how much things change, huh?"

I put my free arm around his waist and led him to my room. "I've been spending a whole lot of time lately thinking about how crazy it is that things stay the same."

"What?"

"Never mind." I shook my head. "Get some sleep and we'll talk tomorrow."

Daniel shucked off his shoes and clothes, and we crawled into bed. "Will those boyfriends of yours lose their minds if we cuddle tonight?" he asked.

"I never said they were my boyfriends."

"You didn't have to." He scooted closer and sniffled. "Please?"

Daniel was normally a happy, upbeat guy. I had never heard him sound so down.

"C'mere," I said.

He was in my arms almost instantly and sobbing just as quickly. At five foot six, I was smaller than just about everyone, but Daniel wasn't much bigger than me, so I was able to hold him while he cried himself to sleep.

I remembered doing the same thing many a night after my breakups with Scott and Adan, but when I thought back to those times, they seemed like a lifetime ago. I remembered how much I had hurt back then, but I could no longer feel the pain, could no longer conceive of the lonely life I'd led for so long.

Maybe Daniel was right about things changing. Or maybe the amazing thing was how much things changed and yet stayed exactly the same.

And that brings me to the next picture in the album: me, Scott, and Adan, cuddled together on my sofa.

Our limbs are all tangled together, our bodies are practically on top of each other's, and our smiles could light up a room. Daniel took the picture Friday evening right after I told them I was going to take the plunge and move in with them and shortly before I went home with them so the three of us could spend the night together for the first time.

Chapter 18

Scott Boone

WITH three potted hydrangeas in hand—one with white flowers, another with pink, and the third with blue—Adan and I knocked on Charlie's door.

"Hi!" He smiled widely when he saw us standing on his doorstep. "You're here early. Did you have a lunch meeting nearby or—" He jerked his gaze from our faces to the hydrangeas. "Are those for me?"

"Yes," Adan said proudly as he stepped inside. "We remember how much you like them."

Charlie bounced into his arms and kissed his chin. "Thank you." He gripped Adan's biceps and his expression turned serious. "I don't want to worry you or anything, but some people might consider the way you're acting to be sweet."

Adan arched his eyebrows. "Are you one of those people?"

"Yeah, I am," Charlie said as he bobbed his head.

"Whew! That's a relief." Adan winked. "I'm glad it's working."

I'd followed them into the apartment and closed the door while they'd been talking. After kissing Adan softly, Charlie gave me one of his amazing hugs.

"Hi, Scotty," he said. He nuzzled my neck. "Thanks for the flowers. I don't know if you remember, but the first time I saw those was—"

"My prom night." I was still holding the plant with one hand, but I cupped his butt with the other and squeezed it. "I remember."

He leaned up to my ear, and whispered, "That was the night you crawled into my window and kissed me." He sighed contentedly and bussed his lips over mine. "Whenever I see those flowers, I remember that night."

I felt a pull in my heart. "I'm sorry I never thought to give you flowers before," I said as I gazed at him.

He shook his head and smiled. "Don't worry about it. It's no big deal."

Adan took the plant from me, kissed my cheek, and walked over to the kitchen counter.

"Sure it is," I said to Charlie as I combed my fingers through his hair. "Thankfully we've got Mr. Sensitive over there"—I tipped my head toward Adan, who was organizing the plants on the already crowded counter—"to keep me in line."

"The day I turn into the sensitive one, we know we're in trouble."

We were all laughing when a voice I'd never heard said, "Chase, do you have any—" All three of us flipped toward the hallway and saw a guy wearing nothing but boxer shorts. "I'm sorry. I didn't realize anybody else was here." He looked down at his body and then turned on his heel. "I'll get dressed and be right out."

My brain went through stages of processing: Who was that guy? Why was he undressed in the middle of the day? Where were his clothes? He said he was going to get dressed, so they must be in the bedroom. He wouldn't be in one of the kids' rooms, so that meant his clothes were in Charlie's room. Why would his clothes be in Charlie's room unless....

That was when I lunged for Adan. Thankfully, he hadn't been far ahead of me in analyzing the situation and I was standing closer to the hallway, so I was able to stop him before he went after Charlie's friend. I'd never seen him look so angry. His face was red, his lips were stretched thin, and his eyes were squinted in a dangerous-looking glare.

"Adan, calm down!" I said desperately. "I'm sure there's a good explanation."

He looked at me appraisingly, jerked his chin down in a rough nod, and sucked in air. "Charlie," he said brokenly as he turned to Charlie. "Explain."

"That's my friend Daniel." Charlie walked over until all three of us were standing close together. "He's in a bad place right now and needed to be with a friend."

"Your friend?" I repeated, feeling some tension drain from my anxious body.

"Yes," he said.

"It looked like he just woke up," Adan pointed out as he squeezed and released his hands hard enough to crack his knuckles. "Did he spend the night?"

"Uh-huh," Charlie answered.

Adan's jaw ticked. "In your bed?" he asked through gritted teeth.

"Yeah, but... wait. Are you jealous?" Charlie sounded a little happier than was wise given Adan's current emotional condition. He looked at me. "What about you, Scotty? How do you feel about—"

"This isn't a game!" Adan snapped.

"No, I know." Charlie put one hand on Adan's chest and the other on my waist. "I didn't mean it like that. I'm glad you didn't think it was hot, that's all."

"Why would we think you cheating is hot, Charlie?" I asked in frustration.

"Not the cheating. Just... Adan's always talking about how hot it'd be to see me with you, and I wasn't sure if—"

"Are you fucking kidding me with this?" Adan threw his arms up in the air as he shouted.

"Charlie, come on, we've been over this!" I added.

"Seeing you with Scott would be hot because it'd be *you* and *Scott*!" Adan's hands shook as he pulled at his hair in frustration. "There's nothing hot about any other guy getting close to you. You're ours, goddamnit!"

Charlie's expression softened. He reached for Adan's hand and then for mine. "I know." He kissed the back of each of our hands and then looked up at us. "I'm sorry. I do know."

"I'm glad," I said, trying to stay calm. "Now, why don't you answer the question before we lose our minds?"

"What's the question?" Charlie asked.

"Did. You. Sleep. With. Him?" Adan said each word slowly, his anger barely contained.

"When?" Charlie asked.

"Seriously?" Adan said incredulously. "You're asking us *when*?"

"Well, yeah, I mean—" He inhaled deeply. "We used to date, a long time ago, and we had sex then. But that was years ago, so if you're asking if I

186

slept with him last night, the answer is no." He paused. "Well, I mean, if you're asking if we had sex last night, the answer is no. But I did *sleep*-sleep with him."

"You slept with him?" I shouted.

"Slept-slept. Not, like, *slept*."

"I'm going to put my head through the wall." Adan rubbed his hands over his face. "Scott, help me out. Did our boyfriend cheat on us?"

"No!" Charlie shouted in horror. He looked up at us. "I'd never do that."

Adan peered at him. "Why not?" he asked.

"Tell us, Charlie. Why wouldn't you cheat?" I repeated.

He jerked his gaze back and forth between us. "Because I love you guys." As soon as the words were out, Charlie blinked rapidly, as if he was surprised by his own admission.

I sighed in relief and cupped Adan's neck. "Well, I guess we finally figured out how to get the guy we love to tell us he loves us back—we need to have a jealous fit."

"Great," Adan said. "Mission accomplished." He rubbed his hand over mine and sighed tiredly. "When's the naked guy getting out of here?"

"His name's Daniel." Charlie crossed his arms over his chest and pursed his lips. "Like I said, he's in a bad place right now, and I'm his friend. That means he can stay as long as he needs."

Adan mirrored his stance, looking every bit as stubborn. "You don't have a spare room and the couch is lumpy. I think your *friend* would be more comfortable in a hotel." He dropped his gaze to Charlie's mouth and added, "And if you keep sticking your bottom lip out like that, baby, I'm going to kiss it."

Charlie whimpered and ran his tongue over his plump lip. "You know, Daniel could stay here tonight with Bobby and Stephi after they fall asleep, which means I can—"

I was on him before he could finish the sentence, holding his cheeks between both hands, pressing my mouth against his, and darting my tongue inside as I shoved my knee between his legs.

"Mmph," he moaned in surprise. It didn't take him long to catch on, and then he held my wrists and sucked on my tongue as he humped my thigh.

I moved one hand around to his nape and shoved the other down the back of his pants, kneading his fine ass.

"Oh!" He tilted his butt up and pushed back against my hand. I dipped my fingers in his crease, and he snapped his gaze up and stared at me wide-eyed. "Scotty," he gasped.

"I want you, Charlie," I rasped.

"Yes." He nodded and gulped. "God, yes." Then he climbed up my body. "Don't stop touching me," he begged right before he licked his way into my mouth.

I held on to him, enjoying his warm, hard body, the silky skin beneath my fingers, and the taste of him in my mouth. I'd just started circling one finger around his rosebud when that voice interrupted again.

"Sorry about that. I'm Daniel Tover. You guys must be… oh!"

I assumed Charlie didn't hear his friend, because he kept moaning and kissing and rubbing against me. The last thing I wanted was to stop making out with him, but the idea of anybody but Adan and me seeing Charlie so uninhibited and in the throes of pleasure didn't sit well.

"Charlie, baby," I said as I pulled away from the kiss and removed my hand from his pants.

"No," he cried out and clutched my shirt. "Please don't stop, Scotty." He looked at me pleadingly. "Need you inside."

I groaned, closed my eyes, and took deep calming breaths.

"Your friend is here, baby," Adan said. I opened my eyes and saw him standing right behind Charlie, caressing his hip as he gazed into my eyes. "You guys are so beautiful together," he whispered. "But I don't want to share that with anybody else, okay? I want to be the only one who gets to see that."

Charlie dropped his forehead on my chest and panted. "Jesus. Sorry." He swallowed a few times and reached down for Adan's hand, squeezing it. "I want you guys so bad. I guess I lost it there for a minute."

"That's a good thing, baby," Adan said as he nuzzled and licked Charlie's ear. "But let's save it for when we're alone, okay?"

After taking another few breaths, Charlie nodded and we moved apart.

"Daniel, this is Scott"—he rubbed my chest—"and Adan." He wrapped his arm around Adan's waist.

"It's great to meet you guys," Daniel said brightly as he walked over. "Charlie talks about you all the time."

"You talk about us, baby?" Adan said with a smirk. "What exactly do you say?"

Charlie blushed and rolled his eyes. "Their egos don't need any more help, Daniel," he mock whispered. "Let's keep the compliments on the down-low."

I kissed Charlie's temple and managed to tear my gaze away from him long enough to tilt my chin up in a greeting to his friend. "It's nice to meet you too," I said.

Adan shook Daniel's hand but his focus remained on Charlie. "You want me to go pick up the kids?" he asked. "They get out of school soon, right?"

"Sure. They'd love that." Charlie grinned. "There you go being sweet again."

Adan goosed Charlie hard, making him jump and shriek. "Ow!" he said as he rubbed his injured backside and glared at Adan.

"See that?" Adan sauntered to the door, rolling his key ring around his fingers. "I'm just as tough as ever."

I hunched down and whispered into Charlie's ear, "Don't worry, baby. Tonight we'll kiss it until it's all better."

WE HUNG out at Charlie's apartment until the kids were asleep, then we thanked his friend for babysitting and drove to our place. All three of us were so ramped up by then we barely said ten words between us.

"We're good without rubbers, right?" I asked Charlie. We'd had the safe-sex talk long before, so I knew the answer, but I wanted to confirm because I had no interest in getting home and then having to run back out.

"Uh-huh," he said as he rapidly tapped his foot. "Can you drive faster?"

Any faster and I'd be risking a ticket, but I figured the question was rhetorical, so I didn't answer. When we finally got home, I rushed to the door and started unlocking it. It seemed Adan and Charlie couldn't wait, because I heard them moaning and kissing behind me.

"Take it inside," I said hoarsely as I pushed the door open.

They didn't separate, but they managed to stumble into the house while they kissed and grabbed at each other's hair, faces, and bodies. I tossed my keys on the side table, kicked the door shut, and watched them.

Adan slammed Charlie against the wall and shoved his thigh between Charlie's knees, grinding it against his balls. Instead of crying out in pain, Charlie threw his head back and moaned.

"Adan! Ungh."

"They're full, aren't they?" Adan asked, his voice sounding dark. He moved his leg up, pressing into Charlie's balls. "Bet they ache."

I'd never heard him talk that way; our dynamic together was completely different. It turned me on so much, I collapsed against the door, tore my pants open, grasped my rigid shaft, and started stroking.

"Yeah," Charlie said breathlessly as he rode Adan's leg. "Need you." He stared at Adan and trembled. "Help me."

Hearing him so turned on, watching his cheeks flush and his blue eyes go wild with passion, had me ready to cum. I squeezed the base of my shaft and groaned.

"Want me to milk your pretty cock?" Adan rasped as he pushed the heel of his hand down the length of Charlie's erection. Charlie gasped. "Bet you do." He moved his free hand to Charlie's nipple and tweaked it.

"Ah!" Charlie yelled.

"That's our boy." Adan slanted his mouth over Charlie's and kissed him hard and fast; then he dropped to his knees, yanked Charlie's pants to his ankles, and went down on his swollen dick.

"Adan!" Charlie yelled. He flailed his hands around before he finally held on to Adan's hair. His chest was heaving, mouth open, and then he turned his head and stared at me. "Scotty?" he said, his voice barely coming out as he held his shaking hand out.

I stumbled over to them, stood behind Adan, and leaned forward, taking Charlie's mouth in a rough kiss. My dick was still sticking out my open pants, so Charlie grabbed it and started pulling and caressing. It was the first time I'd felt his touch in years and it almost brought me to my knees.

We kissed each other sloppily, licking and tasting. I took his nipples between my fingers and squeezed them, making his back arch and his eyes fly open. All the while, I felt Adan's head bumping against my leg as he bobbed up and down, sucking Charlie off. I heard his moans, the distinctive slurping sounds that came with what he was doing, and the slide of his palm over his own dick.

Charlie came first, stretching his neck and shouting.

I pushed my dick through his fist one last time and yelled out, "Ah! Ah! Ah!" as I pulsed over and over again.

Between us, I could hear Adan's muffled cries letting me know he came as he swallowed down Charlie's offering.

It seemed to last forever—the sounds, the scents, the pleasure—but it was over way too soon. Charlie and I crumpled to the floor, and the three of us stayed there, tangled together, touching and kissing whatever parts of each other we could reach.

"Love you," Charlie said tiredly.

Both of us moved to kiss him. It was strange at first, three mouths connecting when I'd been used to two. But it didn't take long for us to find the right angles and then we were joined together in a new way, melding our lips and tongues and mouths.

"This floor's hard," I said eventually. "Let's get in bed."

"'Kay." Charlie let out a loud breath. "I think we need a shower first, though. We're all sweaty and sticky."

Adan nuzzled Charlie's neck and caressed my balls, which he had been cupping. "We're going to get you sweaty and sticky all over again once we go to bed, baby."

"But think of all the fun we can have getting him cleaned up," I reminded Adan as I massaged his thigh.

"Excellent point."

Adan stood up, fastened his pants, and reached a hand down to each of us, then pulled us to our feet.

"I don't think my legs work," Charlie said as he leaned against me. "I'm all wobbly from that orgasm."

Adan smirked. "Good one, was it?"

Charlie rolled his eyes and chuckled. "Yeah, yeah, yeah. Good job."

"Hey, now," Adan said. "Don't mock the mouth that sucks you."

I shook my head at their antics as I did up my pants, then swooped Charlie up into my arms.

He threw his hands around my neck and asked, "What're you doing?"

191

"Carrying you into the shower. I want to make sure you get your strength back." I kissed his cheek. "I have a lot of plans for tonight, and we're just getting started."

"Plans?" Charlie said.

"Uh-huh." I moved the hand cupping his butt so my thumb slid between his muscular globes. "Plans."

"Oh God." Charlie dropped his forehead on my shoulder. "I've been dreaming about you fucking me for years, Scotty."

I almost stumbled. "Me too, baby. And tonight we're going to turn that dream into a memory."

We walked into the bathroom and started shedding clothes.

"So how's it work between you two?" Charlie asked. He stepped out of his pants and stripped off his shirt.

"What do you mean?" Adan said.

I turned on the water and adjusted the temperature.

"Well, you only top," Charlie said to Adan. "I already know that. So Scotty's versatile, is that it?"

"I bottom with him sometimes," Adan replied.

I turned around in time to see Charlie's eyebrows shoot up in surprise. "Huh. I didn't see that coming."

"Yeah, well, neither did I." Adan shrugged. "But I love Scott, so we made it work. He does the same for me."

"He does the same...." Charlie straightened his posture. "Wait. Let me make sure I'm getting this." He pointed at each of us. "Neither of you likes to bottom?"

"It's fine," I said.

At the same time, Adan said, "It's okay."

"Yeah, yeah." He waved his hand dismissively. "But as far as what you like, you're tops? Both of you?"

I wasn't sure where Charlie was going with that question, so I looked at Adan worriedly. He chewed on his bottom lip and darted his gaze toward me, raising his eyebrows. I knew he was thinking the same things I was.

We were terrified Charlie would think we only wanted him around because we couldn't fulfill each other sexually, which wasn't true. Adan and I had always had a good sex life. Neither of us would say it was perfect; we were both honest enough to admit that. But we'd never wanted an open relationship, never wanted to bring some guy into our bedroom just so we could fuck him. What we wanted was Charlie in every aspect of our lives, bedroom included. But the key to that was Charlie—he was who we wanted. Not a third. *Charlie*.

"Holy fucking shit," Charlie gasped.

We both moved toward him, hoping to relieve whatever anxiety he was suddenly under.

"I'm the luckiest guy ever," he said. He moved his gaze from Adan's naked groin to mine and groaned. "Ever."

"Charlie?" I said.

"Are you okay, baby?" Adan asked.

"You're both tops?" Charlie said.

We both nodded hesitantly.

"Luckiest. Guy. Ever."

Chapter 19

INTRODUCTION

Charlie ("Chase") Rhodes

HOW great was my life? I mean, really, how great? I had the only two guys I'd ever wanted back by my side. And, as if that wasn't amazing enough, both of them wanted me as much as I wanted them.

The first night we spent together was unreal. I knew things would taper off at some point, but after being apart for so long, wanting each other so much, we were all so damn horny we went at it over and over again until we collapsed. When I finally fell asleep that night, I knew that was it for me, for all of us. I knew I was done searching, done struggling—I'd hit the end of the line. Together, the three of us, we were home.

After living with two children for half a year, my internal clock was set to wake up at what I used to consider the ass crack of dawn. I wanted to get home before Bobby and Stephi woke up, so that worked out well. I managed to get out of bed without waking either Adan or Scott, took a fast shower, and got dressed.

When I returned to the bedroom, I saw them lying together in the center of their bed. The sheets were tangled around their waists. Adan was on his belly, his face turned toward Scotty, who was on his side with one arm thrown across Adan's waist. The sunlight filtered in through the window, casting a glow over both of them, and they looked beautiful. They were beautiful.

I said a silent thanks to whatever deity had seen fit to grace me with both Scott and Adan. Then I got my phone, snapped a few pictures, and woke them up so we could go spend the day with the rest of our family.

Chapter 19

Scott Boone

OUR shower wasn't big enough for all three of us, but we squeezed in anyway. We enjoyed washing and touching and kissing each other until we were hard again. Then we dried off and went into the bedroom.

"Is there something in particular you want?" I asked Charlie once we'd crawled into bed.

"Kiss me?" he said.

He was lying on his back with Adan and me on either side of him. We both leaned forward in response to his request. I covered Charlie's mouth with mine while Adan kissed his neck and suckled on his ear. Then, by unspoken agreement, we switched places.

While we kissed, I moved my hands over Charlie's body—his nipples, his dick, and eventually his ass. He spread wide for me and canted his hips up, giving me lots of room to play. I rubbed my thumbs up and down his crack, and then pushed one into his hole.

"Mngh!" he moaned. I shoved my other thumb alongside it, and he arched his back. "Scotty!"

"Turn over, baby," I said hoarsely. "I want to taste that pretty butt."

Adan held on to Charlie and rolled them over so Adan was lying flat on the bed and Charlie was prone on top of him. I ran my hand down his back and over his firm ass. Then I took hold of his thighs and spread his legs wide, placing his knees on either side of Adan's hips.

Charlie was completely exposed to me in that position, and I couldn't wait any longer. I dipped forward and swiped my tongue over his pink hole.

"Oh God!" he cried out.

"That's it, sweet baby," Adan said. "Let Scott make you feel good."

What I was doing felt amazing to me too. I held on to Charlie's cheeks and buried my face between them, flicking my tongue over his hole before darting it in and out.

I was so focused on the feeling of Charlie's silky heat, the way his body trembled, and the noises he made, that I didn't notice Adan moving until I heard slurping sounds and looked up. Adan was sitting with his back against the headboard, and Charlie was noisily sucking his dick. I groaned and went back to tongue-fucking Charlie.

I could have stayed there all night, tasting and touching, making him feel good. But eventually he popped off Adan's dick and said, "Scotty, please. I need you."

At some point, Adan must have thought to get the lube, because when he heard what Charlie said, he tossed it over to me. I took a few calming breaths so I wouldn't go off before I got inside him. Then I drizzled lube down Charlie's crack, coated my dick, and pressed my crown against his opening.

I crouched over him, my chest against his back, and kissed the side of his neck. "I love you, Charlie," I whispered into his ear as I pushed my way into his body. "Always have, always will."

"Scotty," he sighed. "Feels so good."

"For me too, baby," I said as I thrust out and then back in. "You feel amazing."

I knelt between his spread legs, held on to his raised hips, and set a good rhythm—fast enough to make him feel good but slow enough to let me last.

"Oh God," he moaned. "Love this." Then he sucked Adan's dick back into this mouth and rocked his body to meet mine, moaning every time I bottomed out deep inside him.

"Ah," Adan grunted.

I raised my eyes and met Adan's pleasure-filled gaze. "Scott," he said as he reached his hand out to me. I kissed his palm then leaned toward him until our mouths connected for a short kiss. "Love you, Adan," I told him as I rocked in and out of Charlie.

"Me too, hon," he said.

Sooner than I would have liked, the pleasure took me to the point of no return. "I'm close," I said as my balls rose up.

I reached around Charlie and took his dick in my hand, wanting to bring him off with me.

He popped his mouth off Adan's cock and gasped, "No, don't. I'm not ready to cum yet."

I released his dick and clutched his hips as I pummeled into him. "Can't stop, baby, can't stop."

"I know," he said. "Want you to cum inside me." He braced his hands on the bed and shoved back against me, taking me in deep. "Then I want Adan to do it too."

"Charlie," I groaned, immeasurably turned on by his words. "Oh God!" I arched my back, closed my eyes, and pressed my groin against his butt as I shot inside his tight, warm body. When my dick finally stopped pulsing, I let out a deep breath and rubbed my hand over his warm skin. "Charlie," I sighed.

"You guys are gorgeous together," Adan rasped. "I knew you would be, but damn."

I looked up and saw his hand flying over his cock as he moved his heated gaze over Charlie and me.

"It's your turn," I said to Adan. "Our boy needs you now."

Adan looked at me and then let go of his shaft and tilted Charlie's chin up. "You sure?" he asked.

Charlie nodded and quietly croaked, "Please."

With a gentle motion, Adan rolled Charlie onto his back and wedged himself between his knees, resting Charlie's thighs over his own. I poured lube onto my hand and rubbed it over Adan's rigid shaft. Then he moved it to Charlie's already slick opening and slowly slid inside.

"Jesus," he said when he bottomed out. He arched his neck and gulped. "You feel even better than I remembered."

Charlie's chest was heaving, his cheeks were flushed, and his dick was red and swollen.

"I can't... I need...." He screwed his eyes shut, tossed his head from side to side, and made a loud keening sound. "Adan, please!"

"I have you, baby," Adan said. "Going to make you feel so good."

With that promise made, Adan held Charlie's legs against his chest and started jackhammering into him. It didn't last long, couldn't last long, not with how turned on they both were.

They grunted and moaned, and then Charlie's eyes fluttered open, so impossibly blue and beautiful, and he looked at me. I leaned over his sweat-slick body and took his dick into my mouth, sucking hard.

"Ah!" Charlie shouted and I felt his dick swell before his hot, bitter seed splashed on my tongue.

"Oh Jesus, yes!" I heard Adan cry out as his balls slapped against Charlie one last time.

When Charlie was finally spent, I moved my mouth off his dick, climbed to my knees, and pulled Adan into a deep kiss, sharing the taste of Charlie's pleasure with him.

"Wow," Charlie said from beneath us, and then he started giggling.

Adan and I separated and smiled at him fondly.

"Do you feel good, baby?" I asked.

He bobbed his head and said, "Best ever."

I lay down on one side of Charlie, Adan settled himself on the other side, and the three of us moved together into a tight hug.

"So," Charlie said after a few minutes of silence. "How much time do you guys need to recharge before we can do that again?"

WE COULDN'T have been asleep more than a couple of hours when Charlie woke us up.

199

"Mmph!" Adan moaned and buried his head under a pillow. I rubbed his back soothingly, and he threw his arm over my hip and cupped my balls.

"Is everything okay?" I asked Charlie, my voice rough. I blinked and tried to make my bleary eyes focus on him. "Why aren't you in bed?" I opened my arms to him. "C'mere, baby, I want to hold you some more."

He shook his head. "If I get in there with you two, I won't get back out."

"That's the idea." I grinned. "Come on. You've got to be beat after last night."

Charlie groaned. "I can still feel you guys inside." His nostrils flared and he gazed at me. "It's so hot."

I felt a tugging in my groin in reaction to his arousal. My dick started to fill, and I heard Adan moan at the same time he moved his hand over my shaft.

"If you get in bed, I can kiss it and make it better," I offered.

Though his breathing became more rapid and he whimpered, Charlie shook his head. "Uh-uh. We need to go." He gulped. "Besides, I like this feeling. Don't want it to stop."

Adan finally joined in our conversation, moving out from underneath the pillow and saying, "It doesn't have to stop. We can kiss it better and then fuck you into the mattress again. Come back to bed."

"I want to get home before Stephi and Bobby wake up," Charlie reminded us.

"Right." I sighed and forced myself to sit up. "Good idea. Give us five minutes to shower and we can take off." When Adan didn't move, I reached back and smacked his butt. "Let's go. The kids are waiting."

"Goddamnit!" Adan shouted. He kicked the blankets off, slid out of bed, and growled, "Fine! But Scott, you need to call the mortgage broker and tell him to speed his shit up. I want us living together under one roof fucking yesterday."

He stomped into the bathroom; I sighed and shook my head fondly.

"I remember Adan wasn't a morning person, but wow," Charlie said as he looked after him, wide-eyed.

I got up, wrapped my arms around Charlie's waist, and pulled him into a hug. "That's, like, 10 percent morning, 10 percent sleep deprivation, and 80 percent Adan wanting you in our life, in our house, and in our bed every day." I kissed his temple. "Can't say I blame him. We miss you when you're not with us, and we've both been on edge for a good six months now, trying to win you back."

"I'm sorry," Charlie said as he squeezed me. "I needed—"

"You needed to know you could trust us. I get it." I nuzzled his neck. "Adan does too. And he realizes it's our fault for messing up before. But you know how he is. Patience is not one of his virtues. He loves you, loves Bobby and Stephi, so he wants you under his roof where he can make sure you're taken care of." I took a deep breath and shrugged. "That's his way."

"Scott! Get your ass in here," Adan shouted from the bathroom. "It's getting late!"

Charlie and I looked at each other and started laughing.

"There's a Starbucks on the way to your apartment," I reminded him as I walked away. "We'll make sure he's civilized before he sees the kids."

Adan was drying off when I walked into the bathroom. "I left the water on for you. Hurry up." He flung his towel over his shoulder and squeezed paste on his toothbrush. "Charlie's right about the kids not waking up without any of us there."

I rolled my eyes, got under the water, and reached for the soap. "It's not like they're alone. Daniel is with them."

"*We* should be with them. Get a move on."

I wasn't going to argue with him, both because he was in no mood for it and also because he was right.

"Hey, Adan," I said as I lathered up. "Before you go out there like a raging bull, try to remember this was the first night we spent with Charlie, the first time we got to wake up all together." I rinsed off, turned off the water, and stepped out of the shower.

"What's your point?" he asked as he handed me my towel.

"No point."

I ran the towel over my body and he started walking out of the bathroom.

201

"A good-morning kiss might be a nice touch, though," I called out after him.

He paused, grunted in acknowledgement, and left. I smiled to myself and reached for my toothbrush.

THE NEXT two weeks passed by in a flash. Daniel stayed in town, so while Adan and I were at work, Charlie and Daniel packed his apartment and our house, which we'd put on the market. And we finally got the financing lined up for the new house, so we were able to close.

Friday morning, while the kids were at school, the movers loaded up the truck and took all of our belongings to the home we'd finally get to share. While the rest of the guys started unpacking, I went for a coffee run. I returned to find Adan sitting on the floor in the family room, surrounded by wires.

"Doing okay?" I asked as I handed him his coffee.

"Yup. Thank you." He took the cup and smiled. "Just getting the TV and the computer hooked up, so Bobby and Stephi can be entertained while we get the house put together this weekend."

"Never thought I'd see you so happy about electronics and unpacking," I said playfully as I sipped my own drink.

"We're finally home. All of us." He reached up and squeezed my hand. "Nothing can get me down."

Well, as long as he was so upbeat.... "Did you ask Charlie what the deal is with Daniel?"

"You mean if he's going to camp out here?" Adan said.

I nodded.

He shook his head. "Nope. The last thing I wanted was to rile him up now that we're here. You know how defensive he is about his depressed friend."

"Yeah, you're right." I sighed. "The house is plenty big and he's a nice enough guy, but it's weird, right? Who shows up out of nowhere for no reason and doesn't leave?"

"Yeah, it's weird. I'm sure there's some reason, but from what Charlie told us, the guy hasn't even told him what happened, so I doubt we'll ever get the scoop."

I took a deep breath. "Well, he's bound to leave eventually, right?"

"Right," Adan said as he dipped his chin. "Give me a kiss and then go deliver those drinks." He tilted his head toward the tray I was holding. "Charlie's unpacking the kids' rooms. He said he wants them all put together by the time they get home from school so they don't feel displaced."

I chuckled fondly and said, "He'll probably have their beds made and their names stenciled on the walls too."

"He's a good dad," Adan agreed.

"So are you," I whispered before squatting down and bussing my lips over Adan's. "I'll go give Charlie and Daniel their drinks and then—" I cleared my throat and used my best Arnold Schwarzenegger voice as I said, "I'll be back."

Whether it was because I was walking quietly, or because the noise from the boxes Charlie and Daniel were ripping open was loud, or because they were so engrossed in their conversation that they weren't paying attention to anything else, I don't know, but for whatever reason, they didn't hear me approach. I, on the other hand, heard them talking, and even though listening in to someone else's conversation is wrong and rude, I'm nosy, so I did it anyway.

"Are you sure you don't need me to stay and help you unpack?" Daniel asked.

"I'm sure." Charlie paused. "You said you're going back to him. Did you change your mind again?"

"I don't know," Daniel whispered.

"You can't run forever, Daniel. We talked about this."

"I know," he answered. "But I wasn't running this time! It wasn't my fault."

I heard Charlie sigh deeply. "Look, you won't tell me what Asher did, but based on the short time I spent with that guy, I'd be willing to bet good money that whatever happened was his fault."

"See? You don't even like him. Why should I go back there?"

"Because I'm not the one who has to live with him, and for whatever reason, you're in love with the guy, Daniel. We both know he's called you a million times. Don't think I haven't seen you listen to his messages over and over again."

"I miss him," Daniel said brokenly.

"Yes, I know. You miss him. He misses you. So get your ass out of my house and on a plane back to San Francisco so you can make up with that hot but personality-challenged asshole."

Neither of them said anything for so long that I thought they were done talking, but just as I was about to walk in, Daniel said, "What if I go back and he... does what he did again?"

"Well, if that happens, you kick him in the nuts or hem his pants."

I swallowed down my laughter.

"Hem his pants?" Daniel asked in confusion.

"Never mind, that's something Scotty said to me one time. Look, does he love you? Whatever else happened, do you believe he loves you?"

"Yes," Daniel said without hesitation. Then he paused and answered again, "Yes."

"Then go home. Set his couch on fire, put a laxative in his brownies, draw on his face in permanent marker when he's sleeping, punish him in whatever way you want, but for fuck's sake, stop running."

My jaw dropped.

"Thanks, Chase. I'll call you later and tell you how it goes."

I was still frozen in shocked horror when Daniel sauntered out of the bedroom. "I wouldn't mess with him if I were you," he said to me as he took his drink from the tray I was holding. "It was nice getting to know you, Scott. I'm sure I'll see you again soon."

He walked down the hallway and then I heard him running down the stairs.

"Are you done eavesdropping?" Charlie called out. "Because I could use some help putting this dollhouse back together."

I shook my head to clear my mind and stumbled into the room. "How long did you know I was out there?"

"Long enough."

I bobbed my head. "So that's why you said that stuff about the laxative and the fire? You were screwing around, right? I mean, it's not like you'd ever actually *do* any of that."

Charlie raised one eyebrow as he picked up his drink and took a sip.

"You're scaring me," I told him.

"Why? Are you planning on doing something to me that would warrant revenge?"

"No!" I shook my head fervently.

He patted my chest. "Well, then we shouldn't have any problems."

Chapter 20

INTRODUCTION

Charlie ("Chase") Rhodes

I LIVE in Las Vegas, Nevada with—count 'em—not one, but two boyfriends. That sounds like the start to a wild and probably pornographic movie, which would be a partially accurate description of our lives, actually. But we also have two children, a puppy, and a fish.

We used to have two fish, one for each of the kids, but then they decided the fish were lonely so they put them in one tank. They were betta fish, otherwise known as Siamese fighting fish. Ever heard of them? They're pretty and colorful, and if you put two of them together, they have a gladiator-style match to the fucking death. It's like a live rendition of the *National Geographic* channel right on your kitchen counter except with screeching, crying children. Awesome.

All joking aside, life is great. The adoption went through, so I'm legally a father. Bobby and Stephi still see the counselor I've been taking them to since I arrived, but she says they're adjusting so well that we're down to monthly visits. And my men give it to me hard and deep on a more than frequent basis. Really, what else could I ask for in life?

Which brings me to the next picture in the album. It's a shot I took on the one-year anniversary of the day we all found each other again. In the picture, Scott and Adan are in our kitchen, surrounded by dirty dishes and who-knows-what on the counters. The air is thick with smoke. Scott is balanced on one foot, wearing oven mitts, and clutching his phone with one hand while gripping his shin with the other. And Adan is holding the landline phone to his ear and yelling.

Ahhh, domestic bliss.

$\mathcal{C}hapter$ 20

Scott Boone

STEPHI had ballet and Bobby had swim lessons on the one-year anniversary of the day Adan and I walked into Charlie's apartment and found everything we needed to complete our family. Adan and I decided to leave work early so we could surprise Charlie by making dinner. Part of our plan worked, the other... not so much.

"What are we going to cook?" Adan asked as we got into the car.

"I printed out a recipe for meatloaf from one of those cooking sites. I figured we'd make that and a salad that comes in a bag. That can't be too hard, right?"

He pulled out of the parking lot and said, "Did you say meatloaf? Charlie won't let us bring dead animals into the house. Are we going back to meat? Did I miss a memo?"

I chuckled at his use of Charlie's terminology. He was adamant about having a vegetarian household, which wasn't a big deal because Adan and I got our fill of meat at lunch. Plus, Charlie cooked every meal at home and he was damn good at it, so it wasn't as if we could complain.

"It's vegetarian meatloaf," I explained.

"Vegetarian meatloaf?" Adan scoffed. "That's an oxymoron. If it's meat, it's not vegetarian and vice versa."

"Thank you for the English lesson," I said sarcastically. "It's got lentils and onions and oats and stuff instead of meat, but the recipe is called vegetarian meatloaf. Deal with it."

"Fine, whatever." Adan rolled his eyes. "Do we need to stop at the store or do we have all the ingredients at home?"

"Uh. I'm not sure." I retrieved the piece of paper from my briefcase. "Do we have—"

"Let me stop you right there," Adan said. "I'm about as familiar with the contents of our pantry as you, so if you don't know, it's a safe bet I don't either."

"Then let's go to the grocery store."

"Okay." Adan nodded.

After a few minutes of silence, I said, "Do you think it makes Charlie mad?"

Adan furrowed his brow. "Do I think what makes Charlie mad?"

"I don't know." I shrugged and chewed my bottom lip. "The fact that we don't ever help with meals."

"Or laundry," Adan added.

"Or laundry," I repeated.

"Or just about anything else having to do with the house," Adan said.

"You know what?" I raised my voice in frustration. "Quit trying to help. You're making it worse."

"I'm not doing anything other than stating the facts."

"Yeah, well, the facts make us look like assholes."

He reached over and squeezed my knee. "Have you ever heard Charlie complain?" he asked.

"Uh, no," I said after giving it some thought.

"How does he usually react when we sit down and eat something he's made?"

I thought about Charlie's proud smile when one or both of us got seconds, which was most nights. "He's happy," I said and sighed in relief.

"Yup. And if he wasn't, he'd tell us and we'd figure out how to change things so they work for all of us. You know that and he does too."

"You're right," I conceded. "Thanks."

"No problem."

209

He pulled up to the grocery store. "Grab the list," he said. "Let's get what we need and hurry home. We don't have that much time to get everything ready."

We hustled into the store and grabbed all the ingredients on the list. Most of them were easy to find, but we walked the entire store three times looking for lentils and still came up empty-handed.

"I think we need to ask someone," Adan finally conceded.

"You're probably right," I agreed.

We took another unsuccessful lap around the store.

"That guy in the red polo shirt works here," Adan pointed out, apparently and inexplicably thinking I'd miss the giant store logo on the man's shirt. "Go ask him."

"You go ask him," I responded.

We walked down every aisle for the fifth time.

"We're wasting time," I said.

"We can ask together," Adan suggested as a compromise.

Asking the question and being walked over to the shelf holding the lentils took all of a minute.

"We must have walked right by these half a dozen times," Adan grumbled.

"At least."

"Next time you should ask so we don't waste any time."

"Yup." I nodded. "You should."

He looked at me and grunted.

I cupped the back of his neck and squeezed it affectionately. "Let's go home and make dinner."

AS IT turned out, making dinner wasn't as easy as we'd expected.

We overcooked the lentils the first time.

"Why is the pot smoking?" Adan asked.

I rushed over to the stove, grabbed the lid, then dropped it and shouted, "Ow! Hot. Hot. Hot." I stuck my fingers in my mouth and shuffled from foot to foot.

"Quit being a baby," Adan said. He came over and looked into the pot. "It's all black and crusty." He darted his gaze toward me. "Is it supposed to be crusty?"

I walked over and stood next to him, shoulder to shoulder. We both looked into the pot. "I don't think so. Maybe we didn't use enough water."

"We have more, right?" he asked.

"Uh-huh," I mumbled around the fingers still in my mouth.

"Get some ice," he said as he reached for the handles on the sides of the pot. "I'll scrape this into the sink and we can try ag—" The pot crashed to floor. "Fuck! Fuck! Fuck!" Adan hopped around and shook his hands. "That's hot!"

I grabbed a couple of towels, dropped ice on them, and handed one to Adan. "We suck."

He nodded, put his fingers on either side of the cold towel, and said, "Seriously."

"Okay," I sighed. "Let's try this again."

We had moderately better luck with the lentils the second time around. They weren't burnt, but they did seem pretty watery.

"Is it supposed to look like soup?" Adan asked as he stared into the pot.

"I don't know." I was standing next to him looking down. "The recipe didn't say."

"Huh, well, maybe we should drain out that water."

"Good idea." I got the oven mitts we'd discovered in one of the drawers and carried the pot over to the sink.

"Uh, Adan?" I asked as I held the pot over the sink.

"Yeah?"

"How am I supposed to drain the water without all the lentils coming out?"

He pursed his lips and furrowed his brow in what I described as his "I'm thinking" look.

"Maybe we can hold the lid over it and tip it. That way just the water will leak out."

"Good idea." I nodded. "Get the lid."

Adan put the lid on the pot and held it in place as I tipped the pot to the side. It worked at first—the water drizzled out of the edge—but when I had to increase the angle of the pot to get to the water on the bottom, the lentils hit the lid, Adan lost his grip, and the entire contents toppled out.

"Shit!" I yelled.

"Goddamnit!" Adan shouted.

"Scoop it up before it goes down the drain! Scoop it up!"

I set the pot down and both of us reached for the lentils and put as much of them as we could retrieve back into the pot.

"You think that'll be enough?" Adan asked, sounding a little breathless after all that excitement.

"I hope so, because we don't have any more we can make."

"Okay," Adan sighed. "Get the rest of the stuff and pour it in here so we can mix it all up."

"I think we're supposed to let it cool first."

"We don't have time."

I handed Adan the bowl we'd used to hold all the other ingredients and he poured it into the pot.

"Is that everything?" he asked.

"Umm, let me get the paper." I looked at the now stained recipe and said, "We need to add a beaten egg and a diced onion."

Adan got the eggs out of the fridge while I looked for a cutting board.

"Just one egg?" he asked as he held it next to the pot.

"Yeah. But you're supposed to beat it first."

"I'll just stir it once it's in here. We have enough to clean up without getting more shit dirty for no reason."

He was right. The kitchen was a disaster. It hadn't even looked that bad the time Charlie and the kids had made a papier-mâché solar system.

"Okay." I found the cutting board, knife, and onion. "This says it's supposed to be diced. What does that mean?"

"I don't know." Adan shrugged as he hit the egg on the side of the pot. "Maybe it's supposed to be shaped like dice."

"Right. That makes sense." I started chopping.

"Shit!" Adan yelled.

I jerked my head to look at him. "What?"

"Some of the eggshell fell in here."

"Oh. Just scoop it out."

"Okay."

I finished cutting the onion and brought it over to him. "Does this look okay? It wasn't easy to get all the little cubes to stay together. Especially with the outside of the onion being so flaky."

He looked appraisingly at the cutting board I was holding. "I think so. Drop it in here."

I scraped the onion into the pot, and Adan stirred everything together.

"Now what?" he asked.

"We're supposed to pour it into a loaf pan."

"What's a loaf pan?"

"I don't know." I dragged my hand through my hair in frustration. "Doesn't matter. Just find a pan and we'll put it in there."

He darted his gaze around the kitchen. "Why can't we just cook it in this? It's metal. It can go in the oven."

I thought about it for a second and nodded. "Yeah, okay, fine. I'll open the door, you slide it in."

"Oh, I like sliding it in," he said, but it was halfhearted at best. We were both so damn tired.

He put the pot in the oven and I closed the door.

"Done." I let out a relieved breath. "How much time is it supposed to cook?"

Adan got the recipe from the counter. "Thirty minutes."

I looked at the clock. "We don't have thirty minutes."

"Just turn up the temperature," he suggested.

"Okay." I turned the dial up. "Now we need to make the salad."

The salad came in a bag. It still took us ten minutes to put it together.

"Charlie's going to be here any second and we haven't cleaned up," Adan pointed out as he looked around the disaster that was once our immaculate kitchen.

I chewed my lip. "How about I turn on the alarm so we hear it beep when he comes in and one of us will run out there and distract him while the other finishes up in here?"

"Good plan," Adan said as he started washing dishes. "Will you find the spray cleaner thing first so I can wipe down the counters?"

I eventually located some Windex in the laundry room. After bringing it to Adan, I hustled over to the alarm panel, which was by the door leading to the garage. I turned it on and had started jogging back to the kitchen when the alarm went off.

"Scott! What the hell?" Adan yelled.

"I'll turn it off! I'll turn it off!" I ran back to the alarm panel, pressed the code, and ended the piercingly loud siren sound. "Sorry," I said as I ran back to the kitchen. "I must have hit a wrong butt—" The air looked cloudy. "Adan?"

"What?" He didn't look up from the dishes.

"I think something's burning."

He sniffed. "Shit."

We'd both turned to look at the oven when the home phone rang.

"I'll get the phone," he said. "You get the meatloaf."

I pulled the oven door open and was hit with a wave of heat and smoke. Thankfully, I remembered to don the oven mitts before reaching for the pot.

"What's our password for the alarm company?" Adan asked frantically.

I looked up to see him holding the phone to his ear. "I don't know. Why?"

"Because you hit the emergency help button or something, and they're going to send the cops if I don't give them the password."

"Shit!"

"Yeah."

"I, uh, think I put the code in my phone." I stood up and left the oven door open as I searched around the kitchen for my cellphone.

Adan tried to get the person from the alarm company to give us more time.

"Do you know where I put my phone?" I asked him.

"How am I supposed to know where you put your phone?" he asked impatiently.

"There it is," I said when I spotted it on the kitchen table. I ran to get it and ran smack into the oven door. "Fuck!" I hopped on one foot and grasped my injured shin with my oven-mitt-covered hand. "Goddamnit!" I limped over to the table, got my phone, and ran back over to him.

"Scott! I need the alarm password."

"It's hydrangea," Charlie said.

Adan and I both spun around to see Charlie, Bobby, and Stephi standing at the edge of the kitchen.

"Uh, hi," I said. "Welcome home."

Adan finished talking to the alarm company and then said, "We made you dinner. Happy anniversary."

WE ENDED up going out to dinner, and when we came home, Charlie got the kids ready for bed while Adan and I cleaned up the kitchen.

"Is everybody sleeping?" I asked Charlie when he walked into our bedroom after doing his nightly check of the house. He always liked to make sure the kids were asleep and everything was in its place before he came into bed.

"Yup."

His brown hair was still damp from his shower, and he was wearing the loose shorts he pretended to sleep in. I say 'pretended' because in the entire six months we'd been living together, he hadn't managed to last even one night with those things on his body. Between Adan and me, there was always someone wanting to play with his gorgeous butt and pretty dick.

"I'm ready for my anniversary present now." He wiggled out of his shorts and climbed onto the bed on all fours.

"Oh, someone wants to have fun tonight," Adan said huskily. He set the book he was reading on the nightstand and held his arms open. "C'mere, baby."

Charlie crawled on top of him and slanted his mouth over Adan's. They licked at each other, pushed their tongues into one another's mouths, and moaned in pleasure.

"Mmm, love kissing you," Adan mumbled and then went back to pressing his lips against Charlie's.

"Me too," Charlie said.

I got the lube out of the nightstand, knee-walked over to them, and set it down. Then I knelt beside them, touching Charlie's butt and pinching my own nipples. I never tired of watching them together. Nothing turned me on faster or made me want more than the sight of the two men I loved loving on each other.

"Scotty?" Charlie said as he spread his legs on either side of Adan's hips and planted his knees on the bed.

"Yes, baby?" I pushed his hair off his face. "What do you need?"

"Want you to fuck me," he said.

I leaned down and kissed him gently before opening the slick and coating us up. While I got us ready, Adan wrapped his big hand around both his dick and Charlie's and started stroking.

"Feels good," Charlie gasped. He dropped his forehead on Adan's chest and pushed into his touch. "Hurry, Scotty. I'm close already."

I pushed both of my thumbs into his butt and slid them in and out while I massaged his firm cheeks. Then I spread him open with one hand and held my dick against his hole with the other.

"Here I come, baby," I said as I pushed inside, watching myself sink into him.

"Ungh! Yes," he hissed. "God, I love that."

Adan moaned. I could hear his hand sliding over their dicks, and he rasped, "How's he feel, Scotty?"

"Tight and hot and perfect," I answered breathlessly as I rocked into Charlie.

"I'm going to take you later, baby," Adan said to Charlie. His shoulder moved faster along with the sliding sounds of his palm. "Won't last right now."

"Me too," Charlie said as he started slamming back against me. "Me too. Me too. Me too!" He yelled out the last word, his entire body stiffened, and his channel tightened around my cock, letting me know he was cumming.

"Ah, Jesus!" Adan shouted. He looked at me desperately, the wet sound his hand made sounded louder and faster. "Cum on me, Scott," he said. "Cum on my cock."

I gasped and circled my hand around the base of my erection, squeezing myself as I pulled out of Charlie. He whimpered and rolled to the side, giving me a full view of Adan's thickly muscular body.

Charlie's semen was already coating Adan's rigid dick and he was pumping himself quickly and desperately. I knelt between his legs, took myself in hand, and stroked hard while I watched Adan's pleasure-filled face and fat cock. It didn't take long before my balls tightened and my shaft swelled.

"Adan!" I yelled as I aimed my pulsing dick at his and shot stream after stream of hot, white seed over his skin.

Whether it was the sound of me calling his name or the extra lubrication added by my ejaculate, I don't know, but Adan arched his back and grunted, "Ah, fuck, yeah!" as he came.

I sat back on my ankles, my spent cock still in my hand, and tried to catch my breath.

"I'm a mess," Adan said with grin as he rubbed his hand over his cum-streaked skin.

"Don't worry," Charlie said. "I'll clean you up."

From the way he was licking his lips and moaning, I knew he wasn't planning on using a towel. I sat back and got ready to enjoy the show, which was sure to be followed by another round. Damn, but did I ever love my life. And based on the smiles gracing my guys' faces, I knew I wasn't alone.

Epilogue

Charlie ("Chase") Rhodes

ALRIGHT, it's time for me to stop scrapbooking for the day and start the chauffeuring portion of my job. Stephi decided to take softball this year and Bobby's in gymnastics, and wouldn't you just figure, they're on the opposite sides of town. Plus, we're short on bread and I'm not happy about how the milk smells, so I need to hit the grocery store.

I'll work more on the scrapbook later, but I'm not in a rush. I mean, it's not as if it'll ever be finished. It's more like a work-in-progress that builds and gets better every time I add another memory to it.

Kind of like life.

CARDENO C.—CC to friends—is a hopeless romantic who wants to add a lot of happiness and a few "awwws" into a reader's day. Writing is a nice break from real life as a corporate type and volunteer work with gay rights organizations. Cardeno's stories range from sweet to intense, contemporary to paranormal, long to short, but they always include strong relationships and walks into the happily-ever-after sunset. Cardeno feels that characters write their own stories and just hopes to find enough time to get those stories on the page.

Cardeno's Home, Family, and Mates series have received awards from Rainbow Awards, the Goodreads M/Romance Group, and various reviewers. But even more special to CC are heartfelt reactions from readers, like, "You bring joy and love and make it part of the every day."

You can learn more about Cardeno's writing at http://www.cardenoc.com/.

The Family Series from CARDENO C.

The Home Series by CARDENO C.

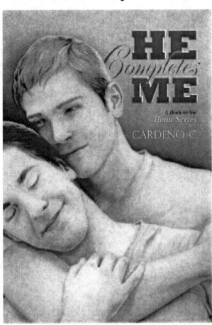

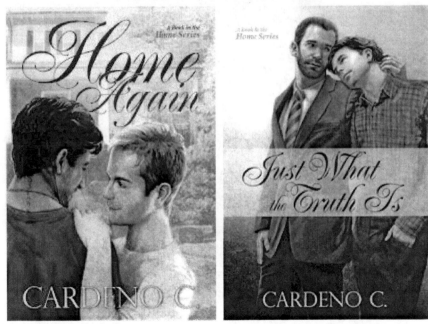

http://www.dreamspinnerpress.com

The Home Series by CARDENO C.

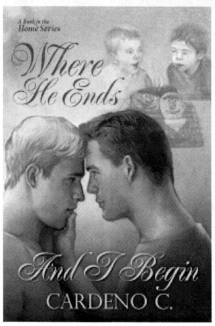

The Mates Series from CARDENO C.

http://www.dreamspinnerpress.com

Also from CARDENO C.

EIGHT DAYS

CARDENO C.

http://www.dreamspinnerpress.com

Also from CARDENO C.

A SHOT AT FORGIVENESS

CARDENO C.

CPSIA information can be obtained at www.ICGtesting.com
Printed in the USA
LVOW12s0705040514

384258LV00007B/36/P